The Art of Mutual Destruction

NEYMAT RABOOBEE

I0564757

This is a work of fiction.

Names, characters, places and incidents are either the product of the author's imagination or, if real, used fictitiously.

ISBN: 978-0-620-79769-6

DEDICATION

To everyone who loved these two enough to ask me about their story – Iman and Adam would be far more of a mystery without your poking and prodding.

PROLOGUE

"I don't know what I did to be saddled with such an ungrateful child," Aasia Rahman snapped irritably, glaring at the child in question.

"Maybe you were cursed," her daughter Iman suggested, pressing her lips together in an effort to suppress her tears. Aasia was *not* worth the headache and swollen eyes a crying jag would give her.

"Probably by your grandfather!" Aasia flung back.

Iman rolled her eyes. "I'll ask him for you," she cooed in a sweet voice, lifting her messenger bag and slinging it over her shoulder.

"Iman, don't you dare go visit that man!" A vein stood out in Aasia's forehead. "I forbid you to go and see him."

"Fine," Iman dropped down in a chair. "Of course, the money he sends will stop if he doesn't see me," she added.

Aasia froze. "What?"

"The money," Iman repeated. The money that was the only

reason she still enjoyed Aasia's dubious hospitality.

"Fine. Go. And stay there for the night," Aasia directed. "I don't want to see you."

Iman squeezed her eyes shut. Taking a deep breath, she called a greeting behind her and slammed the front door.

The urge to go back inside and shriek until her mother finally apologized was overwhelming. But Iman knew it would be futile. In the twenty years Iman had been alive, Aasia's behaviour had not changed once.

Iman looked at the lovely three-storey house. At first glance, it looked like a dream house. But when you looked closer, the cracks began to show. Just like Aasia's little dream family, the facade wasn't good enough to hold up under scrutiny.

I need to get out of here. Fast.

-

There was blood on his sleeve. How long had that been there?

Revolted, Adam yanked his shirt over his head, tossing it to the floor and went in search of another.

A closer examination of himself in the mirror revealed that it had gotten onto the strap of his holster too. Scowling, Adam unbuckled that too, removing the gun and tossing it onto his bed on his way to the bathroom.

A quick shower later and Adam was ready to finish cleaning up. The shirt went in a pile to be burned and the holster was dunked in a bucket of peroxide, as usual.

The routine of the actions struck him and Adam's scowl returned. He was getting too used to being sloppy. Maybe it was time to take a break and brush up on his training, he mused.

There was a twinge of pain as he twisted and Adam looked down at the bandages circling his torso. It was definitely time for a break. Before he killed himself by accident rather than design.

CHAPTER ONE

Ibrahim Khan was, by all accounts, a horrible person. He'd killed many and ruined the lives of more. But for all his faults, he still adored his granddaughter. And though she loathed his lifestyle and the world he'd chosen for himself, Iman still adored him with the pure, enduring love of the little girl she'd once been.

He'd tried to keep her away from him, tried to distance himself when it became clear that his unsavoury lifestyle was starting to affect her. He'd failed royally. The little girl had held his heart in her chubby fist and the young woman she'd become still had possession of it. Even sending her away to her mother hadn't worked, not least because Aasia was a harpy who'd been more of a reluctant carrier than anything else to Iman.

Ibrahim could still remember the day they'd found out Aasia was pregnant and the tantrums that had been thrown as a result of the discovery. She'd consented to keep the baby only after days of arguments, bribery and even outright threats. But Aasia had never forgiven Iman for the crime of existing, nor for the indignities that her body had put her through during her pregnancy.

The little girl had been raised first by staff and then by Ibrahim himself once he'd realized just how starved for attention his beautiful grandchild was. She'd been a lovely child, quiet at first but adorably mischievous once she'd gotten comfortable. He'd let her get closer to him than any other living human being, even his own son.

And then he'd had to push her away. Ibrahim sighed heavily, remembering the day Iman had left. The tears had been atrocious. No matter how hard he'd tried to make her understand that she was being sent away for her own good, all Iman could see that yet another person was abandoning her.

He'd broken something that day. Even now, he could see that she was far from whole. She smiled and laughed and hid her pain, believing him fragile and unable to handle it. But Ibrahim knew his little girl. He saw the emotions she tried to hide, heard the false note in the lies she tried to live.

But what could he do? He had power in spades, more money than he could ever spend. But he couldn't buy safety. He couldn't command his granddaughter's happiness. The work of over half a century was worthless here.

Ibrahim buried his head in his hands, feeling every one of his seventy six years. He was in the same position when Iman burst in fifteen minutes later.

Her entrance made the door to his study bang hard against the wall and caused Ibrahim's head to snap up.

"What's wrong?" he demanded, jumping to his feet. Her face was ashen and she held herself as though braced for a hit. Protective fury welled within him. Who had hurt her? He would make them pay for every moment of sadness they'd caused his little girl.

Even as Ibrahim watched, Iman tried to regain control of

herself. "It's nothing," she hiccuped, reaching up to wipe at her eyes. "Just more of the usual."

The usual? Aasia. Her mother had done this.

"You're not going back there," Ibrahim found himself saying without conscious thought.

Iman's face lit up and common sense came rushing back, making him hurriedly qualify his statement. "Not tonight, at least."

"She wants me gone for the weekend," Iman mumbled. "Is that okay?"

Ibrahim's heart ached. "Of course it is. You're always welcome here."

Iman's mouth twitched. "Just not as anything more than a guest." Her voice wobbled and Ibrahim cursed silently, recognizing the 'about to cry' expression that hadn't changed since she was a toddler.

"I'm sorry," he said helplessly.

Iman sniffled. "I'm going to go unpack."

Ibrahim let her go, knowing that he couldn't comfort her. *He* was the one forcing her to stay away, after all. Or so she thought.

The truth was that Aasia Rahman had gotten used to the large sums of money she received whenever she demanded them in exchange for sheltering her daughter. Once, in a moment of weakness, Ibrahim *had* attempted to take Iman back. But he'd been met with an unyielding brick wall.

It appeared that not only had the harpy become accustomed to her regularly provided pound of flesh, she'd also discovered that while she begrudged Iman the girl's place in her home, she relished the ability to cause Ibrahim pain. And with a politician for a second husband – one who was ready to do her bidding no less, Aasia had all the cards.

Even if he wanted to, Ibrahim couldn't take Iman back without first waging war. And he didn't have it in him. Not any more. He was old, heartsick and decrepit. In no shape for even a little skirmish.

He had no way to help his little girl. Not any more.

-

Home. Finally. The tension drained from Iman's shoulders as she walked into her bedroom. Everything had been left exactly as she liked it, untouched besides what was necessary to keep the room clean and devoid of dust.

There was the jewellery box she hadn't dared to let come within breathing distance of her mother's greed. The fairy lights she'd adored as a little girl were still coiled neatly in a drawer, too old to work but too precious to be parted with. How many times had she fallen asleep with the end of those lights wrapped around her fist?

Iman smiled nostalgically, running a finger over them before turning her attention to the last treasure she'd kept safe and away from herself. An ornately carved box sat in pride of place next to her bed.

She lifted the lid carefully and reached inside with gentle fingers, pulling out the first of a thick stack of letters.

She'd long since memorized them, quite without meaning to. These letters had been her bedtime stories for months after she'd received them before eventually being put away and pulled back out only when she felt truly awful.

Iman unfolded the first letter and began to read the familiar words.

My dearest daughter...

-

As was the norm after she'd spent the night reading her father's letters, Iman woke with a pounding headache and a sense of melancholy she could not shake. Her grandfather eyed her knowingly over breakfast, by now familiar with the signs.

Iman knew that he was itching to say something, and knew just as well that he wouldn't. She sighed in frustration and played with her eggs. She couldn't understand what had happened to her beloved grandfather. One day everything had been fine in Iman's little world and the next, Ibrahim seemed to have retreated behind a wall. It was then that things had begun to go wrong for Iman.

She'd lost the closest thing to a parent that she knew and then had had her family and home taken from her as well.

It would have been easier, she reflected, if she could understand *why*. Or if she could bring herself to hate Ibrahim for his actions. But it wasn't that simple. For all that he'd broken her heart, he'd been there for her for so long. Iman loved tenaciously and even she couldn't make her heart detach itself from the old man.

And so here they sat across one another at a table, eating in complete silence where only a few short years ago she would have long since moved herself next to him and been chattering away nineteen to the dozen about anything that came into her head.

"Is something wrong with the eggs, sweetheart?" Iman looked up in shock at the familiar, beloved voice.

A tall brunette in her thirties was looking at Iman with open concern in her brown eyes. Iman jumped to her feet and tackled the new arrival. Her eyes widened as she threw herself against Shaida and made an interesting discovery. Almost immediately, she pulled back and placed her hands on Shaida's middle. "You're having a baby?" she squealed with delight.

Shaida laughed. "Yes, you'll finally have the little playmate you always nagged me for."

Iman blushed at the reminder. Shaida had been nineteen and Iman seven when they'd met and she'd regularly begged Shaida to get married and have a baby so that she, Iman, would have a baby to play with.

"That's not quite what I had in mind when I was seven," she teased lightly. "But I'll take it."

Shaida reached out and patted her cheek. "There," she said with satisfaction. "Now there's some colour in your cheeks and you look less like a ghost."

Iman leaned into the touch happily, soaking up the now-rare affection. "I missed you," she whispered miserably.

Shaida sobered. "I know, sweetheart. We miss you too."

There was the sound of a throat clearing behind them and Shaida pulled away as though she'd been burned. "I have to go," she said regretfully, glancing at Ibrahim out of the corner of her eye. "I love you, sweetheart."

Iman retook her seat and bent her head, trying to control her anger. Exploding wouldn't help anything, she reminded herself. She'd lost count of how many times she'd done it before and it had never done anything besides make everyone miserable.

"Iman?"

She focused on her breathing. *Calm down. Don't spoil things. Stay calm.*

"Iman? Look at me, please."

"Iman!"

"What?" she snapped.

Ibrahim drew back, startled. "I'm sorry you're upset," he said softly.

"But not for doing what you've done," Iman pointed out, in no mood to accept hollow apologies.

"No," Ibrahim agreed. "I'm not sorry for that."

Iman pushed herself away from the table. "Excuse me," she muttered. "I don't have an appetite any more."

"Iman..." Ibrahim sounded pained. "I'm sorry it has to be this way."

Iman pressed a hand over her eyes. Her temples throbbed and her jaw ached from the force with which she was gritting her teeth. "It doesn't," she hissed. "It doesn't have to be this way! Why can't you just..."

Her grandfather's defeated expression told her all she needed to know and Iman swiped at her eyes, furiously trying to regain her composure. "Never mind," she said wearily, suddenly exhausted. "It doesn't even matter. You made up your mind and you're not gonna change it. No matter how hard I try." *'Or how hard I cry,'* she thought to herself bitterly as she walked out of the dining room.

-

Still sat in front of his breakfast, Ibrahim tossed down his utensils and buried his head in his hands. His heart ached for

10

Iman and he longed to go and comfort his sweet girl but he knew she wouldn't accept it. In her eyes, he could fix everything if he really wanted to.

She'd never grown out of the childish certainty that her grandfather was a superhero who could fix any one of her problems, small or big, if only she asked nicely enough.

But this one problem which hurt her more than any other was one of the few even the great Ibrahim Khan could not fix. Worse still, this problem had come about entirely due to his own actions.

She was right to be furious with him. He'd taken away her home and forbade any of the people she'd come to regard as family from contacting her. There had been no other way to ensure her safety. At the time, he'd thought he was doing what was best.

But now, as he compared the Iman he'd caught a glimpse of when she'd been laughing with Shaida to the Iman who walked around like a little ghost, now he wasn't so sure.

He still didn't know how he was going to get Iman out from Aasia's clutches, or how he was going to keep her safe. But at the very least, Ibrahim decided, he needed to explain everything to his granddaughter. She needed to know that he hadn't wanted to send her away.

Ibrahim made his way slowly up the stairs to Iman's bedroom and knocked lightly on the blue door. "Iman? May I come in?"

There was no answer but he heard a few muffled sniffs. Ibrahim sighed and turned away. He'd talk to her later.

-

Iman didn't remember her father. He'd been gone before she'd taken her first steps and all she had of him were what she'd been able to piece together between remarks from people who'd known him and the letters he'd written her.

Faizal Khan had been a quiet, logical man and he'd seen no point in hiding from the inevitable when five separate specialists had informed him of his impending death. Instead, he'd used the little time he'd had remaining on the Earth to set his affairs in order and make sure his infant daughter would have something of him, some small token that attempted to fill the hole his absence would leave.

There were over two hundred letters in the gorgeous chest – Faizal had written her at least one a day from the day he'd gotten his diagnosis almost to the day he'd died, right until the strength had faded from his hands and he'd no longer been able to hold a pen.

Despite herself, Iman wondered where she'd be if he hadn't died. The man who'd written to her daily for over six months would surely have loved her, even a little. Such dedication could not be anything but the result of love. But would love have been enough?

Faizal Khan had left her before she'd been capable of truly feeling the wound of it. But he'd had no choice. Would he still have left had his fate been in his own hands? Or would he have kept her close?

Iman didn't know. When she was younger, she'd adored her grandfather even more for never having left her. She'd felt secure in the knowledge that he was the only person in the world who'd never leave, the one man who loved her too much to even think about it.

And yet he had. Or rather, he'd made Iman leave, abandoning her to the clutches of her mother.

Thinking about Aasia made Iman's temples throb. There were

times when she hated the woman who'd borne her so fiercely it was an effort to keep the vilest curses behind her teeth.

Aasia had never been a mother to her, not truly. Iman had always known that her mother hated her, for Aasia had never bothered to hide it. She'd always made it perfectly clear that Iman had been an unfortunate accident, a mistake that had never been rectified only because Faizal had threatened to divorce her and Ibrahim had offered enough of a bribe to make her go through with the pregnancy.

And tomorrow, Iman would be forced to go back to the house that felt more like a hotel than any kind of home at all.

-

Hours later, Iman woke with a start. She looked around, trying to ascertain what had woken her so suddenly.

"Iman?" her grandfather called through the door. "Are you coming down for lunch?"

Lunch. The thought of food made Iman's stomach growl angrily. "I'll be there in a few minutes," she decided, making a beeline for the bathroom to wake herself up a bit more.

Ibrahim was still standing in the hallway when she pulled open the door five minutes later.

He smiled tentatively at her and a thread of guilt closed Iman's throat when she noticed his drawn features. Her grandfather looked frailer every time she saw him.

Impulsively, she crossed the distance between them and hugged him close, smiling despite herself at the familiar scent that always took her back to sleepy naps and afternoons sat in an office, colouring away happily while her living chair busied himself with boring black and white papers.

Iman pulled back with an only half-faked scowl and narrowed her eyes at her grandfather. "You've been smoking again," she accused. She'd smelled it on his clothes.

Ibrahim feigned outrage. "Of course not! I quit smoking years ago."

Iman folded her arms across her chest. "I can smell the smoke," she said flatly.

"Ah," Ibrahim winced. "Today *was* very stressful."

"You promised." He had promised. Years ago. Iman had cried incessantly and refused to eat for three days until her beloved grandfather had promised her he would stop smoking 'cancer-sticks'.

The teacher who'd decided to explain the dangers of smoking to Iman's class had received an earful from Ibrahim but he'd been helpless when faced with Iman's genuine fear that he would die and every ashtray, cigarette and pipe had disappeared from the house immediately.

The memory made Iman's eyes shine and Ibrahim's face grew alarmed. "It was just one little cigarette," he assured her. "I'm not going to die from it!"

"I know," Iman blinked furiously to clear her eyes. She tried to find words to explain her sadness and faltered, shaking her head wordlessly.

Ibrahim sighed and reached into the inside pocket of his jacket. "Here." He handed over a box of cigarettes. "Better now?"

Iman nodded silently.

Twenty minutes later, Iman was almost done demolishing her pasta and her grandfather was still eyeing her cautiously.

Surely he didn't think she was still upset about his smoking?

Before she could ask, and reassure him, Ibrahim spoke. "Are you done eating? I'd like to talk to you about something."

Iman looked down at her plate. There were roughly two bites of pasta left on it and she quickly loaded up her fork, stuffing the lot in her mouth.

"Don't choke," Ibrahim cautioned automatically. "And chew properly!"

"What do you want to talk about?"

Ibrahim sighed. "I know you're unhappy," he started. "I know that you're angry with me."

Iman opened her mouth to deny it, shame colouring her cheeks. But her grandfather held up a hand.

"It's alright," he told her gently. "I understand."

"I just don't understand why," Iman said helplessly. "You never even told me what I'd done! You just – you just made me leave."

"You didn't do anything wrong."

Iman shook her head, disbelieving. "Then why did you make me leave?"

"I had to," her grandfather said simply. "It was the only way to keep you alive."

CHAPTER TWO

Iman's eyes widened. "What?!" she gasped, reeling.

"There are certain... codes that we follow," Ibrahim explained. "As a child, they protected you from being used against me. But as you grew, that protection began to evaporate. I had no choice but to distance myself if I wanted to keep my enemies from using you against me."

"Why didn't you tell me?" was all Iman could think to ask.

Ibrahim pinched the bridge of his nose, looking pained. "I didn't want to scare you." He met Iman's eyes. "I'm so sorry."

Iman looked away, swallowing hard. "You should have told me."

Her grandfather nodded. "Yes, I should have. I should have told you a lot of things. Will you let me tell them to you now?"

A small, petty part of Iman wanted to get to her feet and refuse. The sting from the numerous times her grandfather had refused to listen to her still lingered and she was tempted to let him feel the way she had whenever he'd denied her the chance to speak.

She fought down the urge and gave a jerky nod. "Tell me."

He did. Ibrahim told her everything. Every sordid little detail, including many that she wished he'd kept to himself.

"So there's no way out?" Iman asked once he'd finally finished, reading the answer in her grandfather's slumped shoulders.

"I haven't found one," he admitted reluctantly. "But," he added when Iman's face fell, "that doesn't mean that there isn't one. We just need to keep looking."

"Right," Iman didn't bother to hide her doubt. "The thirty fourth time's the charm."

"It may well be," Ibrahim insisted. "You've spent time with your mother recently, you'll know far more about her current weak spots than I do."

Iman shrugged her shoulders. Aasia Rahman's weak spot was the same as it had always been – vanity. She said as much and Ibrahim nodded, frowning thoughtfully.

"It would be easy enough for you to leave by yourself – you're not a minor any more. But I cannot let you live on your own, Iman. It's far too dangerous and I don't have the people to spare to keep a proper watch on you."

Iman scowled as pieces of a puzzle fit into place. "You sabotaged my job interviews!" she cried, outraged.

"I couldn't let you find a way to leave."

"All this time, I just thought I was incompetent," Iman muttered, shaking her head. "But I'm not."

"Of course you're not," Ibrahim's eyes narrowed. "Who told you such a thing?"

"It doesn't matter."

Ibrahim reached for her hand, rubbing it soothingly. "Of course it does."

Iman pulled her hand away. "I don't understand why my mother won't let me leave," she said miserably. "She's never happy when I'm around."

"Your mother is a very... vindictive woman," Ibrahim explained. "The chance to make me miserable is too good to pass up."

"And me," Iman whispered. "She gets to make me miserable too."

Iman knew that more than the money Ibrahim paid her, more than anything else, was what motivated Aasia to keep her around.

-

Back to the dragon's den, Iman thought grumpily as she parked her car. Despite sitting together and brainstorming for the better part of two days, neither she nor her grandfather had managed to come up with any kind of plan and returning to her mother's home had felt an awful lot like giving up.

She sat there in her car until her thighs went numb, dreading the moment she'd have to go inside and deal with Aasia. Maybe she could just sleep in the car. She'd be inside the gates and within the guard patrol's perimeter...

Before she could further consider the wild idea, there was a screech that made her jump and drove all thoughts of sleeping out of her mind.

"What are you doing sitting there?" Aasia demanded, her manicured nails tapping on the glass. "Are you mentally sub-normal? Get out and go to your room!"

She yanked on the door handle hard. It didn't open. "Hurry

up!" Aasia snapped.

Iman nodded dumbly, waiting for her mother to move out of the way.

Aasia just looked at her. "What are you waiting for?"

"You're in the way," Iman said simply, motioning to indicate that Aasia needed to move back.

"Open the door! Stupid girl." Aasia tugged on the handle again ineffectively.

Iman's eyes narrowed. She *hated* being called stupid. Well, Aasia had asked her to open the door. So open it, Iman would.

She pulled on the handle, letting Aasia's tugging do the rest of the work. There was a high-pitched squeal and her mother wobbled, her arms wind-milling as she tried to regain her balance.

"You did that on purpose!" the blonde shrieked.

"You were in the way," Iman repeated, grabbing her backpack from the back seat.

Long nails closed around her arm, biting deep and Iman winced.

"My friends are coming over," Aasia told her in a sugary sweet voice. "And I don't want to have to deal with the shame of having to admit to who you are. So just stay upstairs and don't come down until they're gone."

"What if I need something?" Iman knew it was stupid to rile Aasia in this mood. But she couldn't help it.

Aasia's beautiful grey eyes had hardened into chips of ice. "Don't," she hissed. "Don't you dare come down those stairs unless you want me to start locking you in your room."

She squeezed Iman's arm harder for a moment, digging deep enough to draw blood.

Despite herself, Iman winced. "I'll stay upstairs," she promised.

"Good," Aasia hissed, unceremoniously shoving her away.

Up in her bedroom, with the door locked on the inside, Iman dropped her duffel bag to the floor and retrieved her first aid kit from the bottom drawer of her closet.

She cleaned the scrapes on her arms with practised hands, eyeing the surprisingly deep little marks with pursed lips. Another set to add to her already large collection, Iman thought with a sigh.

-

"IMAN! Get down here right now!" The enraged shriek seemed to bounce off the walls.

Iman looked up from the book in her lap, marking her place quickly before laying it down with the rest under her bed.

"Yes?" she asked, pausing at the top of the stairs. "What is it?"

"Come here," her mother demanded, pointing to the floor directly in front of her.

"Did you want something?" Iman asked innocently as she walked down. She came to a stop, carefully keeping herself out of Aasia's range.

"Come *here*," Aasia said again.

Iman inched closer, wondering how far she could push her luck.

Not far enough, it seemed.

Aasia's hand shot out and she grabbed the ends of Iman's long hair, yanking hard. Iman stumbled forward, fetching up right against her. "I told you to *come here!*" Aasia shouted, her pretty face flushing crimson.

"Let go!" Iman cried, tears of pain springing to her eyes.

Aasia yanked harder. "Why don't you *listen?*"

Iman gasped, reaching up to try and ease the pressure. It felt like her hair was about to be torn from the roots. "I'm sorry," she gasped. "I'm sorry! Please let go."

"There," Aasia cooed. "Was that so hard?" Several strands of light brown hair remained in her grasp even after Iman had pulled away.

"What did you call me for?" Iman asked, fighting to keep her voice level.

"My friends were here," Aasia reminded her daughter. "They came with lovely news. One of them has a new grandchild. The other one is due to set off on a trip to travel three different continents in two weeks once her youngest gets married."

She paused expectantly, lifting a perfectly plucked eyebrow.

"That's... nice," Iman said hesitantly.

"Yes," Aasia agreed poisonously. "It *is* nice. But do you know what isn't nice?"

Iman felt a sense of foreboding. "What?" she whispered.

"*My* life. My daughter isn't getting married or having a baby. All *you* are doing is sitting in your bedroom and weighing me down like the world's ugliest milestone. Well, it stops now!"

Iman's eyes widened. Was Aasia about to throw her out. Hurriedly, she put a hand over her mouth, trying to conceal the smile that was creeping over her face.

She needn't have bothered. Aasia's next words wiped it clean from her face.

"It's time you got married," her mother announced.

"What?!"

"Don't you dare raise your voice at me!" Aasia snapped. "I said it's time you got married and clearly, it is. How rude can you be?"

"But... to who? I'm not dating anyone."

"Don't you worry about that. *I* will pick your husband. It'll be fun," Aasia smirked. "I know exactly what you need." She patted Iman's cheek reassuringly and Iman had to work to keep herself from flinching away from those long nails.

"I'll take care of everything." Aasia grinned unpleasantly. "Just you wait."

-

Married. To a man of Aasia's choosing. Iman's legs felt weak. She didn't know how she'd gotten back up to the bedroom. She vaguely remembered stuttering something faint to Aasia but she had no idea how she'd come to be sitting on the floor of her shower with the water pouring over her head.

The water in her en-suite was set to her favourite temperature but for some reason today it wasn't heating up properly. She could see the steam in the air but it was still too cold. Impatiently, she turned it up as hot as it could go and settled in, leaning her cheek against the cold tile.

It still wasn't hot enough. Eventually, she gave up, shutting off the taps and reaching for her towel to cocoon her dripping hair within it. Vaguely, she became aware of a stinging sensation on her back.

What had she done?

Looking in the mirror made her gasp. The skin from her neck to hips was cherry red. Had the water really been that hot? But she hadn't felt it at all...

She reached behind herself, carefully touching the skin and winced at the sharp pain. She'd burned herself... In the shower?

Her back began to throb in earnest and Iman winced, making a beeline for the painkillers in her first aid kit. Checking the supply made her wince again. She was running low. She'd need to be more careful about how she used them until she could get more.

She swallowed two of the pills, bending over the sink for water to wash them down.

As always, a wave of tiredness hit her and she had just enough time to shrug on the softest clothing she had – an old dressing gown long since beaten into submission by the washing machine.

Hours later, she woke when the door to her bedroom creaked open. Her stepfather stood in the doorway, an odd expression on his face.

Iman sat up, suddenly very aware that her gown had slipped off one shoulder. She pulled it back into place quickly, belting the gown firmly around herself.

"Did you need something?" she asked wearily.

He smiled widely and a shiver ran down Iman's spine. She slid a hand underneath the sheets, groping in the space between her mattress and the bed frame for the knife she'd stashed there months ago.

"I just wanted to check if you were alright," her stepfather said in a casual voice, coming into the bedroom. He shut the door behind him with a click.

Iman squeezed the knife. "I'm fine," she squeaked.

"Are you sure?" He came closer and leaned over her in the bed, making to sit down.

"Yeah," Iman insisted, throwing the covers back. "But I really need to use the bathroom."

She darted into her en suite and slammed the door shut behind herself, breathing hard. Groping blindly, she locked the door, wincing at the loud click it made.

She didn't know how long he stayed in her room waiting, but eventually, she heard the creak of her door shutting behind him from where she stood with her ear pressed against the door.

Quietly, she crept back out. She stayed awake the rest of the night, despite the locked door and the knife that had made its way to a new home underneath her pillow.

CHAPTER THREE

"I can't *take* this any longer! *When* will we find her a husband?" Aasia sank down onto a conveniently placed chair.

Her husband patted her shoulder sympathetically. "It is getting quite tiresome. Perhaps Iman is just not ready for marriage?" He eyed the girl in question speculatively and Iman had to fight the urge to gag.

"Of course she's ready! She's twenty two, for God's sake!"

Iman was twenty but she knew pointing this out would make no difference. "Maybe you're not looking in the right place?" she suggested, trying to seem helpful.

Aasia frowned at her in confusion. "Where else should we look? I've spoken to my friends and your father has spoken to his colleagues. There's no one else."

Step father, Iman corrected silently. "I don't know," she admitted. "But my grandfather might."

"Your... grandfather?" Aasia made a face like she'd just bitten into a piece of rotten fruit.

"He does know a lot of people," Iman pointed out, trying to seem off-hand. "I could ask him?"

"Alright," her mother agreed slowly. "You might as well. I doubt he'll find a suitable candidate though. The people *he* associates with are far beneath us."

"Thank God for that," Iman muttered.

"What was that?" Aasia asked sharply.

"Nothing. I'll go call him."

Iman was halfway up the stairs when Aasia called her back. "Go and stay there," the woman instructed. "I don't want you around, you've caused me enough stress these past few weeks."

Iman hid a smile. "I'm very sorry," she said humbly. "How long will it take you to recover?"

"A week," Aasia decided.

"A *week*?" Iman repeated gleefully.

"Actually, make it three days," Aasia corrected.

She'd been too excited, Iman realized. "Thank you so much for not making it longer," she gushed, trying to rectify the situation.

She packed for a week, hoping that her ploy had worked. Sure enough, as she was lifting her suitcase into the trunk, Aasia came tottering down the driveway on her heels.

"I changed my mind!" the woman called, a vindictive gleam in her eyes. "Stay for a week."

Iman nodded submissively, waiting until she'd gotten into the car – and driven a good five minutes for good measure – to let her glee show. A week! Seven whole days where she wouldn't have to watch what she said or listen to an endlessly long list of her faults.

A week of freedom. And, if they plotted well enough, that week would soon turn into months.

-

"I want to get married," Iman announced to her grandfather that night over supper.

Ibrahim choked on his mouthful of coffee and began to cough. "You want to *what*?" he asked incredulously.

Iman handed over a glass of water. "I want to get married," she repeated calmly.

"You will get married," Ibrahim assured her, beginning to calm down. "In five or ten years, we'll find you a lovely boy to settle down and make my great grandchildren with."

Iman rolled her eyes. "I want to get married now," she clarified.

"No," her grandfather said simply.

"What? Why not?"

"Never mind why not, I said no. That's it."

"But-" Iman began.

"No buts." Ibrahim put down his cup. "Now, let's change the subject, hmm?"

"No," Iman insisted stubbornly. "This is a good idea. Will you just listen?"

"A good idea?" Ibrahim repeated. "What do you mean a good idea? Marriage isn't an idea, it's a life choice. You see, you don't even know what it's about. You're far too young for these kinds of things."

Iman huffed. "I know that. I meant, it's a good idea to get me away from my mother."

Her grandfather stared at her, speechless.

"It is!"

"It's a *terrible* idea and I won't allow it!"

"Then she'll just marry me off to someone she wants!" Iman snapped, fed up. She crossed her arms over her chest irritably and glared at the table.

"What do you mean?"

Iman sighed. "She's been trying to find me a husband for the past three weeks. I've already met twelve different guys. And they're all terrible! I've been trying to drive them off but they take one look at me – and my step father's bank balance – and they're already halfway to proposing! It's getting harder and harder to find a way to repulse them."

"Why didn't you tell me as soon as this started, Iman?"

"You know my mother reviews the camera footage. I didn't want her to stop me from coming to see you." Iman tucked a strand of hair behind her ear. "I just thought that if I got married, it might make things better. And if you helped me find someone, I could make sure I wasn't trading one set of chains for another."

"Surely it isn't that bad?" Ibrahim asked worriedly, reaching out to cup her cheek.

"It is sometimes." Iman looked at the floor, unable to bear seeing the heartbroken look on her grandfather's face. "I'm sorry, I shouldn't have told you."

"You should have told me a long time ago," Ibrahim corrected in a thick voice. "You were trying to spare my feelings, weren't you?"

Iman nodded. "So, do you agree with me?" she asked hopefully.

"I need to think about it," was the non-committal answer.

Iman's face fell and Ibrahim reached out to poke her cheek. "I didn't say no," he reminded her gently.

"You didn't say yes either."

Ibrahim nodded, getting to his feet. "It's a complicated situation, sweetheart. I won't say yes or no until I've thought about all the possibilities. You should know that."

Iman did know that. Her grandfather had always been the type to analyse every situation to death before making a single move.

"Could you hurry?" she asked impishly, copying the response she'd always given to explanations of this sort when she'd been little.

Ibrahim laughed, recognizing the line. "Of course," he agreed, putting an arm around her. "You're here for a week, right?"

Iman nodded happily.

"Well, you'll have an answer by the end of the week then, alright? Now, let's talk about something else."

They spent the rest of the evening trying and failing to discuss the book Iman had just finished reading. Eventually, Iman gave up and made her excuses, resigning herself to an early night spent worrying about her future.

-

She wanted to get married. His twenty year old granddaughter wanted to get married. It was absurd! She was barely more than a child, for pity's sake. Marriage at her age...

Ibrahim conveniently overlooked the fact that his wife had been nineteen on their wedding day. Iman was too young. She wasn't ready. *He* wasn't ready.

They would find another way.

Six days of frantic searching later, Ibrahim had run out of time. But he refused to admit defeat.

His granddaughter watched him with an indulgent look on her face, waiting for him to bring forth yet another outlandish plan that she'd patiently shred to pieces.

He didn't have one.

Iman's eyes glittered with triumph and Ibrahim tried a last-ditch attempt to make her see sense. "Iman, this is foolish," he began patiently.

"I know!" she shouted.

Ibrahim jerked in surprise at the unexpected noise.

"I know," she repeated softly. "I know it's foolish."

"Then why do you persist in doing it?" Ibrahim snapped, his own temper beginning to fray.

"Because there's no other choice!" Iman cried, springing to her feet. "I don't have any other choices."

"Yes, you do." Why didn't she see it? Ibrahim huffed out an exasperated breath. "Sit down."

Iman ignored him. "What choices?" she challenged.

"Patience," Ibrahim suggested. If she could just wait a little longer...

Iman looked disappointed. "That's not a choice," she whispered. "Not any more. Why don't you see that?"

"Why? Why are you in such a rush?"

"Because I want at least a little bit of a choice!" Tears began to spill down Iman's cheeks.

"What?" Ibrahim reached out a hand and tugged her down to sit with him, the way she had when she'd been little.

"That doesn't make any sense, Iman."

She sniffed hard and turned away from him. Ibrahim began to rub her back, falling back into the familiar routine. "Explain it to me," he offered, trying to calm her.

Iman sent a watery glare up at him. "You're pandering to me."

"No," Ibrahim denied. He wasn't *pandering*. He was distracting.

Iman frowned at him for a few moments longer before visibly giving in. "I told you," she whispered at her lap, so softly that Ibrahim had to strain to hear her. "My mother is trying to get me married."

"Yes," Ibrahim agreed. "You also told me that you've made sure nothing could go ahead."

Iman nodded. "It's getting harder." She shuddered, "Some of them, they way they *look* at me. It's disgusting."

Ibrahim tightened his arms around her protectively. "Have you told your mother?"

Iman laughed mirthlessly. "It doesn't matter to her. She told me I should be flattered."

"I'm sorry that it's been hard, sweetheart. But it will die down soon enough."

Iman pulled away. "No, it won't," she said miserably. "She'll keep trying until she finds someone who doesn't care."

"Then you'll need to say no." Ibrahim fixed his granddaughter with a serious look. "I know your mother is hard to live with but you just need to be firm with her."

Iman looked incredulously at him. "What?"

"I know it's hard but you need to stand up to her. Shying away and letting her walk all over you is not going to help things," Ibrahim lectured.

Iman yanked out of his hold, backing away until she hit the wall. "You – how could you say something like that?"

Dread washed over him. He'd seen reactions like this in the past. "Iman," he said, fighting to keep his voice level. "What did she do to you?"

Some of the betrayal faded from his granddaughter's expression. "You know what she's done. You're the one who made her stop when I was little."

Ibrahim's veins filled with ice. The day he'd discovered Aasia slapping her tiny daughter was still one of the worst of his life. "When you were little?" he repeated tightly.

Iman nodded silently.

"But not now." What hell had he sent his little girl into?

Iman shook her head. "You didn't know? I thought... I mean, not the worst of it, I knew you wouldn't let her do anything that awful to me... But you really didn't know about any of it?"

"Of course not." Ibrahim reached out for his granddaughter before thinking better of it and dropping his hand.

"Oh," Iman whispered. "I-" Her face crumpled.

Ibrahim stood and crossed the distance between them, stopping just short of actually hugging Iman. "If I had known," he told her, his voice thick with emotion. "I would have done whatever I had to do to get you back. I am so sorry."

Iman laid her head against his chest. "I should have told you," she said dully. "I didn't think it would make any difference but I should have done it anyway."

Ibrahim flinched like he'd been struck. Iman looked up at him contritely. "I'm sorry."

"I am sorry. I should have seen it." He'd always prided himself on his perceptiveness. It had aided him for decades, being able to see people's secrets. But this one secret, more important than all the rest combined... This secret had evaded him.

Iman yawned unexpectedly, belatedly bringing her hand up to cover her mouth and Ibrahim was shaken out of his miserable thoughts. "You need a nap," he told Iman, the sight of her blinking and rubbing at her eyes with the sleeves of her sweater almost too precious to bear.

How was he going to help his little girl? He knew now that he needed to get her out immediately. But who could he trust with her?

Iman tilted her head at him curiously. "Are you plotting to murder my parents?" she asked lightly.

"I hadn't even thought about it," Ibrahim admitted. Surely she didn't want him to? Iman had always been so soft-hearted...

But abuse victims – and even thinking it about his granddaughter made his heart ache – often abandoned their morals when it came to their abusers. And understandably so.

Iman's eyes widened at the question. "I-"

Ibrahim was about to assure her that she didn't need to answer him immediately when she spoke again.

"No," she said firmly. "I don't want you to kill them."

Just like his son, Ibrahim thought fondly. Stronger than he ever could be. "If you change your mind," he reminded her.

Iman nodded slowly, a little smile beginning to tug at her lips. "You'll take care of it for me," she finished.

And he would, if she asked.

CHAPTER FOUR

The name Ibrahim Khan struck fear into the hearts of many. He was ruthless and terrifying and the people he'd surrounded himself with were equally so. Adam had been warned more than once to steer clear of Khan and his mercurial moods and at first, he'd bought in to the rumours and hysteria.

But a year ago, that had changed. Adam had finally come face to face with Khan, in the most undignified way possible.

He'd been sleep-deprived and ill, in no condition to be doing anything but curling up in a ball and waiting the sickness out. But he'd been arrogant and stubborn and had chosen to work instead.

It should have cost him his life. If not for Ibrahim Khan, it would have.

And now, it seemed the debt he owed was being called due. The summons had come this morning in the form of a letter that had been pushed under his door. He'd opened it to find a single sheet of thick cream paper, more suited to a wedding invitation than a message from a killer.

The message had been short and to the point. His presence

was requested by Mr. Ibrahim Khan to discuss the repayment of a favour. He hadn't recognized the address printed below but a quick search had provided the directions he needed.

There had been no time on the letter but Adam had a feeling that if he delayed much longer, the two strange guys who'd been standing outside his apartment all day would be attempting to physically fetch him for their master.

No point in overcomplicating things for himself, Adam thought with a mental shrug. The rules were clear – he owed Ibrahim Khan his life. Erasing that debt took precedent over absolutely everything. Even delaying in answering Khan's summons too long would give the man a justifiable reason to have Adam's throat slit.

There might be some grumbling about overreactions but no one would truly object. So if Adam wanted to keep breathing for the foreseeable future, he would get off his butt, get the name of his new target and get the job done – fast.

But first, he had to get ready. There was a duffel bag in the trunk of his car with everything he needed for a short trip – two passports, clothing, ammunition and a decent amount of cash. All he really needed to do was leave a message that he'd be gone and make sure that the Will he'd had drawn up years ago was put in its usual place while he was gone – dead centre on an empty desk in his office.

Fifteen minutes later, Adam was ready to go. He'd cleaned up automatically on his way out, his mother's voice echoing in his ears. *Never leave your house in a state! Just imagine how embarrassing it would be to have people know you lived in filth if you ended up dying while you were out?*

She'd told him that at least once a week until he'd stopped living with her. Somehow she'd never appreciated him pointing out that dead people weren't likely to feel embarrassment.

Even now, years after he'd moved out, he still cleaned before he headed out on a job. He was half-convinced that if he did end up dying and leaving a dirty home behind, she'd come to the after-life just to scold him.

She'd probably kill him herself if she knew that he'd landed himself in enough danger to be paying back a debt like this, never mind that she was about half his size.

Adam shuddered just imagining it. With a little luck, he'd finish this job quickly and his tiny mother would remain none the wiser about how careless he'd been getting.

Later, as he sat in Ibrahim Khan's library, he'd wonder if he'd somehow jinxed himself with this thought.

–

"I want you to marry my granddaughter," Ibrahim Khan announced matter-of-factly, once Adam had settled into a chair across from him.

Adam choked on the mouthful of water he'd just drank. "I'm sorry, what?" he croaked, in between coughs.

"You heard me," Khan said calmly. "I'm calling in the debt you owe me. I've decided that you will do well for my granddaughter, if she approves of you."

Adam laughed uneasily. "This is a joke, right?"

Khan didn't smile. "No," he said shortly. "It is not."

He'd lost it. Ibrahim Khan had gone senile. It was actually quite a shame, Adam thought, slightly hysterical. By all accounts, the man had had a brilliant mind before he'd gone and lost it all.

Did debts still count if they were owed to insane people? Adam didn't know.

"I am not insane."

Adam's head jerked up. How?

"You're very easy to read." Khan said, answering his unasked question. "I am not insane, just practical. My granddaughter would like to get married and I find you acceptable."

"But... that's not how it works." Adam blurted out.

Khan tilted his head. "I beg your pardon?"

"I owe you a life. You're meant to ask me to kill someone." He felt foolish, explaining such a fundamental concept to a man who'd known it longer than he'd been born.

"I can ask you to kill yourself instead," Khan offered pleasantly.

Adam's mouth went dry. He swallowed hard, trying to calm his suddenly racing pulse.

"You owe me *your* life," Khan reminded him. "I can ask you to do whatever I'd like and you're bound to fulfil the request."

"But... why?" was all Adam could think to ask. "Why can't she just find herself a husband the normal way?"

"That is unimportant. As for why I chose you... I have a large number of enemies. My granddaughter's husband will need to be a man who is capable of keeping her safe from those enemies *and* indebted to me enough that he will never even think of betraying either her or myself. You fulfil my requirements."

"I don't have any choice, do I?" Adam said slowly.

Khan shook his head. "None. If you decline, you've broken the most important rule of our business."

"And the penalty for that is death," Adam finished unnecessarily. He closed his eyes for a moment, taking in a deep breath. "So, when do I get to meet her?"

"I'm so glad you've decided to be co-operative."

Adam scowled. "Death threats tend to make people compliant."

Khan's eyes flashed and he got to his feet. "Wait here," Adam was instructed.

Adam had been alone for barely a minute when he heard the creak of a door. But there was something strange – it hadn't come from behind him but rather to his left. Movement out of the corner of his eye told him where to look a split second before she entered.

At first glance, Adam thought he was looking at a child. She was tiny, with long blonde hair that was more commonly seen on the head of a toddler than that of a grown woman. The only clue to her actual age was the chest she was currently half-hiding with a stack of books.

She stopped short at the sight of him, her cheeks turning a pale pink. "Oh, sorry. I didn't realize anyone was in here." She gave him a curious once-over. "I don't recognize you, are you new?"

"Very. I've never been here before."

The girl's eyes gleamed in recognition. "Oh, you're the lunch meeting!"

Adam nodded. "That's right."

"What are you here for?" she asked curiously.

"The spoilt princess has demanded a new toy and I'm what her grandfather has decided to give her." Even as he said it, Adam knew he was being unfair. For all he knew, Khan's granddaughter was as unwilling a participant in this farce as he himself was.

"I see." The girl clutched her books tighter to her chest.

"What do you do here?" Adam asked. Surely she wasn't a mercenary too. They generally didn't look adorable or dress in pastels and lug story books around.

"I play at being a princess," she said in a voice sweet as syrup.

Adam's eyes widened. This was Khan's granddaughter? He thought of the big man with his tanned skin and brown eyes. They couldn't look more different if they tried!

Then what he'd said came back to him and he cringed. "Uh..." he started. "Look, I didn't mean..."

She held up a dainty hand. "Don't worry about it. The opinions of toys don't particularly faze me."

Adam winced. He'd deserved that. Before he could try to apologize again, she'd left.

Was it even worth it to try and leave? He had no weapons on him and he was under no illusions about the fact that he'd just signed his own death warrant. No doubt the girl – Iman – was on her way to her grandfather right now, demanding his head.

Stupid!

He really should have just kept his mouth shut.

-

He'd called her a spoilt princess! This was the man her grandfather was sure she'd want to marry?

Iman was so distracted she almost walked straight into Ibrahim.

"Oh, there you are," he said with a smile. "Come with me," Ibrahim held out a hand. "You can meet Adam while he's still here."

Iman shook her head immediately. "I've already met him."

"Oh, good." Ibrahim led her to the window seat. "What did you think?"

Iman shrugged her shoulders as she sat. She'd thought he was gorgeous – until he opened his mouth. "He's attractive. Actually, he's prettier than I am."

Ibrahim wrinkled his nose. "I've changed my mind, you can marry Waseem."

Iman giggled. "Waseem changed my diapers," she reminded her grandfather.

"Yes, exactly," he agreed with a nod. "He's like an uncle to you."

"Don't you want grandchildren?"

"Not for several more years," Ibrahim said decisively. "Are you sure you don't want to say anything more to Adam? The two of you could only have spoken for a few moments."

Iman shook her head. "I'm sure."

"Alright. Wait here, I'll be back now."

"What are you going to tell him?"

"That we'll give him your decision when you're ready." Ibrahim said simply.

It seemed a bit unfair to make the man wait. But he *had* called her spoilt. Maybe it wasn't so bad to make him sweat for a few days before letting him off the hook.

-

Two days later, Iman was glad that she hadn't rejected Adam on the spot. The rude young man was looking better and better compared to the men her grandfather had been introducing her to. He'd been the only one who hadn't talked directly to her chest, for God's sake!

Iman sighed wearily, pulling off the stilettos she'd worn to give herself a little more height. "Who's next?" she asked Waseem expectantly.

The portly man shook his head. "That was the last one. You really didn't like any of them?"

"Not a one. Isn't there anyone else?"

"No," Waseem said sorrowfully. "You've rejected them all."

"Not quite all," Iman muttered, thinking of broad shoulders and dark hair.

Waseem frowned down at his clipboard in confusion. "Who... Ah, yes. Adam. You didn't reject him. Was that an oversight?"

"No," Iman's cheeks burned. "It wasn't."

Waseem smiled brightly. "Wonderful! I'll tell your grandfather you've made a decision."

Iman's eyes widened. "What?" she squeaked. "No I haven't."

"But I thought you hadn't rejected this one?"

"I haven't," Iman agreed. "But that doesn't mean I've accepted him!

Look," she said. "There must be someone else. Just... check again."

Waseem sighed. "Stubborn child," he lamented, in a perfectly audible voice.

"I heard that," Iman called after him.

"Good," he replied over his shoulder. "Maybe it will help you see sense."

Was she being nonsensical? Maybe. She only had a day left before she had to return to her mother's home – Aasia had only agreed to let her stay an extra week – and returning any later without a single bit of progress was a terrible idea that guaranteed pain.

But... silly though it was, she'd hoped to find someone who was nice. Or even just civil. Was that really so much to ask?

Iman sighed. She still had one day left. If she didn't find someone else by midday tomorrow, she'd pick the only option she had left. But until then, she'd hold out hope for a miracle.

Surely she was due one by now?

CHAPTER FIVE

The second summons was identical to the first. A pretty white sheet of paper requesting his presence. The fancy design struck him again and Adam laughed bitterly. It had been and still was far more appropriate than he'd originally realized. He wondered if Khan had deliberately chosen the cards as some kind of sick joke. It seemed like the kind of thing the crazy old man would do.

Adam looked at the large bag of food he'd carried in with him and felt ill. He'd discovered the card on the way back in from picking up some lunch and now he was deeply regretting the decision to open the dumb letter before eating.

He sighed, getting to his feet and picking up the still hot sack of food. He'd give it to a beggar. There was no way he was going to eat it. Not after opening that letter.

He took a cab this time and didn't bother arming himself before leaving. His weapons had been taken from him the last time and there was no point carrying them just to have to surrender them to a stranger at the door again.

He arrived all too soon and, once again, was escorted to the same library.

"Congratulations," Ibrahim Khan told him, a twisted smile on his thin lips. "You've been chosen."

The old man was stood behind the same heavy desk he'd sat at before. "Sit," he instructed, gesturing at the chair opposite him.

Adam didn't move. "I think I prefer to stand."

Khan shrugged. "Suit yourself." He picked up a folder from the desk. "This is a list of all the people who will become your enemies as soon as your marriage to Iman is made public. You should memorize it."

Adam moved forward to take it. "It's thick," he remarked, eyeing the many pages.

"I have a lot of enemies," Khan said blandly.

"And when's the...thing," Adam finished lamely, the word wedding getting stuck in his throat. He still couldn't believe this was happening.

"Immediately."

"What?!"

Khan arched an eyebrow. "Is there a problem?" he asked mildly.

"Yes!" Adam said savagely. "Yes, there's a problem. I can't get married right now! If I had it my way, I wouldn't be getting married at all... But never mind that. I can't get married without telling my family about it first." Though *how* he was going to tell his family was still unclear.

"Of course," Khan nodded decisively. "That's fine. You can do that in the week."

Adam blinked. "Thanks," he said cautiously.

"The ceremony will take place on Saturday then."

"Right," Adam nodded. "Wait, that's six days away."

"Yes. Is that too far away?"

Adam caught the veiled threat. "No! No, it's fine." Six days. This was madness.

"Good. Now, a few ground rules," Khan paused. "Are you sure you don't want to sit down? We'll be here for a while."

"Ground rules?"

"Yes. You didn't think I'd let you have my granddaughter without putting some rules in place, did you?"

"What was I thinking?" Adam said sarcastically, just barely refraining from rolling his eyes. He was beginning to wish that Khan had just shot him in the head that day. It would have been more merciful than these insane mind games.

-

Sitting comfortably behind the second door to the library, leaning her head against the thin piece of wood, Iman heard every word exchanged between Ibrahim and Adam.

Some of the topics made her cheeks burn with embarrassment and still others made her giggle. By the time they were done, her stomach was growling in complaint and her butt was numb. But she felt a rush of love towards her grandfather for being so thoroughly protective of her.

Iman knew that Ibrahim hadn't forgiven himself for making her leave and his behaviour stemmed largely from guilt. But she would take what she could get.

It was so nice to be taken care of again that she didn't particularly care why it was being done. She was too busy appreciating the fact that it was happening at all.

Iman wasn't aware of falling asleep. It felt like she'd just closed her eyes for a second and her grandfather was there, leaning over here and shaking her shoulder.

"An armchair is a terrible place to fall asleep," he told her as he straightened up. "Go up to your room."

Iman nodded blearily, stretching her arms above her head.

"Oh, and congratulations," Ibrahim added with a sad smile.

Iman smothered a yawn with her sleeve. "Thanks," she mumbled. "When's the wedding?"

"Saturday."

A shock jolted through her. "This Saturday?"

Ibrahim sighed. "I need to get you out of there as soon as possible. We won't be able to have a huge event but they're a nightmare to try and secure anyway. I know this isn't necessarily what you wanted but it's the only practical option. And I don't want you in your mother's house a second longer than necessary."

Her mother. Would Aasia be pleased that Iman was leaving so soon or would she throw a fit at not being consulted? Knowing Aasia, she would do both.

"Iman? I'm sorry." Her grandfather was looking sadly down at her.

"It's fine. I always wanted a tiny little wedding anyway," Iman lied.

From the look he gave her, Ibrahim knew she wasn't being truthful but he let it go. "I'll call your mother in the morning before you leave. That way she can get the worst of her mood out of the way before you get there."

If only it was that easy. "Don't tell her," Iman said, surprising both of them. "I'll do it."

Ibrahim looked down at her, frowning in concern. "Iman... Is that really a good idea?"

Probably not. "It'll be fine. This is good news for her, she'll be happy to hear it."

Ibrahim's lips pursed and he shook his head. "I don't think-"

"I need to do this," Iman interrupted. "I want to do it. I promise, it will be fine." She reached up and kissed her grandfather on the cheek. "Trust me."

-

It wasn't fine. Iman ducked to avoid a gorgeous porcelain vase, wondering how long this was going to go on. She'd never seen Aasia quite so out of control before. If she were a cartoon character, she'd have steam pouring out of her ears.

"Honey?" Iman's stepfather said cautiously, poking his head into the room. "Don't you think that's enough?"

Aasia rounded on him. "Excuse me?" she hissed. "What did you just say?"

He backed up, holding his hands up in surrender. "It's just... you might scar her face like this. We wouldn't want that, right?"

Iman backed away instinctively as her mother came towards her. She hit the wall and shrank back, half-wishing that she could just sink through it. Aasia seized her chin roughly in one hand. "You're beautiful," she said, giving Iman a once-over. "Exquisite features."

Iman said nothing and Aasia squeezed harder. "But no manners. What do you say when someone compliments you?"

"Ow," Iman winced. "Thank you!"

"That's better. It really is a shame," Aasia tutted. "You are *so* beautiful."

Before Iman could even wonder exactly what was a shame, Aasia struck. Her manicured nails raked across Iman's cheek, tearing deep enough that blood immediately began to well up in their wake.

She caught the hand Iman had raised to try and protect herself, pinning it to the wall, and studied the damage she'd done. "Almost. But not deep enough, I think."

Again, her nails dug in. Iman screamed. "Let go of me!" Aasia let go of her arm in order to scratch her again and Iman used this to her advantage, bringing both her hands up and shoving as hard as she could.

Aasia stumbled back and Iman ran, pushing past her stepfather and not stopping until she'd gotten to her bedroom and locked the door behind her. She left the key in the lock so it couldn't be turned from the other side and propped her desk chair under the handle for good measure.

Only then did she allow herself to look at the damage.

There were four deep gouges stretching from just below her eye socket all the way down to her jaw line. The entire left side of her face throbbed angrily. Would she have scars? Aasia's nails were sharp enough to do lasting damage, her arms were proof of that.

Iman turned away from the mirror. There was no point in worrying about that now. A compress would help with the pain. She reached for the little cloth that hung on the towel rail and promptly dropped it, her fingers fumbling to catch it before it hit the floor.

She looked down at her hands. They were shaking. She balled them into fists and waited, willing the shaking to stop. She took a deep breath and scooped up the cloth from the floor, clutching it so tightly that her fingers started to hurt.

She held it under the running tap and messily squeezed out the excess water before slapping it onto her face. The impact made tears spring to her eyes and she sniffed hard.

Don't cry. Don't cry, don't cry, don't cry! It wasn't her own voice that she heard but Aasia's. It had always enraged her whenever Iman had started to cry. Iman had eventually learned to stop herself, after several occasions where crying had resulted in screaming and a good few slaps or pinches from Aasia until she'd stopped.

The conditioning had worked incredibly well. Even now, Iman hated crying. It made her feel like she was doing something wrong that she had to hide. And it always gave her a raging headache.

It took several moments of pressing the palms of her hands hard against her eyes but finally, Iman conquered the tears. She wanted nothing more than to curl up in her sheets and sleep the day away but experience had taught her that the sleep she'd get would be plagued with nightmares.

It was better to stay awake and tire herself out enough that her body forced her to sleep when she was too tired to resist it any longer. That way she'd at least have fewer nightmares.

She'd never found a way to get rid of them completely.

-

Mom, I'm getting married.

It wasn't that hard to say. In theory.

In practice, it was a little bit different. Adam had been sitting at his mother's dining table for the past forty-five minutes, trying to force the words out and he'd gotten no further than 'Mom' before chickening out. Twice.

He knew that the longer he took to tell her, the worse it would make things for him.

It was three little words. All he had to do was open his mouth and say them. Surely he could do that.

A door slammed and his stepfather strode in, a filthy look on his face. He walked straight up to the table, stopping when he stood opposite Adam, and leaned his weight on his hands. "When were you going to tell us that you're engaged to *Ibrahim Khan's* only granddaughter?"

Or someone else could say it for him.

"Adam, is this true?"

Adam looked at his mother. "Yes," he said simply. "It's true."

She let out a squeal and jumped out of her chair, rounding the table to take his face in her hands and kiss him soundly. "Congratulations! But wait..." she frowned. "I thought you didn't want to get married?" She crossed her arms. "I've been trying to find a nice girl for you to settle down with for the past six months! If you already had a girlfriend, all you had to do was tell me," she scolded, looking vaguely hurt.

"I don't want to get married," Adam grumbled, pulling away from his mother's soft hands. "And I didn't – don't – have a girlfriend."

"What? Then how are you getting married?" Lina looked crestfallen. "Is your father mistaken? No, you said he's not."

"Stepfather," Adam corrected automatically.

Lina flapped her hands at him. "Same thing."

Adam ignored this. "It's complicated. All you need to know is that I'm getting married on Saturday, okay?"

"Saturday?! What's the rush?"

Adam sighed. He should have just sent a text. "It's-"

"Don't you dare tell me 'it's complicated', young man! Uncomplicate it! And quickly." Lina fixed him with a stern look. "What is going on?"

Adam glanced at his stepfather. As always, Ali was no help at all. "Well, answer your mother," he said, tilting his head at Lina. "She's waiting."

"Mom, sit down." Adam waited until she had before continuing. "Do you remember last year, when I was sick?"

Lina nodded immediately. "Of course. It was awful." She reached out a hand and smoothed his hair. "You were in bed for three days." It would have been longer if she'd had her way but Adam was just as stubborn as the mother he'd inherited the trait from and was not above using her worry for him to his advantage. Lina had let him do as he pleased, worried that he would strain himself if he kept arguing so viciously.

"I was on a job right before that. And I messed up." There was no way he'd tell her exactly how badly. She'd wrap him up in cotton wool and refuse to let him out of her sight. "Ibrahim Khan saved my life."

Lina's skin took on a sickly grey tinge. "Why didn't you tell me?" she shouted, springing to her feet and flinging her arms around his neck.

Adam choked. "Mom, let go." He leaned away in an effort to loosen the tight grip. Lina ignored him. She was trembling, Adam realized guiltily. He shot a pointed look at his stepfather. *Do something!*

Ali got to his feet. "He can't breathe, Li." He put his arms around Adam's mother's shoulders and guided her back to her seat, keeping hold of her hand as he sat himself next to her. "How did a debt turn into a marriage proposal? You met his granddaughter and fell in love?"

Lina brightened. "Is that what happened?" she asked eagerly.

"Not quite," Adam admitted reluctantly.

"Then what happened?" The panic was back on his mother's face.

"We're not in love," Adam hedged.

Lina gave her husband a filthy look. "He gets this from you." She turned back to Adam. "You're marrying her, yes?"

Adam nodded cautiously. "Yes, but-" He stopped again. He didn't want to tell her.

His conscience pricked. Was he really going to lie to his mother?

"Adam? What's wrong?"

"We're not in love," Adam repeated.

Lina rolled her eyes. "Alright," she said, clearly humouring him. "You're not in love. Anything else?"

I'm only marrying her to get rid of a debt. I don't actually want to. And I don't exactly have a choice in all this.

"No. Nothing else."

"Li, do you know where I left my car keys?"

Lina turned, distracted. "What?"

"My keys. I don't have them on me and I have that meeting to get to just now."

Lina left the room, grumbling about absent-minded men and Adam sank back in his chair, letting out a deep breath. A moment later, he straightened back up. "Your keys have been in your hand this entire time."

Ali glared at him. "Took you long enough to notice. You're getting sloppy."

"Forgive me for being just a little bit distracted!" Adam could feel the blood rushing to his cheeks. The criticism rankled. Ali was right. He had gotten sloppy. He'd said as much to himself more than once. But what he yelled at himself in the privacy of his own head and what he heard from the man who trained him were two different things.

"You   did   the   right   thing."
"What?"

Ali glanced at the open doorway. "Lying to your mother," he elaborated. "You know she's a romantic. It would have broken her heart to know that you're marrying this girl to repay a debt."

"You did know." Adam scowled. He should have expected it. Ali Cassim always knew more than he should have done. It was one of the most infuriating things about him and the reason his nose was so crooked – more than one man had swung a punch directly at Ali's infuriatingly smug face upon hearing his own secrets revealed in that annoying matter of fact tone.

"I didn't," Ali corrected. "Not until you brought up Paris." He shifted forward and gave Adam a once-over. "I knew you were leaving things out when you reported back to me but I would never have expected something like this."

Adam looked away. He thought that he'd gotten away with the small deception but it seemed Ali had seen straight through him. As always.

"I should smack you," his stepfather grumbled.

"When has that ever helped?"

Ali nodded, conceding the point. "If you had just told me, we could have found a way to fix it."

"How?" There was no way to *fix* a debt like this. Nothing trumped it.

"I don't know," Ali admitted, shaking his head. "This is a bigger mess than all the others you ever got yourself into. Combined." He reached into his suit, pulling out a box of cigarettes and a lighter.

The box was offered to Adam who declined, wrinkling his nose. He hated cigarettes. "Mom will kill you for smoking inside."

"She can't mind it that much, there's an ashtray right here." Ali indicated the one in the middle of the table.

"Do you want to have her killed?" Ali asked when he was halfway done with his cigarette.

"That won't be obvious at all!" He couldn't kill her. And he couldn't leave her unprotected either. Her grandfather had been *explicit* in his instructions. Adam was trapped. And trying to find a way out only emphasized just how unbreakable the trap was.

"If you'd just listened to me and avoided him..." Ali ground out the rest of his cigarette viciously. "But when have you ever listened to me?"

"Could you just *stop*?" Adam shouted, surprising even himself. "Don't make this about your problems with me! I am having a really hard time right now and I don't need you pointing out to me what a big mess this is – I know! Better than you do. But there's nothing that I can do. And there was nothing that I could do back then either. I didn't go waltzing up to Ibrahim Khan, I ran into him. By accident. On a job *you* sent me on." He fell silent, panting.

Ali's eyes had narrowed into slits and his face had hardened. "If you want to do it by yourself," he said icily, extending a graceful hand toward the door. "Be my guest."

Adam took the hint.

CHAPTER SIX

There were raised voices outside her door and Iman was curled up in a ball in the bathroom. She *hated* this. Her chest was tight and her eyes stung and she hated that almost as much as she hated the way her shoulders were drawn up almost to her ears.

It was stupid to crouch on the floor like this, she knew. She couldn't lock herself in this room forever. Eventually, her food would run out and she would need to come out. Hiding like this would just make it worse when she was finally forced out.

But Iman couldn't bring herself to stand. Her limbs wouldn't obey her. She was... she was terrified. The shame of admitting it, even to herself, made her cheeks burn. She was a grown woman and she was afraid of her mother.

She couldn't even face leaving her room and risking the *possibility* of running into her mother.

Pathetic.

A series of chimes sounded and Iman lifted her head. Her phone? It was in the bedroom, in the bag she still hadn't unpacked four days after returning. To answer it, she'd have to go right up to the door where the bag lay.

Iman considered ignoring it, letting it ring until the person on the other end gave up. But there was only one person who ever called her any more. She couldn't leave her grandfather to worry about her.

Quietly, she crept toward the door. She was so focused on not making a noise, she didn't even notice that the shouting had stopped. An eternity later, she had the phone pressed to her ear. "Hello?" she whispered, a hand cupped in front of her face to muffle the sound.

"Iman?" The voice hadn't come from the device pressed to her ear but from outside, Iman realized.

"Shaida?" Iman experienced a moment of extreme confusion. What was her babysitter doing in her mother's house?

The doorknob rattled and she jumped.

"Open the door, please," Shaida called from the hallway.

Iman hesitated for a split-second before turning the key in the lock. "It's open," she said quietly.

The door was being yanked open before she'd finished speaking.

"Thank goodness! Didn't you hear us calling you?" Shaida came into the room. "And why is it so dark in here?" She touched the light switch on the wall and Iman flinched, squinting at the sudden brightness.

Shaida's eyes widened in horror and she gasped. "What happened to you?"

How terrible did she look? Shaida looked like she was about to cry. "I haven't been sleeping well," Iman admitted.

"No," Shaida hissed, her cheeks red with anger. She stepped forward and raised a hand, stopping just short of actually touching Iman. "What happened to your *face?*"

"An accident," Iman lied, touching light fingers to the bandage that covered the scratches. "It's not as bad as it looks," she reassured the older woman. "I probably overdid it with the bandage."

Shaida's face softened. "Here, let me take a look," she offered.

"No!" Iman jerked away. "I – it's still a little sore," she said lamely.

Shaida pursed her lips. "Alright," she said softly. "We'll leave it for now."

"What are you doing here?" Iman asked, trying to keep her voice casual.

"I thought I would help you pack. But it looks like you're pretty much done." Shaida indicated the suitcases lined up neatly in the middle of the room. She frowned. "Is that all you have?"

"Yeah," Iman glanced at the three suitcases. "That's all of it." It wasn't, but if it would get Shaida to leave and stop looking at her like the woman could read her soul, Iman would lie.

Shaida nodded decisively. "Alright, here." She handed the smallest case to Iman. "Take this one and your purse."

Iman took the handle. "Shaida, I'm not really up to going out today."

"We're not going out."

"Then why do I need my purse?"

Shaida took control of the two remaining suitcases. "Because," she fixed Iman with a serious look. "You're not coming back

59

here."

At first, Iman thought that she'd gotten the days wrong. A quick look at her phone assured her that it was still only Thursday. "Of course I am. It's only Thursday."

"You'll stay at your grandfather's until the wedding."

Longing filled Iman and she was hit with the urge to walk straight out. But...

Shaida read the disappointed look on her face perfectly. "Your mother-" She sighed. "She wasn't particularly pleasant, as I'm sure you heard. I informed her that you were leaving today."

"And she agreed?"

Shaida misread the bewildered delight in her voice and gave her a sympathetic look. "I'm sorry, sweetheart. It took a while for her to agree," she added, clearly trying to make Iman feel better.

"She agreed to let me go?" Iman repeated, still marvelling. Could it really be that easy?

"Yes."

Iman could feel a smile spreading over her face. "Let's go!"

-

"What the hell?" A tall brunette stood waiting in the entry way to Adam's apartment. Her hands were on her hips and the look of fury on her face was so icy, Adam imagined he could almost feel the chill.

"Hey," he said automatically.

Her chest heaved. "'Hey'? Is that all you have to say to me?"

Adam closed his eyes and counted to ten. Twice. "Can I get in the door before you start interrogating me?"

"Fine." She turned on her heel and headed for the lounge, her heels clicking as she walked.

Adam took his time putting away the groceries he'd just purchased. He was debating making coffee when he heard the sound of heels clicking rapidly.

'Typical,' he thought fondly.

"Aren't you done yet?"

"No, Kat, I'm not. And since you ambushed me in *my* apartment, you can wait til I'm done."

"Sorry," she said begrudgingly. "Your Mom told me and I headed straight over. What are you busy with?"

"Nothing," Adam admitted.

Kat's mouth dropped open and she gaped at him for a moment before smacking him on the arm. "Mean!" she scolded.

"You deserved it. How many times have I told you not to just barge in?"

Kat rolled her eyes. "Whatever. Stop avoiding the subject. When were you going to tell me that you're *getting married*?" She said it like most people would say *jumping off a cliff.*

There went his plans for a nice, quiet evening. "It's a long story, Kat."

"I have time." She looked expectantly at him.

Just how many times was he going to have to tell this story? "Last year..."

-

Adam sat and watched Kat pace. He'd debated telling her the same lie he had told his mother but had decided against it. Kat knew him far too well to be fooled by a hasty lie like that. And she of all people deserved to know the truth.

Kat had been the first friend Adam had made after his mother spontaneously decided to uproot them and marry Ali all those years ago. She had been with Ali since she was tiny and Adam had heard the whispers that Kat was the daughter Ali had conceived with a prostitute and that she had been left on her father's doorstep because her mother wasn't willing to raise her.

Kat was the only one who hadn't tried to suck up to him to get into Ali's good books. And later, when Adam had begun to join in on training sessions, she'd been the only one who hadn't resented the personal attention he'd gotten from his stepfather.

They'd promised one another long ago that there would be no lies between them – a rarity in the profession they were in. Adam wasn't going to break that promise.

He waited for Kat to run out of steam but ten minutes later, she was still going strong, the heels of her knee-high leather boots clicking rhythmically as she walked. Her hands were on her hips and her lips moved quickly as she muttered to herself.

Finally, Adam couldn't take the clicking any longer. He took himself off to the kitchen and made the coffee he'd been craving all night. As he'd expected, the scent eventually lured Kat into the kitchen and he handed her the small mug he'd fixed for her before picking up his own and taking a long drink.

They sipped in silence for a while before Kat finally spoke. "This really sucks."

Adam snorted. "Way to state the obvious." He drained his mug and immediately poured a second.

"There's nothing else to say. I can't think of a single way to get you out of this that doesn't involve faking your death and running far and fast. And we both know you'll never leave your mother."

"And she'll never leave my stepfather," Adam added bitterly.

"It might not be so bad."

Adam snorted and Kat bit her lip. "Really," she insisted, despite the disbelieving look in her own eyes. "I've heard about Iman Khan. She's supposed to be gorgeous."

"She is," Adam admitted, thinking back to fair skin and delicate features. "She's also supposed to be a spoilt little brat." He'd heard rumours of her antics himself and the laundry list of orders her grandfather had unloaded on him had only cemented his belief that he was marrying a spoilt brat.

"This really sucks," Kat repeated. "I wish there was a way we could fix it."

"Are you coming tomorrow?"

"To the wedding?" Kat frowned. "Do you want me to?"

"It would be nice to know someone other than the Khans."

"Your parents aren't coming?" Kat winced. "I mean-"

"I know what you mean," Adam cut her off. Much like his mother, Kat was in the habit of referring to Ali as Adam's father. Unlike his mother though, she listened when he asked her to stop. For the most part, at least.

Adam knew that the constant corrections sounded petulant. People even called him ungrateful for refusing to call his mother's husband 'Father'. But it was the truth. Ali *wasn't* his father, for all that the man had tried to parent him. Adam's father was dead and no amount of pretending otherwise would change that truth.

Kat recognized the sour look on his face and made a production of checking the time on her phone. "Well, it's getting late. I should go."

Adam reached out and grabbed her arm. "No, it's okay. You don't have to go just because I'm grumpy."

"Maybe I don't want to deal with you when you're grumpy." Kat leaned up and kissed his cheek. "I'll be there tomorrow. And I'll bring your mother with me."

"Don't. It's never good when both of us are in his bad books at the same time."

Kat smiled secretively. "I wasn't planning on telling Ali where we were going."

"He'll find out," Adam warned. "He always does."

"By that time, he'll have gotten over it. You know he's just being obstinate right now because he's feeling possessive."

Adam felt a need to defend his stepfather. "I told him I could deal with it on my own," he explained.

Kat fixed him with an unimpressed look. "You've been doing that since the day you met him. It's never driven him up the wall like this before. Trust me, he's just sore because this happened without his approval, that's all."

Controlling and petulant. That *did* sound like his stepfather. "Do you think he'll ever let us go?"

"No," Kat said softly. "I don't."

Neither did Adam.

The people who worked for Ali didn't leave unless it was in body bags. Those who tried were quickly shown the error of their ways.

Adam sighed. The day he'd come to fully understand just what working under his stepfather meant, he'd sworn that he'd never be ensnared like that again.

But he had been. And it had taken a little over a year to realize it. Adam's only comfort was that it had taken more than twice that the last time. He was getting faster at noticing the traps even if he still hadn't learned how to avoid them.

He looked down at his left hand. From tomorrow, it would be different. There would be a band of platinum there, reminding him every time he looked down at his hand that he belonged to someone.

His stomach churned and bile rose in his throat. There was nothing in his stomach but he still rushed to the kitchen sink and braced himself over it, deliberately breathing through his nose and swallowing hard.

I wish there was a way we could fix it, Kat's voice whispered in his head.

Adam wished there was a way to fix it too.

CHAPTER SEVEN

Iman examined herself critically in the mirror. She had no idea where the wedding gown had come from but it had been waiting for her when she woke up that morning. It was a gorgeous, full-skirted thing that fit her perfectly and she knew that it must have cost a fortune to alter so fast.

It was a shame that only a handful of people would get to see it.

Shaida came in, carefully balancing a stack of velvet boxes in her arms. "I completely forgot about jewellery! I just grabbed a few things that I thought would go well but we still have time to go looking if you don't like any of them."

"I'm sure it'll be fine." Iman took the stack, dropping most of it unceremoniously on her bed. She kept a single box, easing it open gently. "Oh!" A set of diamonds and emeralds lay nestled within, sparkling attractively.

"Are those emeralds? You've always looked lovely in green." Shaida lifted the bracelet out and began to fasten it on Iman's wrist. "What do you think?"

"It's beautiful." The bracelet was exquisite. Iman looked at her reflection again.

Shaida straightened up. "What's that face for?" She touched the frown lines on Iman's forehead. "Today's supposed to be a good day, remember?"

"I-" Iman sighed and shook her head. "I'm being silly."

"Are you nervous?" Shaida's eyes softened in understanding. "It's normal with arranged matches like this. But you'll be alright. Your grandfather thinks highly of Adam, I know." She smiled wickedly, adding: "He's very attractive too."

Iman blushed. "It's more than that," she admitted.

Shaida sat down on the bed and took Iman's hands in her own. "What else is it?"

"It just feels like a lot of fuss. The dress, the caterers... It's not like this is a real marriage anyway."

"What?"

Iman shrugged, tugging at the beading on her gown. "I'm not in love with him."

"I'd be a little worried if you thought you were, after two meetings," Shaida laughed. "There are many successful marriages that start with nothing more than mutual respect and many more where the initial passion fades."

She nudged Iman gently. "That's not all. What else is bothering you?"

"What if I picked the wrong guy? I only picked him because I wanted to be the one to pick and he was the best of a bad lot. What if it turns out to be awful?"

"Immy..." Shaida looked pained. "You can't marry someone who doesn't know what kind of world we live in. It's too dangerous. You need to be with someone who can protect you and who we know is loyal to your grandfather. I know it limits the pool but... the alternative just isn't an option. It's too dangerous."

"I know. Papa told me about all this when he was explaining why I couldn't live here." Ibrahim had been frighteningly candid about his own waning power and the unexpected protection that living with her important politician of a stepfather had afforded Iman for the past two years.

It made sense when Iman thought about it. Her stepfather had enough clout to make Ibrahim Khan step warily. Of course the Khans' enemies would be just as hesitant to make an enemy of him. If only Iman could still lay claim to that protection *without* having to be anywhere near her slimy stepfather.

Shaida rubbed Iman's thigh comfortingly. "I'm sorry you're limited like this, sweetheart," she said regretfully.

Iman flushed guiltily. "Don't feel bad. It's a pretty small problem, in the grand scheme of things. I guess... I guess I just wanted a little more fantasy and a little less reality."

"Do you want to call things off?" Shaida asked delicately.

Iman opened her mouth and she held up a hand. "Wait, let me finish. I don't want you to call things off. However inconvenient and uncomfortable marrying Adam may be, it's still your only real way to get away from your mother, sweetheart. She can't touch you if you're legally married. Even if she gets you declared as incompetent, she doesn't have a claim on you, if you're married."

"But you got her to back off the other day," Iman argued. "Can't we just use whatever it was that worked the other day to make her stay away?"

Shaida winced. "I bluffed," she admitted. "And if your mother weren't so intimidated by me, she would have realized it on the spot. She *will* have figured it out by now and it won't work again."

Iman's heart sank. She had thought she was resigned to this farce of a relationship but it seemed she'd still held onto a tiny spark of hope. Until now, that was.

"What do you want to do?"

Iman looked up at the closest thing to a mother she'd ever had. "Finish getting ready," she said, reaching for a necklace.

Shaida squeezed her shoulders comfortingly. "I'm sorry there isn't a better way."

"I should have guessed there wasn't," Iman admitted. "Papa's been going over it for long enough. If there were anything else, he would have seen it."

"This marriage will at least be good for one thing – lowering your Papa's stress levels. God knows, he's been frantic about you. Knowing that you'll finally be safe and in trusted hands has already made him start to look better."

Iman cocked her head in confusion. "He has been looking lighter," she agreed. "I thought he'd still be worried because I lose my stepfather's guards but he seems fine."

"Adam's capable of protecting you if need be. And he's important to some very powerful people. That protection falls over you now too. You'll be nearly as safe as you have been these past few years."

"Safer, if he doesn't try to hit me," Iman muttered.

Shaida scowled furiously and put a protective hand over her stomach. "If I wasn't pregnant, I would have taught your mother a lesson on Thursday. She sorely needs it."

Iman privately thanked God that Shaida *was* pregnant. She knew that her old babysitter was completely serious. "It wasn't that bad," she said weakly.

"It was bad enough that you still have a bandage on your face. Thank God we got you out of there before things could get even worse."

This Iman could agree with fully. "I'm not out quite just yet," she said ruefully. "It's not legal until we sign, right?"

"Then we'd better get you downstairs." Shaida clapped her hands decisively and headed to the door.

Iman said a silent prayer, smoothed her dress down one last time and followed her.

-

Adam couldn't remember when last he'd felt so on edge. The room was filled with Ibrahim Khan's closest friends and allies, none of whom seemed too impressed by him. He couldn't shake the feeling that he was being sized up and found wanting.

It was a familiar feeling. He'd been paraded around like this for months after Ali had adopted him. Just like then, the interest today was anything but innocent. Adam knew quite well that every single person in the room was loyal to the Khans. One wrong move and he'd have an army ready to take him down.

His stepfather had been right. This mess was worse than all the others combined.

As though thinking about him had summoned the man, Ali came into view just then. His stepfather was as on edge as Adam had ever seen him. His jaw was clenched and he held himself stiffly, standing half in front of Adam's mother as though to shield her.

Adam headed towards them immediately, not even bothering to excuse himself from whoever it was Khan had just been trying to introduce him to. Earlier in the day, he'd resented their absence but now that he saw them, saw his *mother* in a room filled with hostile killers, he wished Ali had kept to his word and stayed away.

"I thought you weren't going to make it?"

Ali winced.

Adam's mother frowned from behind her husband. "Don't be ridiculous, Adam. Of course we weren't going to miss your wedding day."

"I was overruled." Ali looked around the room. "And I maintain that I was right. I'm not happy with you being here, Lina."

Adam's mother ignored this. "Where's Iman? I can't wait to meet her."

Adam had no idea where his bride was. She'd been whisked away the second they'd finished signing their names and he hadn't seen her since.

"I think she's upstairs," he said uncertainly.

"Iman will be down in a few minutes, I'm sure." Khan put an arm on Adam's back and he tensed. How did such an old man move so quietly? If he didn't know better, he'd think the man was doing it just to make him jump.

There was an awkward pause. Adam's mother cleared her throat. "I don't think we've met." She extended a hand. "I'm Lina Cassim, Adam's mother and this," she indicated Ali, "is his father."

Khan took it. "I am Iman's grandfather, Ibrahim. A pleasure to meet you. Please excuse me, I need to see where Iman has got to." He disappeared up the stairs.

"Lost your bride?" Ali asked sardonically.

Adam grunted.

"Not much of a loss."

Lina smacked his arm. "Ali!" she said sharply. "Honestly, I don't know what's gotten into you these past few days."

"I'm not going to pretend to condone this nonsense." Ali turned his attention to Adam. "Look after your mother." With that, he stalked off. Adam could see him already pulling out his lighter.

Lina stared after her husband. "Where is he going?" she asked, baffled.

"To smoke."

Adam's mother sighed. "Of course," she said ruefully. "I don't suppose you want to introduce me to some of these people?"

Adam grimaced. He could just imagine how terribly that would go. Lina was a friendly woman by nature and not even years of being married to a mercenary had taught her reticence. She'd be giving away sensitive information before he could blink.

She misread his hesitation and sighed. "You know, one day, you're going to stop being ashamed of me."

"Mom!" Adam looked down at her wide-eyed. "I'm not ashamed of you!" How could he be? His mother was warm and sweet. He wasn't ashamed of her, he was scared *for* her. She couldn't hold her own here, amongst a crowd that prized being sharp and deadly. They'd tear her to shreds.

It was useless trying to explain this to Lina, however. She clung to the illusion that people were nice and kind, just as she was. If he told her to be wary, she'd scold him for being paranoid and rude.

"You just don't want anyone to know about me."

Adam winced. She was right, but she had the reasoning all wrong. He sighed. "Mom, I don't know them myself."

She tilted her head, distracted. "Are you being antisocial again?"

Adam laughed. "Yeah, Mom. That's exactly it."

"Oh, honey, you need to be more social. How many times have I told you, you need to make an effort with people!"

"I know, Mom."

"Remember when you were younger? You only had Kat as a friend because you just wouldn't be nice to the other kids when they tried to make friends with you. That was so hard on you. I don't want that happening again."

Adam chose not to mention that the 'other kids' had been looking for information about both him and her to use against them as her husband had trained them to. Much like this crowd would, if given half a chance.

"I'm fine, Mom. Where is Kat, anyway?" At first he'd assumed that she hadn't been able to get away from Ali but his stepfather was here. And Kat had promised to come.

Lina bit her lip. "I asked her not to come," she admitted.

"What? Why would you do that?" Adam was puzzled. His mother liked Kat almost as much as she liked him.

Lina looked pained. "Honey," she said in a low voice. "It's a little inappropriate."

"What? Inappropriate how?"

His mother made an impatient noise. "Kat is a beautiful young woman," she said pointedly.

Adam looked at the crowd. "You think she would have been hassled? She can take care of herself, Mom."

"I think," Lina said delicately. "That Iman might not like it."

Adam was appalled. "You can't be serious?"

Lina didn't budge.

"Mom, it's Kat! I've known her for almost a decade. She's the closest thing to a sister I've ever had."

"Still, honey. Women feel insecure."

Adam fought the urge to bang his head against the wall. "Mom, it's not an issue. I have to call Kat."

He didn't get the chance. At that moment, everyone's attention went to the staircase. It seemed Adam's bride was making her big entrance.

-

There was a strange woman hugging her. And she didn't seem particularly inclined to let go any time soon. Iman looked over the woman's shoulder for help and found Adam – her husband, she reminded herself – standing close by with a pinched look on his face. Their eyes met and he sighed.

He came forward and put his hands on the woman's shoulders, gently easing her away. "Mom, let her breathe." *Mom?* Iman looked at the woman with interest. This was her mother in law? But why was she being so pleasant to a woman who'd trapped her son?

Adam's mother smiled apologetically at her. "I'm sorry, I guess I'm just a little excited. I've been waiting for this day for such a long time, you see," she explained. "But I'll confess, I *did* think I'd be meeting my daughter in law *before* the wedding day."

Iman squirmed. "I'm sorry," she found herself whispering.

"Oh no, honey, I don't blame you." Iman's arm was patted reassuringly. "I blame Adam. He's always been a secretive child. I should be used to it by now, but... Well, a mother does have dreams."

Adam looked so pained even Iman began to feel sorry for him. "Mrs. Cassim," she began helplessly.

"Oh, none of that! Call me Lina – we're family now, after all."

"Alright, Lina. It hasn't really been Adam's fault," Iman pointed out uncomfortably.

Lina smiled. "You're sweet to defend him. And now's not the time for all of that anyway." She tucked Iman's arm into her own. "We've got today to make up for lost time, at least. Come on, you can tell me all about yourself."

Iman found herself being led to one of the many tables that had been set up. As an afterthought, Lina turned and called at Adam, "Honey, go find your father, please!"

When Adam pulled out his phone, she added. "Walk, don't text!"

"That boy," she said fondly, shaking her head at her son's retreating back. "So antisocial. And you seem shy as well."

Iman smiled uncomfortably. "I am, a bit."

"Well, you won't have much to worry about with Adam. He's always been very private. No matter what I tried to make him a bit more social, nothing stuck."

Iman said nothing.

Lina continued, undaunted. "Where are your parents? I can't wait to meet them either."

Iman froze. "They're, they're not-" she stuttered, shaking her head.

"Oh, no. I'm so sorry," Lina's face fell. "I didn't mean to bring up a sensitive subject."

Iman was saved from further questioning by the arrival of her grandfather. "There you are. A lot of people still want to congratulate you, you know."

"Oh, I'm sorry. I'm the one to blame for that."

Ibrahim turned to Lina. "Perfectly understandable," he assured her. "But Iman, it would be rude for you to ignore the rest of the guests."

"Right." Iman took the hand he extended and got to her feet. "Of course."

Ibrahim guided her to an alcove. "What happened? You looked ready to bolt."

"She's very... enthusiastic."

Ibrahim smiled. "Yes, I saw that. It's better than apathy, sweetheart. Just remind yourself that when it gets a bit overwhelming."

"Right," Iman agreed unenthusiastically, making a face.

"And have an escape route easily available," Ibrahim added.

"Is that what that was? You were giving me an escape?"

"Yes and no. Your guests *do* want to speak to you." Ibrahim frowned. "I thought you'd be happy to see so many old faces."

"It would be easier if they were all nice faces." Iman cast a wary eye around the room.

Ibrahim sighed. "*We* have to keep our enemies within reach," he lamented. "If only you'd been born someone else's granddaughter."

"I'd be worse off."

Ibrahim laughed. "A worse liar, definitely."

Iman held out a hand. "Come on. Help me remember all the names."

"You don't have to talk to the ones who scare you."

"The only ones who really scare me aren't here today."

Ibrahim's face hardened and he reached up to touch her cheek. She'd kept the bandage on despite no longer truly needing it, preferring to keep the marks hidden. "Yet another thing I failed to keep you safe from," he said regretfully. Then he shook himself. "But now's not the time for that."

He looked around the room and brightened, extending a hand to point over her shoulder. "There's someone you'll be happy to see again."

Iman looked to where he'd pointed and felt a grin spread across her face. The next moment, she was hurrying forward, her pace kept slower than a run only by the heavy dress she wore.

He saw her coming and grinned, holding out his arms invitingly and Iman flung herself into them without a second thought, burying her face in his shoulder and breathing in his familiar scent. "I can't believe you're here!" she cried happily.

James Blackwell looked affectionately down at her. "I wouldn't miss your wedding! Though, to be honest, I *was* hoping to be playing a different role."

Iman smacked his shoulder. "Don't be a tease," she scolded. There was no heat in her voice. She was too happy to see him to even pretend convincingly to be cross. James had been a constant fixture in her life ever since he'd come to work under her grandfather. Eleven years older than Iman, he'd been around to see her through all the most embarrassing stages of her life.

She'd had the most ridiculous crush on him when she was younger and he'd known it full well. He'd been kind to her, though. He'd teased – it wasn't in his nature to resist! – but he'd never made her feel stupid or unworthy. He'd left when she was fifteen and she hadn't seen him since.

Until now, that was.

"How long are you here?"

"A while," James replied, grinning infuriatingly. Then he took pity on her. "I'm back for good. Your grandfather's been asking for a while and I figured I'd better make the move before asking turned into ordering."

"Good choice." Ibrahim Khan gave his people more leeway than most. But he was known for expecting immediate compliance when he eventually did shorten their leashes.

Unable to help herself, Iman hugged James again. "I really missed you," she whispered. "I'm glad you're back."

CHAPTER EIGHT

"You look like a hobo." Adam said as he wrinkled his nose and waved away the cloud of cigarette smoke. In a suit that cost more than some families lived on in a year, there was as much difference between Ali and a hobo as there was between a private jet and a skateboard, but the comment still made the corner of his mouth twitch.

"It's times like this when I remember fondly the days when men could drown annoying little brats."

"I'm a good swimmer."

"That's what the cement is for." Ali dropped his cigarette to the floor. "Did you need something or are you just here to remind me how very annoying you are?"

"You're needed inside. Mom sent me to get you."

Ali straightened up. "Needed for what? Is she alright?"

Adam levelled his stepfather with an unimpressed look. "Do you think I would have left if she wasn't? She wants to introduce you. She's... with Iman."

Ali groaned. "You cannot be serious. You left your mother with the woman who *bought* you? Willingly? Where is your head, boy?"

Adam bristled. "I didn't exactly have any other options. What was I supposed to tell her? 'Sorry, Mom, I can't leave you alone with your new daughter in law because she's a little snake?' She has no idea what's going on here, remember?"

Ali put a hand to his temples. "I should never have agreed to come today."

"Why did you, anyway?"

Ali pursed his lips. "It *is* your wedding day."

"*You're* being sentimental?" It was entirely out of character and Adam cast a worried look at his stepfather out of the corner of his eye. "Did you get hit in the head or something?"

"Very funny," Ali said drily. "Joking about head trauma, how original."

Adam couldn't let it go. "Seriously, why do you care?"

"Because I care about you. Despite what you seem to think." With that, Ali stalked back inside, leaving Adam to stand in the cold and gape at his retreating back.

What had *that* been?

-

Iman had been feeling less and less confident about her choices as the day went on. Now, in a car with a man who clearly did not like her, it was difficult to remember the very good reasons she'd had for the choices she'd made.

The reality of the situation was beginning to sink in. She'd gotten married to a virtual stranger. And yes, if he hurt her, he'd be dead in short order.

But it wouldn't do her much good if she were lying in a ditch somewhere by the time anyone caught up to him.

Iman peeked at Adam out of the corner of her eye and couldn't suppress a slight shudder. He was so big! She hadn't realized it properly before. Of course, she'd known he was large. But it hadn't truly sunk in until today when he'd put his arms around her.

The folded knife Shaida had slipped inside her sleeve, with a whispered *just in case* lay heavy against her arm and she scowled resentfully at the feel of it. It was a slim thing – it had had to be to fit under the sleeve of her gown – and was the cause of her current unease.

She had been happily oblivious to the fact that Adam was more than capable of killing her, that he'd made a career out of killing people far more dangerous than she could ever be, but the shock of cold steel against her skin was an abrupt reminder that she *wasn't* home safe. She still needed to watch herself.

There was the sound of someone clearing their throat pointedly and Iman started at the unexpected noise. She looked around for the source of it and found Adam leaning into the car with an irritated look on his face. Iman hadn't even noticed the car stop.

"We're here," he snapped unnecessarily. "Are you planning to get out or should I bring you a pillow?"

Iman got out of the car so quickly she tripped on the hem of her gown. There was an unpleasant ripping noise and she winced. Looking around, she quickly forgot the dress. "Where are we?"

Adam looked at her like she was an idiot. "The parking garage."

"You live in an apartment?"

Adam nodded impatiently. "Looks like it."

"But... isn't that hard to secure?" Looking around at the number of cars, it was obvious that dozens of people came in and out each day.

"Don't worry, you'll be safe."

Iman bristled at the patronizing tone and bit down a retort. "Could you open up the back?" she said instead, waiting until the car let out a happy beep to lift the lid. She reached in to pull out her bags and was just grabbing the handle of the first one when a much bigger hand closed over her own.

"I've got it," Adam told her brusquely.

Iman backed away hesitantly. "I can do it."

Adam eyed her disbelievingly. "Good for you. I've got it." He lifted both bags out easily.

"Thanks."

Iman trailed after Adam silently all the way up to his front door and inside the apartment. Once there, he dropped her bags in a sparsely decorated bedroom with a thump and headed out the door without another word to her.

In the silence, Iman had nothing to distract her when her shoulders began to throb. Her gown's heavy skirts had been biting into them all day and Iman was more than ready to yank the entire mess of tulle and silk above her head and throw it in a corner.

There was just one slight problem. She couldn't unzip it. The gown was cut tight enough that trying to get her arms behind her was a struggle that she was fairly certain would end in ripped seams if she kept trying.

Iman struggled in vain for a good few minutes before finally admitting defeat. She needed help.

Finding Adam was easy enough. It only took a few moments of wandering and poking her head into doorways before she found him sprawled on a couch.

"I need your help," she said, not looking at him.

He straightened up immediately. "What's wrong?"

"I – I can't reach my zip."

"What?"

"My zip. The gown is too tight for me to reach it."

Adam looked blankly at her.

"I need you to unzip me."

He got to his feet and came up behind her, dragging the zip down slowly.

The hairs on the back of Iman's neck stood on end and she reached back to stop him the moment the gown loosened enough for her to move. "Thanks, I should be able to get it the rest of the way."

There was a thunk and they both looked down. The velcro strap on the knife she'd been wearing had somehow come loose.

Adam picked it up and held it out to her. "I didn't take you for the type to use knives," he commented. "It's cute. Not particularly useful, but cute."

Iman took it. "Thanks for the help," she mumbled, and fled. If he said anything in reply, she didn't hear it.

Back in the bedroom, with the door firmly closed behind her, she cursed her gown, its zip and velcro in general before firmly putting the entire incident out of her head.

-

Adam stared after Iman's retreating back and felt a slight twinge of guilt. He knew that he made her uncomfortable, and probably scared her too – it had been written plain on her face. But he couldn't bring himself to feel too bad. What had she expected, honestly?

He dreaded to think of how she would react when she found out he only had one bedroom. Well, Iman was just going to have to deal with it. Adam had no plans to give up his bed and ruin his back. If she was that uncomfortable, *she* could sleep on the couch.

Adam ignored the voice in his head that shrieked in dismay at letting a woman sleep on a couch while he took a bed. It wasn't his fault, he reasoned grumpily. He hadn't made her live with him.

The next thing he was aware of was a strange feeling of weightlessness before he toppled head first to the floor. There was a loud crack that just barely drowned out the sound of his yell.

Adam lay there for a minute, cheek to the floor, and cursed his life. He could keep his feet in a fight but crippled himself rolling over on a couch. He sat there for a moment and let himself be furious before he took a deep breath, pushed himself to his feet and stalked toward the bedroom, ready to do battle with the tiny woman currently occupying it.

She was asleep. And she'd forgotten to close the curtains. The light pollution from the city was bright enough that he could make out her features clearly from where he stood in the doorway.

She was even tinier asleep, with her knees tucked up against herself. She fit neatly in the far corner of the bed, leaving the majority of it empty. There was space for even his big frame, with enough left over that they'd still have a decent gap between them.

Adam wrestled with himself, giving in when his head gave a particularly nasty throb. If she had a problem, he'd deal with it in the morning, he decided as he settled himself, carefully making sure he didn't touch her.

-

Iman woke slowly. She couldn't remember the last time she'd slept that well. She propped herself up with one arm and swept the hair from her eyes with the other. Her eyes landed on the mattress in front of her, and, more importantly, the man sprawled across it.

Her reaction was immediate and instinctive. She shrieked and scrambled away from him, stopping only when her back hit the wall.

Adam's head jerked up and he glared blearily at her.

"What are you *doing?*" she demanded, her voice embarrassingly shrill.

Adam lazily scrubbed a hand across his face. "I *was* sleeping."

"Why in here?" Iman asked shakily. She folded her arms around herself and her right hand came into contact with the holster she'd refastened around her arm earlier. She glanced down at it, startled.

Adam snorted. "I told you, that won't kill anyone."

"I wasn't-" Iman tried to defend herself. But he wasn't listening. She watched as he got to his feet and made his way to a chest of drawers on the far side of the room.

He tossed something on the bed. "If you want to stab someone," he said in a patronizing voice, "you need something a bit bigger. See?"

Iman glanced at the knife on the bed. "Yeah," she squeaked, scooting even further against the wall. "I see."

"Keep it," Adam offered.

"No, thank you." She was liable to hurt herself rather than anyone else with something like that.

Adam rolled his eyes, looking impatient. He grabbed the knife, then took her arm. "Keep it," he repeated, sliding the holster up her arm and tightening the strap.

Iman shook her head stubbornly. "No." She unfastened the big knife and held it out awkwardly. She did *not* want to keep that thing.

"There's only one bedroom."

"What?" Iman furrowed her brow in confusion. What was he talking about?

"There's only one bedroom," Adam repeated. "That's what I was doing in here. I'm not sleeping on the couch, it was uncomfortable enough for the few hours I did it last night. You can sleep there or you can keep the knife and sleep in here."

"I'm not going to do anything to you either way," he added. "Keep the knife or don't. Sleep in the bed or don't. It makes no difference. I just don't want you waking me up with the screaming."

That was... fair, Iman had to admit. Still... The fear she'd been grappling with since the previous day raised its head.

"Will it even make a difference?"

"What?"

"The knife," Iman elaborated. "If you wanted to hurt me..." She looked him straight in the eyes. "Would it make a difference?"

"Yes," he said calmly. "It would."

"Enough to stop you?" Iman pressed.

"No," Adam admitted. "Probably not. But," he added, "it would probably hurt a lot."

Iman couldn't decide whether to be scared or amused.

Adam yawned then and she eyed him guiltily. "Sorry."

"Don't do it again." He stretched. "Are you going back to sleep?"

Not with him in there!

"No," Iman scrambled off the bed. "I'll just... go somewhere else."

She snatched up her shoes and hurried out. It was only later that she realized she'd kept a hold on the knife.

Iman regretted her decision as soon as she lay down. Adam's couch was the most uncomfortable thing she'd ever felt. She was almost sure that the floor wouldn't be as uncomfortable.

After an indeterminable amount of time shifting around trying to find an at least less *un*comfortable position, she finally gave up. It was dawn, she may as well accept that she was done sleeping for the night.

But what was she going to do for the next few hours? All she had with her were her shoes and a heavy, scary knife.

She studied the doorway. Was it rude to go exploring? It wasn't her apartment... But she was going to be living there for the foreseeable future.

It wasn't *really* an invasion of privacy if she didn't start opening cupboards, right?

-

"What are you doing?"

Iman jumped, letting out a shout. She spun around, her hand pressed against her heart. "You scared me!"

Adam stood in the doorway, his arms crossed against his chest. "What are you doing?" he repeated icily. His eyes were hard.

"Your couch is terrible," Iman stalled.

"What does that have to do with you being in my office?"

"I couldn't sleep." Iman glanced at Adam out of the corner of her eye. His face was impassive. "I got bored."

Adam said nothing.

Iman squirmed uncomfortably and started to babble. "I'm sorry, I know it's an invasion of privacy. I was just really bored. I didn't touch anything! I was just looking."

Still nothing.

"I – I'll leave. Sorry."

"Wait!" Adam grabbed her arm.

"What?" Iman looked up.

"You didn't read anything?"

Iman shook her head vigorously. "No, I was just looking."

Adam frowned harder. "Looking at what?"

"The rooms? I was really bored." Iman bit her lip. "I know, it's kind of rude. I'm sorry," she added hopefully.

"That's it?" Adam checked.

"Yeah," Iman confirmed nervously. He still had hold of her arm.

"Don't do it again," he said simply. "If you're bored, go somewhere else."

"Okay," Iman agreed immediately.

He let go of her. "You're sure you didn't read anything?"

"I'm sure!"

"*If* you did-" Adam took hold of her shoulders and looked seriously at her.

"I didn't!"

"*If you did,*" Adam repeated, as though she hadn't spoken, "keep whatever it is to yourself. Do you understand me? Don't tell anyone. Not even your grandfather."

"O-okay," Iman said shakily. "I won't tell anyone. I promise." He let go of her. "Okay. Don't come in here again."

"I won't." Her voice wobbled. Iman pressed her lips together.

Adam sighed. "Don't cry."

Easier said than done. Iman nodded silently and slipped past Adam. She heard him swear loudly behind her and her shoulders hunched involuntarily at the violent sound.

-

She'd been *in his office.* Adam resisted the urge to swear again. He didn't want to make her cry harder. What the hell had she been doing in his office?

He dropped into his desk chair and buried his face in his hands. He wasn't angry at her, not really. He was angry at himself. He couldn't believe he'd left the door unlocked. He knew better.

It was one thing when he was being sloppy with his own life. But the information in his files, on his laptop... it was important to other people. Being careless with that put *them* at risk.

He'd thought he'd left that kind of stupidity behind when he was fifteen. It was jarring to know that he hadn't.

Well, what are you going to do about it, brat? Ali's voice rang in his ears. It was the same thing he'd asked Adam upon hearing of the disaster Adam's first job had been.

Adam had fixed it then. And he'd fix it now too.

He got to his feet and began to gather up files. Fifteen minutes later, he was done. His office was spotless. *Everything* had been locked away, from the smallest scrap of paper to the thickest file.

There.

The tension that had been knotting his shoulders since he'd discovered Iman in his office finally began to drain.

Iman.

He'd scared her again. Had made her cry, if he wasn't mistaken.

She'd been in the wrong. She shouldn't have come into his office.

He wanted to apologize to her anyway. The thought of her

crying – because of him, because of something he'd done – sat ill with him. Besides, her grandfather would skin him if the old man found out.

Adam sighed yet again. How had his life gotten so complicated? In the space of a few weeks, no less.

He got to his feet and went in search of her – of his wife.

He found her in the lounge, curled up on his uncomfortable couch with her feet tucked underneath her. She looked like a kicked puppy and Adam was hit with the feeling that he'd done something inexcusable.

She curled up even further as he came near. God, she was fragile! Was it because she'd been coddled? The gauze on her face didn't help either.

Adam pushed these thoughts away. It didn't particularly matter *why* she was the way she was. It was the way she was and he was the idiot unfortunate enough to have to deal with it.

"I'm... sorry," he said uncomfortably. "I didn't mean to make you cry."

Iman stared at him. "What?" she said blankly.

"I'm sorry," Adam repeated.

"Oh." She sounded surprised. "It... it's okay."

"Don't go in my office again."

"I won't."

Adam nodded decisively. "Right. Good."

They stared at each other awkwardly.

"Um-"

"I-"

Iman's stomach growled loudly. She gasped and then began to giggle. "Sorry! I – didn't eat much yesterday."

"Breakfast." He could do breakfast. "Do you like eggs?"

Iman nodded.

Adam disappeared gratefully into the kitchen.

-

Iman shuddered and dropped her forehead on her knees. That could have gone a *lot* worse. Idiot.

She'd relaxed. God knew why but she had. How stupid could she get?

She had been sure, for a moment there, that Adam was going to hit her. He'd been angry, she knew that. There had been no screaming. He hadn't even been rough when he grabbed her. But he had been furious.

He'd scared her more than her mother ever had. Iman could get away from Aasia. She'd never fought back, but she could run. It had saved her more than once.

But Adam... She'd tried to run and he'd caught her. With barely any effort.

What the hell had she gotten herself into?

Her eyes blurred with tears and she sniffed hard, shifting.

Something dug into her thigh and she looked down. The knife Adam had tossed her that morning.

"Would it make a difference?"

"Yes, it would."

Iman pulled the heavy piece of steel out of its holster and looked at it. Earlier, the weight had unnerved her. Now, it felt comforting.

CHAPTER NINE

There was a weight on her chest, making it hard to breathe. Iman didn't bother to open her eyes as she planted her hands firmly and shoved. There was an irritated grumble and the pressure eased.

It was strange, how quickly they'd adjusted to sharing a bed. Adam had a tendency to sprawl out and roll on top of her in the night which had initially been fairly alarming. Iman had screamed so loudly the first night she'd woken up surrounded by darkness and pinned underneath Adam's considerable weight that his immediate reaction had been to grab the gun he kept next to the bed.

Now, just over a week later, the weight barely fazed her. She'd grown accustomed to it, just as she was growing accustomed to Adam. The apartment was large but sharing a bedroom should have had them bumping into one another. Instead, Adam manoeuvred around her so smoothly it felt like coincidence at first.

He used the guest bathroom and left the en suite to her, then spent the rest of the day holed up in his office. Iman still didn't understand how the apartment had two fully equipped bathrooms but only one bedroom.

The only time they interacted outside of the bedroom was during meals. Every day without fail, Adam would cook, then come and find her. Iman's stomach growled just thinking about it. Every meal she'd eaten in the past week had been fantastic.

She was pulled out of her daydreaming by an insistent buzzing. It sounded like a large, angry insect. The bed shifted and Iman followed Adam's outstretched arm to the source of the noise; his vibrating smart phone.

She watched him answer sleepily, then abruptly throw the covers off and leave the room, pulling the door closed behind him.

What was going on?

-

Adam was not having a good day. As was becoming the norm, he'd been shoved awake at the crack of dawn by dainty little hands.

Fair enough. He'd rolled on top of Iman and squashed her. He couldn't exactly hold a grudge against her for wanting to breathe.

But unlike every other day this week, today Adam *hadn't* been able to just roll over and drop back off.

Today, he'd been just about to fall back asleep when he was rudely awakened by the buzzing of his cellphone. And now, he stood yawning and shivering as his stepfather played his favourite game of babbling nonsense in between hinting at actual important news.

"Could you just get to the point?" he snapped finally, now

thoroughly annoyed.

There was silence on the other end of the line for a moment. When Ali spoke again, his voice was poisonously sweet.

"Do you have something more important to be doing than *listening to your employer?*"

Adam suppressed the urge to bang his head against the wall. "At six in the morning? Yeah, I do. It's called sleep-"

"Don't be uncouth!" he was admonished.

Huh? Adam frowned down at his phone.

"Everyone is well aware of what you're doing with your wife right now. Mentioning it is tacky."

"That's – that's not-! Oh, my God." Adam put his face in his hands. "That's *not* what I meant. We're not even-"

He took a deep breath. "Why did you call me?"

"You're 'not even' what? Are you having problems in the bedroom?" Ali sounded genuinely concerned.

"I thought it was uncouth to talk about," Adam said innocently.

Ali growled. "Adam, don't be a little brat. Is something wrong? Do I need to call you a doctor?" Adam experienced a moment of horror. Ali *would* call a doctor and he'd be as obnoxious about the whole thing as possible. Adam would have an entire compound of people commenting on his *capabilities* by noon. He shuddered. "Nothing is wrong!" "Are you sure?"

"Yes!"

"There's nothing to be ashamed of."

"I know!" Adam yelled. "Why did you call me?"

"Hmm? Oh, yes. You have a new assignment. I need you here to discuss the details."

"Why can't you just send a file?"

"I don't feel like it," Ali said blandly. "Be here by nine."

Adam pulled the phone away from his ear and checked the time. "I'll have to leave *right now* to make that."

"Yes," Ali agreed. "Get going."

Adam scrunched his eyes shut and worked on not screaming. "Fine," he hissed, through gritted teeth. "Anything else?"

"Yes."

"What?"

"Bring Iman. Your mother would like to see her."

Adam gaped at the phone. "Wh-No!" It was too late. Ali had already hung up.

He growled in frustration. Ali was petty enough to send him right back into the city if Adam tried to arrive without Iman. His stepfather was the world's most obnoxious control freak.

He should have just let the stupid call go to voicemail.

-

Iman was still awake when Adam returned, the scowl on his face so deep it looked permanent. "You need to get dressed," he told her. "Quickly." The corner of his mouth twisted. "We're already late."

"What are we late for?" Iman climbed out of bed and went to her side of Adam's closet.

"Breakfast."

Iman glanced at her phone. It was barely seven.

"We're driving for a while," Adam elaborated, answering her silent question. "To my mother's house."

He came over to the closet and reached over her head. "Try to be ready in the next ten minutes," he requested. "The later we are, the longer my headache will be once we get there."

He sounded so put out about being scolded, it made Iman giggle.

"What?" Adam glanced down at her.

"I'm sorry." She pressed her lips together. "Nothing."

"You're laughing at me?"

"No!" Iman lied, trying to suppress the laughter. She hiccuped.

"You *are* laughing at me." Adam frowned at her. "What's so funny?"

"You're pretty worried about your Mom yelling at you."

The lines of Adam's face softened. "I'm not worried about my Mom. I'm worried about my stepfather. And," he leaned forward, starting to grin. "I'm not worried about him yelling at me, I'm worried about him shooting at me. Don't forget, ten minutes." With that reminder, he grabbed the little stack of clothing he'd been accumulating and headed for the door.

Iman gaped after him.

-

Adam glanced over at the tiny blonde in his passenger seat. She'd been asleep for the past hour, making an almost offensively cute little snuffling sound with every breath. Peacefully asleep, she looked even tinier than normal and

Adam was forcibly reminded of the day they'd first met.

He'd thought she was a child initially. A proper look at her chest had told him different. But he'd still thought she was adorable. Until he'd found out who she was, at least.

He had been watching her all week, waiting for the tantrums and demands to start. But she didn't act like a princess. In fact, from the way she skulked around sometimes, it felt almost like *he'd* been the one to trap *her*.

He couldn't figure her out. Was she a naive girl? A manipulative woman? Something else entirely?

Adam didn't know and it was driving him insane. He *hated* puzzles. They nagged at him until he'd unravelled them, distracting him from everything else until he found the solution.

He looked at Iman again. She was the most infuriating puzzle he'd ever seen. He only had a fraction of the pieces and he had a nasty feeling that the few he did have were somehow upside down.

It was almost half past nine. He'd been waiting for her to wake up for the past ten minutes. Ali was probably spitting mad and pacing.

Adam reached over. No point in putting it off even longer. "Iman? Iman, wake up."

She started then blinked up at him sleepily. "Mhm? Wha's matter?"

"We're here."

-

It was like he'd thrown a bucket of ice water over her head. Any last vestiges of sleepiness that had been clinging to Iman fled.

99

She was suddenly wide awake and experiencing all the nerves that came along with being properly present in the moment.

Adam looked bemused. "That was quick."

"Abject terror's good for an energy boost," Iman snapped, before she could think better of it.

Adam looked taken aback. "Terror?"

"Terror's maybe a little bit of an exaggeration," Iman admitted. "Just a little though."

"Uh huh. What is it that's so terrifying?"

Iman fidgeted with her seatbelt. "I'm really bad with new people. And your mom's, she's really sweet but she's kind of like a-a." She faltered, unable to think of a word to describe Adam's mother that wasn't either offensive or completely inaccurate.

"A pit bull?"

"Yes!" Iman agreed fervently. Then her brain caught up to her mouth. "No! I mean... yes. But... a nice pit bull?" She buried her face in her hands and groaned. A pit bull. That wasn't offensive at all.

She braced herself, waiting for the yelling to start. Nothing happened.

Iman lifted her head warily.

Adam was staring at her with a strange look on his face. Their eyes met and he shook his head lightly, as though to clear it. "My mother has no idea how we met or why we got married. As far as she's concerned, I liked the look of you and proposed."

"Oh. But wait, then-" Certain things she'd heard on her wedding day had begun to make a lot more sense. Iman winced guiltily. She'd thought Lina was absurdly friendly, even a bit ridiculous. In truth, she'd been lied to.

"I know it sounds ridiculous. But it's more plausible than what actually happened."

More plausible than being contacted by a man who could just barely be called an acquaintance and being coerced into marrying her a few days later? That wasn't exactly hard.

Iman frowned. "How long does your mother think we've known each other?"

Adam thought for a minute. "A few months? I wasn't specific." He opened his door. "Come on, we should get inside."

A thought occurred to Iman and she paused. "We don't know anything about each other."

Adam shrugged. "I'm a private person."

Iman couldn't shake the feeling that something was about to go horribly wrong.

-

There was a crack in the ceiling right above her. Iman followed it with her eyes and tried to guess its length.

She'd been waiting for Adam to resurface from his private and seemingly very intense conversation with a stunning, willowy brunette for long enough that she was beginning to feel stiff from standing in one position for so long.

It showed no sign of letting up any time soon.

Iman wondered who the brunette was. Adam had made a beeline for her as soon as he'd caught sight of her and they'd been absorbed in one another ever since. She was gorgeous, whoever she was, with a kind of intensity that drew attention.

She certainly seemed to be drawing *Adam's* attention. The catty thought made Iman do a mental double take. Had she really thought that?

Her cheeks burned. She had. It *bothered* her that Adam was so fascinated by this woman. But why? She had no real claim to his attention. He hadn't married her out of any particular desire to do so.

What was happening to her? A week ago she'd been worried about keeping Adam from killing her and now she was fretting about who he was *attracted* to?

The sound of her name being called made Iman jump. Adam and his friend were both staring at her. They looked wonderful together, she couldn't help but notice. Both tall and dark, they seemed to fit beautifully together.

"Sorry, I was just-" Iman faltered. "Never mind. What were you saying?"

Adam had been making introductions, it seemed. He repeated them quickly. The brunette's name was Kat. She was his oldest friend.

"Interesting to meet you," Kat said coolly, examining Iman in a way that somehow managed to make her feel every one of her flaws all at once.

"Likewise." Iman dredged up a smile. As *interesting* as she imagined coming face to face with a crocodile would be.

"Are we going inside?" she asked Adam.

Kat reached out and took her hand and Iman fought the urge to yank it back. "We are. Adam has some things to see to. Come on, I can't wait to hear all about you."

CHAPTER TEN

Adam headed to the den, turning over the conversation he had just had with Kat in his mind as he went. She'd been cryptic, mindful of Iman who was hovering nearby, but the underlying message had been clear: big trouble. Someone had done something and now Adam was being called upon to clean up their mess.

He met no one along the way. He'd initially assumed that Ali had called a full meeting and everyone was waiting but Kat had told him different. They were all gone. Apart from the men at the gate, the compound was deserted.

It was unnerving.

He found Ali in the corner of the dark room, just where Kat had said he would be. He had a laptop open in front of him and two empty coffee cups at his elbow.

A look of relief briefly flitted over his face at the sight of Adam before being replaced with a scowl. "You forget how to tell time?"

Adam ignored the jab. "What's going on?"

"Connor is dead. I received these," Ali handed a folder over to Adam, "in the mail today."

Adam glanced at the photos and grimaced. "Someone made a mess." He couldn't even make out exactly how Connor had died but it was clear that the man's death had been painful.

He hadn't liked Connor in the slightest. He'd been rude and condescending and the way he'd leered at both Kat and Adam's mother had ensured they were never friends. But Adam felt a stab of pity for the dead man nonetheless. No one deserved to die so painfully.

"I want you to find out who killed him."

"Do you think they're planning to keep going?"

"It might just be a simple dispute. It's not the first time there's been a killing over a double booked job." Ali pinched the bridge of his nose. "It might even be something personal. Connor was... abrasive. I don't know. But there's no harm in finding out."

"Where am I going?"

"Italy. You leave this evening." Ali shut the laptop and got to his feet. "Your mother is furious with me."

"Is that why we're here for breakfast?"

"In part," Ali allowed. "I may have hoped that another chance to interrogate your wife would put her in a better mood. We'll see if it worked."

Adam glanced around as they walked through the silent house. "Where is everyone?"

"I was not in the best mood when I got the mail this morning."

Translation – Ali had terrified everyone into disappearing so they weren't at risk of irritating him into shooting them.

"Any casualties?" he asked facetiously.

"Just one. A trainee. He wasn't much of a loss, all things considered."

"What?" Adam stopped dead. He couldn't have heard right. Could he?

"You *killed* a trainee?" This had to be a joke. A very unfunny, slightly worrisome joke. Adam knew all too well that his stepfather had a hideous temper. But murdering trainees? That was extreme.

Ali had the grace to look chagrined. "I choked a trainee," he corrected. "He's still alive. But, understandably, not particularly interested in staying around."

"Oh." Adam could feel his heartbeat beginning to slow. "Poor guy."

Ali waved a hand dismissively. "I'm sure he'll get over it."

-

Iman's head was spinning and her throat was dry. She'd never talked so much in her life.

"Iman, what did you say your parents did, dear?" Lina asked sweetly.

Iman hadn't mentioned her parents at all.

She was saved from having to answer by the arrival of Adam and his stepfather and it was all she could do to not sigh in relief.

Lina was immediately distracted. "Oh, there you are!" She squeezed Adam around the neck then levelled him with a disapproving look. "How many times have I told you to come and greet me before you disappear with your father! Well, never mind. At least you're here now. And we have all day together before you leave!" She petted his cheeks.

All day? Iman prayed that wasn't true. Fifteen minutes with the tiny woman had left her hoarse, she couldn't even imagine what a whole day would be like.

"Actually, Mom, we're going to need to leave pretty soon."

Lina looked scandalized. "What? But your flight isn't until tonight!"

"I need to drop Iman off at her grandfather's."

Iman tried to look like this wasn't news to her.

Adam's stepfather took that moment to intervene. He leaned down and whispered something into his wife's ear and Lina's frown immediately smoothed out. "Oh. Oh! Well, alright then."

Iman glanced curiously at him, wondering what he'd said to cut his wife off so neatly. This was the man Adam had said would shoot at him? He seemed so friendly... She continued watching him as they ate, trying to make the conflicting images reconcile themselves. She was fairly certain Adam *hadn't* been joking, but even still, she couldn't see the charming, handsome man seated across from her holding a gun.

She'd just about decided that Adam *had* been joking and she'd just missed it – which was reasonable, she'd only known him for a little while – and then Ali Cassim looked at her.

Iman shivered involuntarily. She'd seen that look several times before. Her mother had worn it just as Aasia had raked her nails across Iman's face. Her stomach churned.

Cassim smiled widely at her and Iman dropped her knife with a clatter.

Lina looked at her in concern. "Iman, is everything alright? You don't look very good."

She didn't feel it either. "I- No," she said unsteadily.

Vaguely, she noticed that Lina had gotten to her feet and was leaning over her. "Come on," the other woman said gently. "Some fresh air might help."

She was guided to her feet and a warm hand settled in the middle of her back, urging her forward. Moments later, she was settled on a porch swing.

"If the swaying makes you nauseous, let me know and I'll have Adam bring you a chair. Do you know what made you feel sick?" Lina settled herself next to Iman, facing her.

Iman did know. Cold, dead eyes. But how was she meant to explain that to her mother in law?

-

"What a delicate little flower," Kat commented as they watched Lina lead Iman away. "I'm gonna go before all of this makes me sick to my stomach. I'm sure your mother wouldn't want me puking on her tiles."

Adam made to follow her. He'd barely gotten halfway out of his seat when a hand closed around his shoulder and pulled him back. "Let her go," Ali advised him. "She's not in any mood to talk right now."

He was right. When Kat ran off, she did it because she wanted to be isolated. He had made the mistake of following her before and all he'd gotten for it was a non-verbal grunt and then, after he'd irritated her enough by his constant questions, a knife thrown at his head.

He still had a tiny scar on his cheek.

"I'm leaving tonight," he grumbled. "If she holes up now, I won't see her until I get back."

"She knows you're leaving, she's the one who booked your flight," Ali countered. "Bugging her now will make things worse. You know this as well as I do."

He frowned at Adam. "Why are you being so erratic? First you were late and now you're being overbearing. Are you deliberately trying to push everyone's buttons today?"

Adam's eyes went involuntarily to Iman's empty seat.

Ali made a sound of comprehension. "I see. Speaking of your wife, why did she keep eyeing me like I was a demon?"

"She did?" Adam hadn't been paying much attention to Iman, distracted as he'd been by his mother.

"Yes, it was quite unnerving, actually."

Adam thought for a moment. There was only one real explanation. "I told her that you shoot at me."

"You deserve it!"

Adam was treated to a narrow-eyed look. "You seem to be getting strangely fond of that new wife of yours."

"She's not as bad as I thought she'd be."

"Be careful not to get *too* fond of her," Ali advised. "A sentimental mercenary is a bad joke and a worse security risk."

"You *love* my mother," Adam pointed out, his cheeks burning.

"I am the boss. Do you know what that means?"

"You get to be a giant hypocrite?"

"Oh, you do know!" Ali smiled, pleased. "That's right. I get to do exactly as I please because I am the one who makes the rules." He leaned over and squeezed Adam's jaw, laughing when the action earned him a sour look and a glare. "You'll get your turn."

Yeah, right. Adam snorted. Chances were high he'd be cold in the ground before Ali Cassim even began to falter. He said as much making his stepfather shake his head.

"You underestimate yourself and overestimate me. You will be in charge one day. Although," he allowed, "it will likely be several decades in the future."

Adam's mother found them laughing minutes later.

Her hands went automatically to her hips at the sight of them and the look she levelled at Adam sobered him instantly.

"Your wife is ill and you're sitting here cracking jokes? Is this how I raised you?" Lina shook her head. "Go and be a good husband. Find out what's wrong and comfort her." she ordered, pointing her hand in the direction of the door.

Adam had a fleeting moment of panic. How was he supposed to do that? Iman was almost as much of a stranger to *him* as she was to Lina. And his mother had no idea that that was the case.

Adam headed out the door, firmly convinced that he was about to make a fool of himself.

Half an hour later, he was still fighting the urge to bang his head against the steering wheel.

At least she hadn't laughed at him.

She hadn't done *anything* except sit there and tremble for a while. If he hadn't known better, he would have said that she was scared, not sick.

It had been murder trying to get anything out of her and eventually, he'd given up trying to figure it out. It was none of his business anyway.

-

"I'm leaving for Italy in a few hours," Adam announced unexpectedly, while they were driving back to his apartment.

"Okay..." Iman glanced at him. "How long will you be gone?"

"It depends. There's no set timeline for what I'm going to do. What are you going to do while I'm gone?"

Iman was caught off-guard by this unexpected question. "I don't know. Is there something I should be doing?"

Adam took his eyes off the road for a moment to stare at her. "I meant, are you going to be staying at the apartment? You'll be by yourself for an unknown amount of time and I don't have guards at the doors to keep you safe," he reminded her.

A spike of fear shot through her. "You think I should stay with my grandfather?"

Adam nodded. "It's the safer option."

"Um, okay. I'll get someone to pick me up." Iman reached for her cellphone.

"Don't. I'll drop you off."

"Oh," Iman didn't know what to say. "Thank you. But... isn't it less convenient?" He'd have to drop her off, then drop his car back at his apartment before getting a taxi to the airport.

"Don't worry about it. Be ready to leave by four, please."

They spent the remainder of the journey in silence. When they got to the apartment Adam headed into his office without a word to her and Iman, bored and still jittery, decided to spend some of her energy packing.

She had kept a substantial amount of her things at her grandfather's home. In truth, she didn't need to pack anything at all besides her handbag and sketchpad. Nonetheless, she wasted over an hour packing and repacking her smaller suitcase before she was done.

There *was* something that she could have been doing. Something that, if she was honest, had needed to be taken care of days ago. But she'd been too afraid to do anything about it.

Aasia. She'd contacted Iman the morning of her wedding to let her know that the Rahmans wouldn't be attending either the ceremony or the little get together that took place afterwards.

Apparently they were on a cruise and wouldn't be back for at least a month. But two days ago, Aasia had demanded that Iman call her immediately. Iman hadn't obeyed. She had instead elected to pretend that she'd never received the message. God only knew how long avoidance would work against Aasia but Iman knew in her gut that she was playing with a bomb no matter what she chose to do.

She picked up her phone and dialled her mother's number. Her thumb hovered over the green call button as she debated what to do.

Fed up with her own fear, Iman made the call, her stomach twisting with nerves.

"Iman!" Aasia's voice was sugary-sweet, a sure sign that she was with other people. "I'm so glad you *finally* called."

There was a rustling noise and then Iman heard, muffled. "My daughter. She's on her honeymoon! Can you imagine? I'm old enough to have a married daughter." Aasia giggled. "I know, I don't look it, do I? I'd better go talk to her, I'll just be a sec so don't you go anywhere!"

A male voice spoke in the background. "I'll be right here waiting for you, sweetheart."

Iman's cheeks burned. Even now, years after being exposed to it for the first time, Aasia's casual infidelity still made her cringe.

"Well," Aasia snapped abruptly, "you certainly took your own sweet time to call me back. Just what was so important that you decided to ignore me?"

"I'm sorry," Iman said dutifully. "I should have called you back faster."

"Yes, you should have. But you've always been a disappointment. I shouldn't even expect more from you by now, you're clearly incapable of it."

Iman bit the inside of her cheek.

"Well, aren't you going to tell me?" her mother demanded shrilly. "Am I supposed to beg you?"

What? What was Aasia talking about?

There was an enraged shriek and Iman realized she'd spoken her thought out loud.

"Have some respect when you talk to me!" The tone made her back stiffen.

"Sorry."

Aasia huffed. "Now tell me about your husband," she demanded. "It's bad enough that you didn't even introduce me to him, you will not embarrass me any more! I refuse to be shown up in front of the people I know because *you* want to be secretive, you ungrateful little brat. Tell me everything I need to know about him, right now!"

"His name is Adam Cassim. He's two years older than me." Iman wished she had the guts to just cut the call.

"Is he rich?"

"No," Iman lied. "He's not." Adam *was* wealthy, of course he was. Mercenaries were paid incredibly well – they risked too much of themselves not to be.

Aasia tsked. "Well, I'm not surprised. Your grandfather associates with terrible people. You *should* have waited and let me choose you a husband, but of course you had to rush and do what you wanted. Well, don't come crying to me if it's hard to live with."

"I won't," Iman snapped, infuriated by the crack against Ibrahim and emboldened by the distance.

"That attitude will do you no favours," Aasia assured her. "And don't think you can come back to my house, after the way you left! You're just going to have to tell that new husband of yours that even your own mother can't stand you. I wonder how long he'll stay with you once he knows that," she hissed vindictively.

Aasia disconnected the call, saving Iman from having to come up with a retort.

Frustration and regret welled within her. She should never have called. Why *had* she called? What had she been thinking, that suddenly her mother was going to change? That Iman leaving would make Aasia treat her better?

Iman squeezed her eyes shut and pressed a hand against them, trying to stop the tears. It didn't work.

Yes.

The stupid little girl inside Iman, the one who'd never truly accepted that her mother didn't love her, had been hoping that somehow, things would be different. Somehow, Aasia would realize that she was hurting her daughter and would change.

Stupid.

She was still so stupid.

-

"Hey, Ms. Newlywed!" James grinned down at her. "What are you doing here?" He glanced behind her. "And with a bag? Trouble in Paradise?"

Iman felt her mood lift immediately and the smile she gave James was almost genuine. "No, Adam has a job," she explained.

"Ah!" James nodded. "So you're gonna be pining away, huh?" He made a comically distraught expression, pressing an imaginary handkerchief to his eyes.

Iman giggled.

"There," James said smugly. "Now you don't look so miserable any more."

Iman winced. Had she really looked that bad?

"Thanks, James."

"Any time," the tall man assured her. "Just think of me as your own personal clown."

"You're everyone's clown, Blackwell," Shaida called as she made her way to them. "Now get out of the way, you're blocking the doorway."

"What? Oh!" James moved to the side, letting Iman in.

"Your grandfather has been waiting for you for over an hour, go put him out of everyone's misery," Shaida ordered as she took Iman's suitcase and handed it to James. "And you, put this upstairs."

Iman gasped in dismay. "I gave him the wrong time?"

"No, you're right on time. Actually, I think you're early. He's just excited to see you."

Shaida put a hand at the middle of her back and urged her forward. "Go on, go see him."

Iman did as she was told.

Moments later, cuddled against her grandfather, Iman finally, finally felt safe again.

He looked dismayed at the sight of her.

She sniffed, unable to help herself and Ibrahim pulled back. "What's wrong? Wh-"

He froze, his eyes hardening and turned her arm over to inspect it. "What the hell is this?" he hissed. "When did this happen?"

Lightly, he touched the scratches Aasia had left. "These don't look new, Iman. Are they? Do I need to hunt down your husband?"

"No," Iman admitted reluctantly, cursing herself. "They're from when I was with my mother."

"She scratched you," Ibrahim said flatly. "Why didn't you *tell* me?" he demanded hotly. "You said you'd scraped up your face, I didn't even know about this!"

"There wasn't any point! Shaida came and got me and it was over! What would telling you have done?"

Ibrahim deflated.

"I just didn't want to think about it again," Iman whispered miserably. "It was over. I wanted to forget it had ever happened."

"Oh sweetheart. It's not that easy."

No, it really wasn't. It wasn't easy in the slightest.

CHAPTER ELEVEN

It had been a difficult job. He thought he had been prepared for it. He knew going in that it would be messy, knew that he'd have to do more than just kill.

Killing was easier. It was quick – when he did it, at least. And he could lie to himself that he was being merciful. He'd made it his calling card – clean, quick murder.

But this was different. He'd had to track down well-hidden information and that had necessitated utilizing his other skills.

He'd needed to butcher people into spilling secrets. There were prettier words for it; interrogation, information gathering, coercion.

None of those meaningless words hid the true, brutal nature of this side of his work. Hiding behind them didn't make him feel any cleaner and it sure as Hell didn't stop their screams from ringing in his ears.

He'd forgotten a million things. Unimportant and important memories alike. But every moment of time that he'd spent making a person scream was etched into his brain.

He would never forget a second of that. Those memories were crystal clear. They'd remain that way until the day he died. It almost felt like his mind's way of punishing him.

He'd accepted it as an unavoidable part of his life just as he'd accepted the violence and gore of the world he had been unwillingly dragged into when his mother had made a choice with her heart instead of her head.

He could do nothing else.

He wasn't brave enough. Wasn't strong enough.

Resistance may not have been futile but it was beyond him.

-

The past two weeks had been bliss. Iman couldn't remember when last she'd been so relaxed. And the constant pampering hadn't hurt either. Between Ibrahim and Shaida, she hadn't been allowed to do much of anything for herself.

Thinking of Shaida made her sigh. The older woman's pregnancy seemed to be making her even more protective than normal, to the extent that she all but refused to leave Iman's side. Iman didn't mean to sound ungrateful but the constant hovering was beginning to chafe a little.

More importantly, Shaida wasn't meant to be in the city any longer at all. She was supposed to have left a week ago to go stay with her own mother and spend the rest of her pregnancy safely away from even the vaguest possibility of any danger. But Shaida had insisted on staying and even though no one had said it outright, Iman knew it was because Shaida didn't want to leave her. They'd all – Iman, her grandfather and even Shaida's husband – given up on arguing with the heavily pregnant woman because it upset her so much that her doctor was concerned about what the extra stress was doing to her baby.

Thankfully, it looked like she'd be leaving before long and perhaps that would ease Shaida's mind enough to allow her old babysitter to leave before she drove her poor husband to distraction. She'd gotten a text from Adam that morning, letting her know that he'd be back in town soon. He hadn't elaborated on when soon was exactly but Iman had taken it to mean in a few days.

She looked out the window and caught sight of the biggest gift her grandfather had given her. A brand new car to replace the one she'd had to leave when she'd left her mother's house. Iman had no doubt that the car and everything else she'd left behind had been discarded within hours.

Aasia had never been the sentimental type and Iman doubted she'd want to keep reminders of an unsatisfactory daughter around. She wouldn't bother to give the things back to Iman either. It wasn't worth the inconvenience.

In direct contrast, not a single thing she'd left in her grandfather's house had been touched unless it was to have it cleaned.

The difference was easy to explain – her grandfather wanted her and her mother... didn't.

-

He was exhausted, sweaty and hungry.

All Adam wanted to do was drive home and dive into a shower where he could scrub himself raw and then pass out for a good few days. Unfortunately, he couldn't. He had to pick up his wife.

His already sour mood worsened every second he got closer to the Khan mansion. The last thing he wanted to do was deal with people when he was this filthy. He didn't even like Kat being around him in this state and she'd seen him in all manner of compromising situations.

Iman... Dealing with her would be hell.

Adam knew he was being unfair. Iman wasn't a killer. And she had no idea what he had been doing for the past two and a half weeks.

He had no doubt that she envisioned his job to be as clean and emotionless as a video game. The details would probably give her nightmares for the rest of her life.

She was sheltered. It wasn't her fault.

He resented her for it anyway.

She got to live in a clean world, with sunshine and rainbows, while he was forced to deal with muck and blood and gore.

And it was his own damn fault too.

That was the worst part. Knowing that he'd dug his own grave by being too spineless to resist and stand his ground.

-

Adam had been locked in the bathroom for over an hour now and Iman had no idea what to do with herself. He was clearly in a horrible mood and he'd looked almost... sickly.

She couldn't decide whether she should leave him alone or go and ask him if he needed anything.

She didn't want to irritate him. And he'd clearly not been feeling good.

But he'd looked so terrible she felt sorry for him.

She'd wait for another five minutes and then check on him. And if he didn't want her help, she'd just leave him alone.

She was well-accustomed to terrible patients – her grandfather seemed to collect them.

She'd lost count of the number of times she'd encountered one of his people in the halls, clearly injured and in need of medical attention and viciously denying that they were in anything but perfect condition.

Perhaps it was a trait they all shared.

Whatever it was, she had never let the grumpiness faze her before. And she wasn't planning to start now.

-

There was an angry, tiny woman in his space.

Adam had no idea how he had landed himself in this situation.

He was stark naked – still – and besides blushing red enough that Adam wondered how her body had enough blood left to circulate through the rest of it, Iman didn't seemed fazed by it.

The rest of him hadn't given her pause either. Scars, muscle and what he knew from the mirror to be a fairly impressive scowl hadn't stopped her from leaning into his space and clucking over the wounds he still hadn't tended to.

Adam couldn't understand why she was bothering to try and fix him. He could take care of himself. And he would, eventually.

He'd said as much to the tiny blonde and she'd had the audacity to roll her eyes at him and enquire in a voice sweet as sugar whether he truly was as dumb as a bag of rocks or whether he just enjoyed pretending.

The laugh that had bubbled in his throat had shocked them both and a small, satisfied smile had curved around her pretty mouth.

Adam glanced down at her now, bent over at the waist and peering at his right hip as she cleaned a long gash, utterly intent on her work. It was a minor enough cut that he wouldn't have even bothered with it but she seemed adamant on going over every inch of him.

The blood in her cheeks was much prettier than the blood he so routinely spilled. In her cheeks, it was pink and covered in smooth, satiny skin. Was it as soft to touch as it looked? His fingers itched to find out.

For all that they'd shared a bed, he'd never actually touched her. He'd woken with her cheek pressed against his chest, felt her feet tangle in the blankets above him, but he had never actually reached out and touched.

The same part of him that revolted whenever he picked up a gun or knife hissed that he wasn't worthy. Touching her would taint her.

He'd get his filth on her and she'd tarnish.

Adam tucked his hands behind him to master the urge.

Iman fixed a final piece of tape to her liking and then stepped back. "There, all done." she announced happily, eyeing him with satisfaction.

Her gaze stopped at his waist and she gasped. "I'll- You should put some clothes on. Yes, that's a good idea. You must be cold, all... naked like that." she said in a rush, staring fixedly at a spot over his head.

There was the embarrassment he'd been expecting. Adam waited but Iman didn't move. "Iman," he prompted. "I need to get my clothes."

"What?" she said in a dazed tone.

"My clothes are in the bedroom. I need to go out there. Past you. You should probably go if you don't want even more of a show."

Iman squeaked and darted out of the bathroom without a backwards glance.

-

She was blushing so hard it was a wonder her skin hadn't peeled off.

Iman leaned over the balcony railing and let the breeze leech the heat from her skin. She'd flushed from head to toe the moment the steam from Adam's excessively long shower had cleared and shown her exactly how much he *wasn't* wearing.

He'd let her patch him up without too much of a fight, thankfully. She couldn't believe that he'd gone so long without properly taking care of the cuts and burns she'd seen on him and she couldn't help wondering what he would have done had she not been there.

Would he even have bothered taking care of himself? He'd left it so long already by the time she'd gotten to him. It was likely, she knew, that he'd scar worse and take longer to heal than if he'd just bothered to take a little bit of care with himself from the start.

Iman felt a familiar frustration. She'd had this exact same argument with nearly a dozen men and women before and it had always ended in them patting her on the head and assuring her that she was being overprotective. That they were big, scary assassins and they could take care of themselves.

Iman buried her face in her hands, feeling an old grief rise up and choke her. So many of them *hadn't* been able to take care of themselves. They'd been arrogant or foolish or just plain careless and they'd paid for it with their lives. She'd attended so many *preventable* funerals. After the last, she'd sworn to herself that she wouldn't let it happen again. Not ever.

And then she'd been pushed out. She'd been exiled to the other side of the city and not one of the people she'd loved with all her heart had bothered to answer her when she'd called for them.

She knew now, had known even then when she was stubbornly refusing to accept it, that her grandfather had been the one to order the lack of contact.

It had still hurt though. It hurt even now that she knew the reasoning behind it and understood that they'd stayed away for her protection, because they couldn't bear to put her in danger.

Adam wasn't the reason that she'd devoured all the information about first aid she could and seriously considered training as a nurse. He wasn't one of the ones she'd wanted to save.

But unlike them, he was here. She *could* help him.

It wasn't what she'd wanted. She'd wanted to save them. It wasn't even close to what she'd intended.

But it was something.

Maybe it would help ease the grief that she carried.

CHAPTER TWELVE

"You *don't* look awful." The look of utter shock on Kat's face made him grin despite himself. She leaned against the door frame, eyeing him curiously.

"It's that much of a surprise?" Adam feigned hurt, hunching his shoulders and shortening his stride as he walked toward her.

"No. That's not. That's not what I meant!" Kat straightened up, dropping her arms to her sides. "It's just, you're usually more awful-looking when you come back. Kind of like a corpse, actually," she said all in a rush.

Like a corpse? Adam frowned. He'd thought he'd been doing a better job of hiding the toll these jobs were taking on him. But apparently not.

Kat misread his expression. "I didn't mean you look like a dead corpse! Just..." She trailed off as she realized her mistake.

"Just an alive one?"

"No!" Kat's cheeks reddened and she crossed her arms with a huff. "Never mind, I give up." She looked up at him, still a little shorter even with the black heeled boots she wore. "I didn't mean to make you feel bad."

Adam reached out and grabbed her around the waist, towing her toward him. "I know, Clumsy-Kat." How long had it been since he'd last called her that? Adam had first used the nickname as a way to rile Kat up when she'd begun training in the ridiculous shoes she insisted on wearing. She'd fallen as often as she breathed for a few weeks there.

Adam thought that she was insane for letting her vanity overcome her common sense and had resorted to needling her every chance he got, after first reasoning and then pleading had no sway. But Kat won in the end. She stuck with it, pigheaded as always and had come away with an almost unnatural sense of balance, reminiscent of the animal that was her namesake. But even now, years later, the nickname still had the power to get her riled.

"I'm not clumsy!" Kat hissed, true to form.

Adam pretended to be confused. "Is there a different way of describing the way you were stumbling all over your words like that?"

Kat let out a shriek of frustration and lunged at him.

They slammed into the wall and Adam winced as his head made contact with the wooden panelling. Kat's fingers dug into his shoulders and she grinned viciously when he winced. "Take it back!" she demanded.

Adam grabbed a fistful of her hair and tugged. "Kat, get off me!"

"Apologize!" Kat pressed her nails in further.

Adam cursed. "Get off!" He wedged his free hand between them and shoved hard.

"Children, what the *hell* do you think you're doing?"

Adam jumped guiltily, feeling oddly like a child again, and turned his head to the side. Ali stood at the end of the hallway, glaring frostily at them.

"Adam, I've been waiting for you. Kat, seeing as you're so in need of a spar, time for some drills." Ali jerked his head to the side. "Go. Now."

Kat glanced between the two of them for a moment, hesitating.

"I'm not going to bite him, Kat. Go." Ali made a shooing motion with his hands.

She left easily then. Adam watched her slim figure as it retreated, her unbound hair swaying gently in time with her steps.

He turned to his stepfather and any amusement he'd been feeling evaporated.

"Come on, let's get this over with." Ali turned around and started to lead the way to his office.

What would happen if Adam refused? If he dug in his heels and announced that he wasn't going and Ali would simply have to live without having a play by play of Adam's depravity.

He already knew the answer to that question. His stepfather would drag him in anyway and would suddenly find himself fascinated by every detail of the entire trip.

Adam would be forced to recount every minute that he'd been gone, over and over again until his stepfather was satisfied that he'd learned his lesson and was aware of just how much worse his reports could be if Ali chose to make them that way.

Controlling bastard.

"Is there anything else?" Ali asked, eons later.

Adam cleared his throat, hoarse from all the talking. He shook his head and reached for the glass in front of him. "Nothing."

Ali put his hands together and thought for a moment.

Adam waited, wondering if it would be sufficient or if he'd be forced to go into even more gruesome detail. He braced himself for the latter, grateful that he hadn't been able to stomach eating for the past day and a half. His stomach was still churning but at least he knew that there was nothing left to bring up.

It seemed Ali was satisfied, however. "You did well," he said simply. "Better than I would have expected."

Adam didn't thank him.

He was given a quick once-over. "You have a month of downtime, barring any real problems."

A month?

Adam didn't realize he'd spoken aloud until Ali nodded at him, the older man's mouth curving up in amusement. "You've earned it. Now get out of here, your face is making everyone feel bad."

Adam was all too happy to do as he was told. A month of downtime was ridiculously generous but he wasn't going to keep questioning it. Why look a gift horse in the mouth?

Later, Adam would recall this moment and remember the answer he'd been given by one of his trainers when he'd once repeated the expression in their presence.

To check for explosives. In our line of work, anything nice is suspicious. Never assume another person's generosity. For most of us, it doesn't exist any more. Suspicion is what will keep you alive and one step ahead. Be too trusting and you've signed your own death certificate.

If only he had remembered those words that day instead of just accepting the unexpected break and not even bothering to wonder at the reasoning behind it.

Things would have been completely different, had he just stopped for a moment to think.

-

There were hands on her. Rough and unwieldy, pawing at her like some kind of animal. Iman struggled to get away, panic closing her throat and silencing her scream.

The bed shifted as the body above her used their knees to pin her to the mattress.

Panic gave her strength and she ripped one of her hands free, hope kindling in her chest, only for it to be extinguished when it was easily recaptured. Her arms were pushed above her, allowing her captor to take both her wrists in one large, filthy hand.

He leaned down and whispered in her ear. "That's it. Keep fighting. It's no fun when you don't."

Tears of fury streamed down her cheeks and she thrashed uselessly.

He laughed. "Just like that," he murmured approvingly, a sick excitement gleaming in his eyes.

He had turned the lights on when he'd come in and she could see the gleeful smile on his face.

Iman squeezed her eyes shut tight, unable to stomach looking at that disgusting face any longer.

There was a pause and then the hand holding her wrists tightened. "Open your eyes," he demanded, panting over her.

She ignored him, vicious satisfaction flooding through her at this one last rebellion.

"Open them!" he hissed furiously, pawing at her face with clumsy fingers.

After a few moments of fruitless struggling, he gave up. "Fine. I'll still get what I want out of you. See if I don't." His tone was so petulant it reminded Iman of a toddler being refused sweets and a bizarre desire to laugh welled within her.

The laughter faded immediately when she felt that remaining hand slide down her body, gripping possessively at her before sliding under her waistband and yanking off her last, feeble protection.

There was a gruff laugh. "How pretty you are. Even more than your mother. I'm going to enjoy this."

Iman sobbed and renewed her efforts to struggle free, bile rising in her throat. No. No! NO!

She screamed and then began to sob in earnest, her eyes still shut tightly as she braced herself, still pulling so hard on her hands that her shoulders burned in agony. He was going to hurt her but she wouldn't make it easy for him. She would resist in whatever small way she could.

"Iman. Iman!"

The pressure eased and she tore her eyes open with a gasp, ready to fight.

There was no one there. Iman looked around wildly, searching for her stepfather, determined that he wouldn't catch her unaware again.

He wasn't there.

"It was just a dream," someone said soothingly to her right.

She knew that voice. Iman looked around the room, blinking rapidly to try and clear her eyes. She wasn't in her mother's house, she realized, and her heartbeat began to slow. She was in the bedroom she shared with Adam and he... There he was, standing off to the side with his hands raised non-threateningly in front of him.

It had been a dream.

Her stomach churned and Iman clapped a hand over her mouth, retching. She tried to get up but fell back, her legs caught in a messy tangle of sheets.

In desperation, she leaned over the side of the bed and emptied her stomach, cringing even as she spat out everything she'd eaten the previous day.

When she was finally done, she straightened up and weakly began to untangle herself, focusing on the sheets as she apologized to Adam. "I'll clean it up," she assured him. "Just give me a second-"

"Leave it," he said softly.

Iman lifted her head, thinking she'd misheard. Adam was watching her with a curious look on his face.

"Leave it," he repeated. He'd retreated to the opposite side of the room but he came closer now as he spoke. Still carefully out of her space, he quickly untangled the sheets.

"Can you get to the bathroom by yourself?"

Iman didn't know. Her legs felt like rubber. She said as much and Adam's mouth tightened. "I can carry you," he offered carefully.

Iman hesitated and Adam drew back. The churning of her stomach decided her finally and she nodded frantically. "Yes, please, now!" she choked out, slapping a hand over her mouth.

The next moment she was in the air and moving.

His hands were gentle, she noticed absently. So different to the rough ones that she could still feel sliding over her. She shuddered and Adam stopped, looking down at her in concern. "You okay?"

"Fine," she rasped. "I'm fine."

He set her down in front of the toilet, carefully letting her regain her balance before he let go and backed out of the room. "If you need anything," he said softly, pausing at the threshold, "just call."

Without another word, he was gone.

Absurdly, she felt worse alone.

Iman woke the next morning to an empty room that smelt heavily of the lemon-scented cleaner Adam's house help favoured.

She frowned in confusion. How had she gotten back to bed? The last thing she remembered was being too tired to lift herself up from the floor and resigning herself to spending the rest of the night lying against the cool tile.

Adam.

He'd carried her to the bathroom and he must have carried her back as well.

She needed to thank him and come up with some kind of explanation for what had caused her meltdown. And soon.

The contents of her dream flashed before Iman's eyes and she shuddered. Her stepfather had never touched her. He'd leered and commented and even once come into her bedroom. But he'd never gotten the chance to touch her.

Had he?

Where had that dream come from?

Iman pushed it out of her mind. Dreams – nightmares – were terrifying and strange. But most of them weren't true. This one *wasn't true*. It couldn't be. It just couldn't.

She was just unhappy about the upcoming dinner Aasia had insisted on.

She didn't want to see either of them again – was angry that Aasia had forced her into accepting the summons that she'd sweetly disguised as an invitation – and that fear had manifested itself as something terrifying. That was all.

It had to be. The alternative... it just wasn't worth considering.

-

Trust your instincts.

It was one of the first lessons he'd ever been taught and he'd obeyed it religiously. Adam knew his instincts were good. He'd been saved by them too often to think otherwise.

Right now, those instincts were blaring, trying to warn him that something was wrong. But what could it be? He wasn't in danger – heck, he wasn't even working.

Instead, he was seated in a large, heavily decorated dining room, politely trying to keep the boredom he felt from showing on his face. He had the sneaking suspicion that he wasn't succeeding, going by the slowly reddening face of the man seated to his right, at the head of the table.

A manicured hand reached across the table to grip his wrist. "Adam, why don't you tell us a bit about yourself?" Iman's mother – Aasia, she'd introduced herself as – suggested. "I'd hope that we could get to know one another before the wedding, but…" she gave a forlorn sigh. "Well, you know what Iman is like. Always in a rush."

Adam made a non-committal noise which was all the invitation the woman sitting across him needed to keep talking.

"I've always said, I don't know how Iman managed to be so different from me. I'm her mother but you wouldn't know it by the way she acts!" Aasia laughed, high and grating, making Adam wince at the ugly sound.

He looked at Iman for help but her eyes were glued to her plate and she didn't seem at all interested in joining the conversation any time soon. Was this revenge for leaving her alone with his mother? It sure as hell felt like it.

Thankfully, his mother in law seemed happy to babble away without any input from anyone else at the table. Aasia talked all the way through their meal about her recent trip, her problems, her friends and her problems.

Adam tuned her out easily enough and judging by the glazed look on her husband's face, he wasn't the only one bored by the mindless chatter. Eventually, once she'd exhausted herself, Mrs. Rahman turned her attention back to him.

Adam felt ice run down his spine and he automatically sat straighter in his seat. For a moment there, the tall, thin woman had almost looked… *sinister.*

He blinked and the unnerving expression vanished, replaced by a look of avid curiosity. "I'm tired of talking all about myself. Adam, why don't you entertain us?" Aasia's tone made it clear that it wasn't a request.

Adam cleared his throat, still puzzling over what he'd just seen. "What do you suggest?"

"Well," Aasia drew out the word as she played with her glass, "what do you do?"

"Security," Iman said succinctly. It was the first thing she'd said all night.

Aasia pounced. "Security? That's lovely! My husband's a politician, you know. We're always looking for more security. Maybe we should be working with you, Adam!"

Iman coloured and opened her mouth to respond but Adam beat her to it. "I don't think you want the type of security I offer," he said blandly, finally understanding. Aasia Rahman may have looked like a porcelain doll but she was a viper.

The woman in question blinked. "Oh, what a shame," she mumbled, disappointed.

A shame that you didn't get to spring your trap, Adam thought cynically.

Aasia got to her feet. "Why don't we go out onto the terrace? It's such a lovely night."

Adam was all too happy to agree. The overly rich food they'd been served sat like a stone in his stomach and the stuffy, overly perfumed room wasn't helping him keep it down. Fresh air sounded wonderful. He followed Aasia without a second thought.

-

It took Iman a moment to get up and follow. She hadn't realized the direction the conversation had turned until she looked up and saw the two figures making their way outside.

That moment cost her dearly.

By the time she'd gotten to the doorway, her stepfather was blocking it, that same ugly, filthy smile on his face as the one she'd seen him wearing in her dream.

Iman's mouth went dry. "Excuse me," she croaked out, trying to get past him.

He smiled.

Animals don't smile, Iman remembered. They bare their teeth to show off their fangs.

That wasn't a smile. It was a threat.

"What's the rush?" he whispered. "Sit and talk with me for a while. The words themselves were innocuous. But the way he looked at her, running his eyes up and down her body slowly, smugly, like she was his for the taking. It made her ill.

Iman shuddered and jerked her eyes to the floor. "Excuse me," she said again, licking her lips to try and moisten them.

Big mistake.

He reached out a hand and took hold of her chin. Iman's left cheek, long since healed, began to ache as she remembered the last time she'd been trapped in a hold like this.

He'd spoken up in her defence then. He had even tried to get her mother to stop, albeit not very hard. And now... She couldn't even finish the thought, her mind rebelling in a last ditch effort to shield her.

He saw the panic in her eyes and chuckled. "Are you scared?" he whispered gleefully. "You are!"

She needed to get away. Now. Before...

Her body wouldn't budge. It was like her feet had grown roots.

Think! You can't move. What next? What else can you do?

Scream! The thought flashed in the forefront of her mind.

Even as she opened her mouth, a large hand slapped over it, trapping the shriek that had been building.

"None of that," he murmured irritably. "We don't want anyone disturbing us, do we?"

Yes, I do! Iman thought hysterically.

Someone, she begged silently. *Please, someone find me!*

Her eyes were glued to the doorway, praying for someone to walk through it and... And what? Save her? No one had ever saved her from Aasia. The staff were too afraid and well-trained to interfere.

Her chest tightened as the realization sank in.

No one was coming to save her.

Iman gasped, fighting to get air into her lungs and the tips of two of those fat fingers slipped into her mouth.

The taste of tobacco and his revolting cologne made her gag.

Disgust and fury made her heart pound. Enough.

His other hand slid between her legs, yanking up the hem of her dress.

Enough!

She couldn't run. She couldn't scream.

She gagged again and his fingers caught on her teeth.

Viciously, she bit down. Once, then when he swore, again.

Blood filled her mouth and he dropped her.

Brutal satisfaction filled her as she heard his scream ring out, the tang of his blood still coating her tongue.

CHAPTER THIRTEEN

Something was wrong. What, he didn't know, but something was definitely wrong. He could feel it even if he couldn't see it.

"Adam?" Aasia came toward him, lifting a hand as if to touch his face. "Is something the matter?"

He stepped back hastily, avoiding her. "Why do you ask?"

"You don't seem to be enjoying yourself." She tilted her head to the side. "Is there something I can do to... help you out?"

At first Adam thought that he'd made a truly awful mistake but when Aasia slowly lowered her gaze down and then licked her lips obscenely, he knew he'd been correct.

His mother in law had just propositioned him. What the Hell?

He opened his mouth to decline her... offer – vehemently – then stopped when he heard a man's scream.

Iman! He'd seen her stepfather get up to follow them but neither he nor Iman had joined them on the terrace. It had been too long to be an innocent delay, and coupled with that scream...

What had happened?

Adam ran, cursing himself as he went. All night he'd been on edge but he hadn't even noticed when two people went missing.

He'd left without a word to Aasia and he could hear her screeching behind him, furious that she'd been rejected. Adam spared a moment to feel ridiculously grateful for his own mother. Lina could be nosy at times and he'd more than once wished that she would be more assertive. But she was nothing, *nothing* like this harpy. And thank God for that.

It was no longer a surprise that they hadn't met before now. If Adam had been in Iman's shoes, he wouldn't have wanted to admit to a relation with Aasia either.

He crossed the threshold to the dining room moments later and for a second couldn't understand what he was seeing.

There were no gunmen or robbers but Adam was less than relieved. Iman lay on the floor, blood dripping from her mouth and her stepfather loomed over her, his features twisted in a scowl.

He had one of his hands clutched to his chest, Adam saw. The hairs on the back of his neck stood up. She'd bit him. What had he done to drive Iman – tiny, delicate Iman – to open her mouth and use those pearly white teeth as a weapon?

"What is going on here?" He barely recognized his own voice, it was so filled with fury.

Iman let out a sob and struggled to get to her feet. The collar of her dress was ripped.

"She's just over-excited," he was told. "Nothing to worry about."

Iman wobbled on her feet as she crept towards him, carefully keeping out of reach of her stepfather.

Adam reached out and offered her a hand, careful not to touch her without permission and she leaned on him heavily, curling into his chest. She was trembling.

It took everything he had in him to stop himself from killing the disgusting man where he stood.

"Did she slip and fall on her mouth?" he asked sarcastically.

He couldn't let go of her – she could barely stand on her own. And much as the odious man deserved to die, Adam refused to kill him in front of Iman.

It would keep. Right now, his priority was his wife. He made himself smile. "Don't worry about it. I'm sure whatever happened, she deserved it."

The pig's eyes brightened and he had the audacity to grin. "You're exactly right. Why don't you sit and let her get cleaned up?"

Adam shook his head. "No, we should get going. Iman's had enough excitement for tonight." he said smoothly, not a hint of his ire showing.

The monster looked like he was about to protest, a petulant look on his face. Like a child being refused a toy.

It nearly killed him but he added, "But we'll be back soon enough. You can have some fun then."

Iman had gone rigid in his arms. His only comfort was that this would be a short deception. They'd get to the car and then he'd be able to explain.

With that in mind, he swept her into his arms and made for the door.

She made a little sound, reaching out, and he looked down. "What is it?"

"My bag," she whispered.

He collected it and then stalked out.

-

Iman had gone numb.

When Adam had arrived, she'd stupidly thought that she was saved. He'd steadied her and she'd thought that the nightmare was over.

But then...

I'm sure whatever happened, she deserved it.

We'll be back soon enough. You can have some fun then.

He'd never touched her himself. Never forced himself onto her.

She'd let herself believe that he was decent.

You can have some fun then.

She needed to get out. There was no way she'd go back to his apartment with him. She'd jump out of the car first.

But how? He was holding her so tightly, there was no way she'd be able to struggle free.

Surely he'd put her down to get in the car?

He didn't. Carefully, he balanced her on one arm while he used the other to unlock the car and pull open the passenger side door.

He settled her in and she took her chance.

Iman was halfway out of the car when he caught her, his hands landing solidly on either side of her waist. "Whoa, easy!"

"Let go!" she sobbed. "Let go." She sagged in defeat, unable to break his grip.

And he put her down.

Iman lifted her head and stared at him. "You put me down," she whispered, unable to believe it.

She waited for him to lift her again, to laugh and snatch away the freedom he'd just dangled.

But all he did was lift his hands and back away. "I'm not going to hurt you," Adam whispered, glancing back towards the house. "But we need to leave, and soon. Please get in the car."

Iman hesitated, studying him. "You're not gonna..." She couldn't say it.

Adam's features twisted and she recoiled. "No," he said coldly. "I am not. I promise you, I'm not going to touch you unless you ask me to. And," he added, looking her directly in the eyes. "I promise I am going to take every bit of pain you felt tonight out of that disgusting man's hide."

Iman got into the car.

It was only when Adam was pulling into the driveway of her grandfather's house that Iman noticed they'd driven in the wrong direction to get to his apartment.

"What are we doing here?" she asked dumbly.

Adam turned to look at her. "I thought you'd want to be somewhere familiar," he said softly.

Iman shook her head. "Not here." Not with her grandfather and Shaida already on a hair trigger.

Adam frowned. "I don't want to leave you alone," he said gently. "And more importantly, you need to get checked out by a doctor."

Iman coloured and ducked her head. "He didn't... he didn't get a chance to *do* anything."

Adam looked relieved. "Good," he said softly. "That's good."

Iman ignored the voice in her head that whispered, *this time.* It had been a dream. It had to have been a dream. She clung to the delusion, refusing to even consider the alternative.

She would have known. If he'd done that... If he'd *raped* her... She would know. She would have felt it.

Adam looked at her in concern. "You're still shaking," he said, again in that soft voice as though she was a frightened animal that needed soothing. "I really think you should see a doctor," he persisted.

"But-"

"Please. If you want it to be a stranger, I'll take you to a hospital. But they'll ask more questions than someone in your grandfather's circle."

He was right.

Traumatic events often result in shock.

A line from one of the many textbooks she'd read on emergency first aid came back to her. Adam thought she was in shock. That was why he was being so persistent.

Was she? Was that why she couldn't seem to think properly? Why the world kept fading in and out of focus?

"Okay," she found herself saying.

Adam put the car in reverse and she automatically put out a hand to stop him.

His arm was so warm. She spent a good few moments just enjoying that warmth, until he cleared his throat softly. "Mmm?"

"I need that arm to drive." He began to tug it away and she let out a sound of protest.

"No, you don't."

Adam's brow furrowed in confusion.

"You don't have to keep driving," Iman explained, slow and careful. "I'll go inside."

"Are you sure?"

Why did he care, Iman wondered.

"Iman?" Adam called her name gently.

He'd asked her a question.

What was it?

She couldn't remember.

Iman nodded her head anyway.

"Okay." Adam unbuckled his seatbelt. "Let's go."

-

Adam looked down at his wife worriedly. She was still unsteady on her feet and he hadn't been able to resist picking her up and holding her to him when she'd stumbled over the gravel.

She was so out of it he was beginning to worry that she'd been drugged. He wouldn't put it past her disgusting excuse for a stepfather to do something so underhanded. The weak bastard probably wouldn't have been able to hold her without drugging her.

Thank God she'd agreed to see a doctor at her grandfather's. Adam would probably have had to kidnap a doctor otherwise. He didn't have any kind of ID for her, real of fake. Yet another clumsy, careless mistake.

The guards at the door took one look at Iman before ushering them through, one of them running to summon someone – probably Khan. It only took a few terse words to the other to get him scurrying away for a doctor after he'd hastily pointed Adam in the direction of Iman's bedroom.

He set her down on the bed and made to leave, wanting to go and find her grandfather before he found them, when her soft voice called him back. "Could you give me my box, please?"

"Box?" Adam scanned the room.

Iman pointed to the table on the other side of the room. "My box," she repeated. "From my Dad."

Adam lifted the carved piece of art and brought it to her. He was struck by the beautiful expression it brought forth in Iman. If this was what it moved her to after such an awful night, what would she look like on a normal day?

He'd never seen her look even remotely this happy before and he couldn't contain his curiosity. "What's in the box?"

"Letters. From my favourite person in the world."

Jealousy choked him, hot and bitter. "Yeah? Maybe I should go get him for you."

That beautiful smile vanished. "You can't," Iman said dully. "He's dead."

Shit.

"He died before I could walk," she continued. "He only just got to see me being born."

Adam had barely opened his mouth to try and apologize when the door was flung open so hard it nearly bounced off its hinges.

A familiar looking woman rushed in, pausing to give him a suspicious once-over before she seated herself next to his wife, taking one of Iman's hands in both of her own. "Sweetheart, what happened?"

She caught sight of Iman's ripped collar and her eyes narrowed in fury. "What the Hell?" she breathed.

She'd sprung to her feet and closed the distance between them moments later. Adam finally noticed her protruding belly and placed her. This was the woman who'd hovered over Iman throughout their wedding day, the one who'd slipped her that knife just before they'd left if he wasn't mistaken.

He'd just braced himself to take the hit – he *refused* to lay a hand on a pregnant woman – when Iman called. "Shaida, leave him alone."

The pregnant woman – Shaida – looked even more furious. "Your dress is ripped and you have blood on your mouth, Iman. The only place I'm leaving him is in a coffin."

Adam recognized an ally when he saw one. Now if only he could convince her that *he* wasn't the enemy.

"It wasn't him," Iman said quietly. "It was... my mother's husband. Adam - he helped me."

Shaida lowered her hands. "You helped her?"

Adam nodded sharply.

"Did you kill the bastard?"

"Not yet. I needed to get her out of there."

Shaida's eyes flashed with something that looked like approval and she gave a nod. "Good."

He knew it was foolish to ask but he needed to check. "You'll take care of her while I go and finish things?"

Shaida, to her credit, controlled her offence. "Of course," she said simply. "Kill him slowly," she instructed, looking back at Iman.

Adam followed her gaze, seeing the bruise that had started forming on Iman's jaw. "It would be my pleasure."

Adam was just a few feet away from Iman's bedroom when a wrinkled hand closed around his arm, yanking him in the opposite direction with surprising strength.

Ibrahim Khan looked at him with murder in his eyes and Adam knew that this was the man he'd been warned to stay away from, the one who haunted people's nightmares and was likened to some kind of demon.

"I'm not the one you need to be hunting right now," he said, feigning a calm he didn't feel.

"No? You are the one who brought me my granddaughter back to me damaged. Why *shouldn't* I gut you?"

Adam's temper, already on a hair trigger, ignited. "You're as responsible for this as I am!"

Khan drew back, honest shock showing on his face for a moment before quickly being replaced by suspicion. "How dare you-"

"How dare you! You told me every single little thing about all of your enemies but conveniently forgot to mention that her parents were monsters! I had no idea going in there that I needed to watch myself and *she* suffered for it!" The fear he'd been keeping buried made him vicious and he couldn't hold back from landing one final attack. "She didn't even want to come here afterwards, did you know that? I had to convince her to come inside to get checked over by a doctor. Why exactly is that?"

Khan drew back as if struck. "I – I had no... She was supposed to be safe there," he whispered, devastated.

"She wasn't." Adam looked pityingly at the older man. "You really had no idea?"

"No." Khan cleared his throat, visibly pulling himself back together. When he spoke again, his tone was distant, almost clinical. "Iman has always been very worried about me. Specifically about my health. I knew that she wasn't particularly happy living with her mother but she kept the extent of the problem from me out of some absurd urge to protect me."

Khan glanced behind him to the still-closed bedroom. "What happened tonight? How badly hurt is she?"

He assumed her mother had hurt her physically. Adam winced internally. He was definitely not the right person to break the truth to Khan. Almost anyone else would be better. But there was no one else. He wasn't going to make Iman do it. And he wasn't going to take her friend away from her either.

Adam took a deep breath. "Her stepfather attacked her. When I found them, she was on the floor and he was bleeding. He-" It was hard to keep his voice steady. "He tried to rape her."

The fury on Ibrahim Khan's face was a sight to behold. "He needs to die," Khan said flatly. "Tonight."

The darkest part of himself – one that he usually kept locked up and tightly suppressed – purred in delight.

"Where did you think I was going?"

Khan grinned savagely. "Good." He looked Adam over then and frowned. "You don't have anything on you."

He was right. Adam had been unarmed all night. He'd planned to stop off and collect some weapons once Iman had been settled. He said as much and Khan shook his head. "No. Take things from here." He extended a hand towards an unobtrusive looking door. "You'll find everything you need in there. If you'll excuse me, I need to see my granddaughter."

-

It had been laughably easy. He'd walked right in, with none of the guards even batting an eye. Either they were too stupid to realize that he'd walked in with weapons or they simply didn't care. Adam didn't stick around to find out.

He found his quarry sprawled out on an armchair in front of a large television with his eyes glued to the screen and a hand stuffed down his pants.

How long would it take for him to be noticed? The little man was so absorbed in his fantasy that even though Adam hadn't bothered to be quiet, he hadn't noticed that he was no longer alone.

It would be the work of a minute to put a bullet in his brain and leave.

No. Adam wanted him to know exactly why he was dying.

He came fully into the room, picking his steps deliberately to ensure they were audible despite the blaring television.

Finally, there was a reaction. The jump and accompanying

squealed oath made him grin.

"What – what the Hell are you doing here?" was the outraged shriek. "I wasn't informed about any of this! And don't you have any sense? How long were you standing there... *watching* like that?"

"Did I make you uncomfortable?"

"Yes! It's incredibly rude of you to take advantage of someone like that!"

"When you were vulnerable, you mean?" Adam pretended to be confused.

"Exactly!"

"I see. It's almost... a crime, isn't it? Taking advantage of vulnerability like that?"

"Well..." the man hesitated. "I wouldn't go that far." He dug a finger beneath his collar, uncomfortable though he didn't know why. His body knew that his breaths were numbered even if his brain wasn't sharp enough to comprehend it.

"I would," Adam purred. "People who take advantage of the vulnerable should be punished. Swiftly." He unsheathed the knife he was carrying.

"What... what do you want? Do you want money? I'm very rich, I can give you whatever you want!" His voice was high and panicked, an animal in distress.

Adam paused, less than a foot away. "Oh? Can you?"

There was a frantic nod.

"I want you to suffer," he said blandly, watching the hope extinguish. "You attacked someone very precious to me tonight. Someone vulnerable who *you* took advantage of. I want you to feel every bit of fear she felt. Every bit of helplessness."

A foul smell filled the air. Adam looked down at the couch cushions. The man had soiled himself in fear. He was trembling and mouthing soundless pleas.

"Don't worry," he said softly. "It'll be over eventually."

And then he set about fulfilling his promise to Iman.

He didn't enjoy it. He never had. But when he was done, there was a lingering sense of satisfaction. He'd taken another life today. He didn't regret it in the least.

CHAPTER FOURTEEN

"I knew leaving was a terrible idea," Shaida grumbled, even as she bustled around the room, fluffing pillows and adjusting the curtains. "I knew you needed me. Thank goodness I insisted on staying."

Iman grimaced apologetically at Fareed who seemed to be taking his wife's bad temper in stride. "I'll bring you something to take for the pain," he said, patting her knee.

"Could you make sure my grandfather sleeps?" He'd been so upset. She'd never seen him that way before.

"Of course." Fareed got to his feet. "I'll be back in a few minutes."

Iman looked at Shaida once he'd left. "You should sleep too."

"I'm not leaving you alone," Shaida said at once. "I'll be fine, don't you worry about me." But Iman could see the exhaustion on her. Shaida had been run off her feet for months now. She should have been relaxing and enjoying being doted on by her own mother but instead she was spending her time mothering Iman.

"I want to sleep myself," Iman lied. "You might as well get some rest. Please? For me?"

Shaida wavered. "I'll wait til you're sleeping," she decided eventually.

"Shae, give her some space. I'm sure Iman will call you if she needs anything." Fareed handed Iman a little cup of pills and a bottle of water then took his wife's hand. "Come on, you need to sleep."

Iman nodded in agreement. "I'll be fine."

Shaida pursed her lips. "You shouldn't be left alone. Let me stay until you fall asleep."

"Honey," Fareed said patiently. "She'll be out in a few minutes with those pills."

"Alright," Shaida relented, letting Fareed tow her behind him gently. "Your phone's next to you if you need it. Call me if there's anything. Anything at all."

"I will," Iman lied, promising herself that she wouldn't.

The door shut with a click and she looked down at the little plastic cup before upending all four of the pills into her mouth.

-

She was fast asleep. Adam looked down at the tiny blonde – dwarfed by her covers, with her hair in a ridiculous state – and found something deep within himself begin to ease.

It was almost dawn.

She'd wake up soon and he'd have to tell her what he'd done. Would she be shocked? Terrified? Or would she understand?

Adam didn't know. Either way, he didn't regret it in the

slightest. There was one less monster on the streets and he'd sleep easier knowing that he wouldn't ever get his hands on Iman again.

He sank into a chair, careful to keep his movements soundless. He didn't doubt that a strange man in her bedroom would terrify her. But leaving her alone was beyond him. He couldn't shake the feeling that if he left her alone, something would happen to her.

So he camped in a chair, to ease his own worries and keep her safe as long as he was able.

-

Iman was groggy when she woke, no doubt a side-effect of the cocktail of pills she'd swallowed. Her wrists throbbed angrily, the pain cutting through the fog in her mind and waking her up enough that she noticed the man slumped in her vanity chair.

Her heart raced until she recognized him. Adam. Had he slept in that chair all night? It didn't even have a back!

As though her errant thought had unbalanced him, he began to list to the side before startling awake and looking around wildly. His eyes met hers and his mouth curved into a smile. "You're awake," he said, sounding pleased.

Iman nodded, suddenly shy.

"How are you feeling?"

She'd meant to say fine, but her mouth betrayed her. "Awful," she admitted.

"That's understandable."

"I don't ever want to see him again." Even as she said it, the thought of encountering *him* made her feel ill. She tightened her arms around her middle, trying to calm the waves of nausea.

"You won't have to."

The conviction in Adam's voice made Iman lift her head and stare at him. "How do you know?" she whispered, horrified.

I am going to take every bit of pain you felt tonight out of that disgusting man's hide.

What had he done?

"I killed him," Adam said softly. "Last night, when I left, I went to make sure he wouldn't ever be a threat again."

No. Oh God, no. Iman stifled a sob with the back of her hand.

"Do you want me to go?" Adam had a resigned look on his face.

What? What was he talking about?

Iman shook her head. "That won't help!"

"What will help then?" he snapped, a frustrated look on his face.

"I don't know!" Panic made her shrill. "Why did you have to kill him?"

"Because he was a monster!" Adam exploded. "He deserved to die!"

"I know that! But it's dangerous!" Somehow, the thought of Adam dying was making her panic even more than the thought of dealing with her stepfather. She could have borne that more easily than this unrelenting anxiety.

"Iman, what are you talking about?" Adam asked softly. "It's not dangerous. This is my job, remember?"

He didn't understand. She shook her head and tried to explain, stuttering out a garbled version of the explanation her grandfather had given her what felt like ages ago.

Adam held up a hand. "Is that all that bothers you?" he asked, a strange hope in his eyes.

What else would it be? Iman voiced the question and Adam stared at her. "You're not afraid of me?"

Iman shook her head.

"Or disgusted by me?"

"Of course not!"

A smile began to make its way across Adam's face. Iman watched, distracted despite herself. She'd never seen him smile like that before. It suited him.

Iman ducked her head in embarrassment and her eyes landed on the bruises that decorated her wrists. Her anxiety came rushing back and she sprang to her feet.

"Iman, calm down," Adam said soothingly, holding out his hands.

"There's nothing to worry about."

He still didn't understand. "Of course there is!" she snapped.

"No, there isn't. I know what I'm doing. I cleaned up after myself."

"There are guards. They would have seen you!"

Adam sighed. "The guards have been threatened and bribed. The body and a car have been moved and will be found in a few days. We've done this before. Many times."

He sounded so sure...

But her grandfather had been just as sure that it was too dangerous. Iman said as much and Adam's mouth firmed into a line. "Your grandfather does things very differently to my stepfather."

What did that mean? Before Iman could ask, the door was flung open.

Shaida burst in, clutching a large gun. Iman gaped at her. "Shaida!"

"I heard the screaming," was all the pregnant woman said in explanation. "What's wrong?"

"I told Iman where I'd been last night," Adam explained. "It upset her."

Shaida scowled. "You couldn't have waited? Or did you just want to brag about your kill like a Neanderthal."

"She was scared. I wanted her to know she didn't have reason to be," Adam said icily.

Shaida gave a begrudging nod. "Well... I suppose you did the right thing."

"I suppose I did."

"You shouldn't have upset her."

"I didn't intend to."

Shaida turned to Iman, who'd been watching them and fighting an absurd urge to laugh. "That's all that happened?"

"Yes, Shaida. I'm alright. Don't worry so much."

They stood silently for a beat. Adam cleared his throat. "I should go talk to your grandfather," he told Iman. "Just in case there's something I missed." He gave her a final smile and then walked out the door.

Shaida looked between her face and the door. "What was that?"

Iman knew she wasn't referring to what Adam had said.

"When did that happen?" she continued. "And why on Earth didn't you tell me?"

Iman shook her head. "I don't know," she said softly. "It just... happened."

She sank down on the edge of her bed. "I can't believe he's gone."

Shaida snorted. "Good riddance. If your mother could only join him, I'd throw a party."

"Shaida," Iman admonished. Even after everything that she'd done, Iman couldn't bring herself to hate Aasia, let alone wish her dead.

Shaida sighed. "I'm sorry, I know. You still love her, even though she doesn't deserve a bit of it."

"Yep." Iman's throat was tight. She knew that the person she loved, the version of Aasia she had in her head and heart, was fake. But she'd never stopped hoping that her mother would turn into that better version of herself that Iman wished she'd be. The one who was kind and loved her daughter.

"Just don't expect me to spit on her if she's on fire." Shaida patted her hand. "You're not stupid for wanting her to be better."

Iman jumped. "How did you..."

Shaida levelled her with an unimpressed look. "I've known you almost all your life," she reminded Iman. "I know when you're thinking dumb things." She gave Iman a hug then slowly got to her feet. "I'd better go before Fareed decides I've jumped out the window."

Iman watched her go, tamping down on the panic that being alone made her feel. *He's dead*, she reminded herself. *He's dead and the dead can't walk.*

-

For the second time in two days, Adam was squaring off against Ibrahim Khan. He'd wandered until he found a guard then asked them to find their boss, not wanting to go poking through the house until he found the right room.

Now, he sat waiting on a sofa, fighting the urge to yawn. He hadn't intended to fall asleep while sitting with Iman but that little nap hadn't been longer than a half hour and he was far from well rested.

It didn't help that the sofa was so soft either.

Adam shook his head to clear it. Focus. He needed to be firing on all cylinders for the upcoming conversation. He had a sneaking suspicion that he was about to hear several things that would make him furious.

-

He'd been right. An hour later and Adam was still fuming. He also had a brand new person on his hit list.

He'd completely underestimated Aasia Rahmaan, clearly. The woman had made Iman's life miserable for years and it seemed no one had been able to stop her. Adam still couldn't understand *why* no one had just slit the woman's throat years ago.

Shaida seemed to adore Iman like her own child and clearly

Ibrahim loved her. But none of them had just gotten rid of the problem. Instead, they'd just stood idly by and left Iman to be *brutalized*.

He'd left without getting any kind of proper answer, too angry to even see straight. Now, an hour later, he'd calmed down enough that he wasn't in danger of screaming himself hoarse and terrifying anyone, he was on his way back to her.

His phone rang and he glanced down at it. Ali. What could he want? Adam was still 'on vacation' for another fortnight, so it wasn't likely to be a job. After the night he'd had, Adam was in no mood to deal with his stepfather if he was just bored but he knew better than to let the call go to voicemail.

"What."

"I see you still haven't regained any manners."

Adam grunted.

Ali got to the point. "What happened last night?"

"I killed someone."

"I'm aware of that. You used my staff to help you deal with the fallout of it. Why did you kill someone out of the blue like that?"

"He was a rapist," Adam explained tersely.

"Oh. You made him suffer?" Ali's voice had hardened considerably.

"Not enough."

"It never is," his stepfather responded. "Good job."

"Thanks." Adam made to disconnect the call when Ali called his name. "Adam... Don't worry about the fallout from this one.

If there is anything, I'll deal with it myself."

"Thanks," Adam repeated. "Was this guy really that powerful?" he asked curiously. "He was a worm."

"No, not particularly. But he was a politician. That's always something that needs monitoring. Don't worry about it, it'll be taken care of."

"Keep me updated," Adam requested.

"Take care of her," his stepfather instructed him before disconnecting the call.

Adam would, for as long as she'd let him.

He turned into the Khans' driveway absent-mindedly and remembered the first time he'd done so. He'd thought he was being sent to kill someone, thought that he'd do the job and that would be that.

He'd been ready to kill when he'd heard the truth. And now... Now, he'd killed for the woman he'd almost considered murdering all those days ago. And he was glad of it.

-

One look at Iman's ashen face and Adam was yet again fighting back panic. She somehow looked even worse than she had the previous night, almost as though a strong wind would be enough to shatter her.

He'd only been gone for an hour. What could have happened to make her this upset?

Adam gave her a quick once over. She didn't seem hurt. He watched as she fiddled with her phone for a moment and then sighed unhappily.

"What's wrong?"

She jumped then looked round at him and attempted a smile. "Adam. I didn't know you were back."

"What's wrong?" Adam repeated. "Are you in pain? Do you need something?"

Iman shook her head. "No. No, *I'm* fine." The way she said it made it clear that someone else wasn't.

"So who isn't?"

Iman hesitated for a moment, clearly unsure.

"Tell me," he urged. "Maybe I can help." Anything to bring some colour back into her cheeks. She looked unnervingly like a corpse.

She hesitated for an instant longer, then relented and explained, growing more upset with each word. By the time she'd finished, Iman was on the verge of tears.

He looked helplessly at her. "Where is Shaida?"

"Lying down upstairs. Fareed's with her." Iman glanced anxiously up at the ceiling. "Everyone's tried talking to her but she just won't listen. And the harder we try, the more stressed she gets. I don't know what to do." She put her face in her hands.

"Can I try?"

Iman lifted her head. "You? But you don't even know her."

"Could it hurt?"

"I guess not. Just... if she starts getting upset..."

"I'll leave," Adam assured her, hoping he wasn't about to make things worse.

"Wait here, okay?" Iman climbed off the window seat. "I'll

163

come get you after I talk to Fareed."

Adam waited, feeling more doubtful with every passing moment. What the Hell was he doing? He was about to interfere in something that was none of his business.

Iman poked her head in over the side of the door. "Come on," she said, looking at him hopefully.

Right. That was why he was doing it. Because this tiny girl had looked so miserable that he couldn't help but try to fix it.

God, what was happening to him?

"Are you ready?" she asked, glancing back at him with her hand on the doorknob.

No.

"Yes."

-

Iman stood outside the large room that functioned as their infirmary, straining her ears to hear what was being said inside. She had no idea what Adam was planning to do, and she had little faith that whatever it was would actually succeed but she was desperate enough to point him in Shaida's direction and pray.

Maybe hearing it coming from a stranger *would* help. Maybe Shaida would accept that they weren't being unreasonable and would agree to slow down.

But probably not. Shaida was insistent that she knew her own limits and nothing anyone said or did seemed to have any effect on her other than to make her dig her heels in more. Fareed was at his wits end, worrying about both his wife and his baby and Iman couldn't bear knowing that she'd been the one to cause the strain.

Seeing her old babysitter's eyes roll back into her head and watching her slump to the floor had been one of the most terrifying things Iman had ever experienced. She'd screamed and five different people had come running into her bedroom immediately to help but those few seconds while they'd been anxiously waiting for Shaida to wake up had been some of the worst in her life.

If something did happen to the baby... Iman would never forgive herself.

-

There was a handgun lying on the night stand. It was smaller than the one Adam had been threatened with that morning and by the way Shaida's hand shook when she took hold of it, he knew that it had been replaced because she could no longer handle the weight.

"Who let you in here?" she asked, instantly suspicious.

"Iman. I heard you caused some chaos a little while ago."

Shaida didn't respond.

"You're supposed to be on bed rest somewhere, aren't you?"

An ugly expression crossed the pregnant woman's face at the words *bed* and *rest*. "I am *supposed* to be right here. Iman needs me," Shaida said with a thread of steel in her voice. "Why are you so interested in the plans of a complete stranger?"

"Because they affect someone I'm bound to."

Shaida's eyes sharpened and she propped herself up on her elbows. "You should be happy that Iman has someone else looking out for her. More protection is never a bad thing."

"In theory," Adam acknowledged, watching the way she sagged

back against her pillows.

"So what's your problem?"

"My problem is that you're being selfish."

Shaida's mouth fell open and her face reddened with anger. "*What* did you just say to me?"

He'd struck a nerve. "You're being selfish," he repeated. "Iman is outside tearing herself up out of worry for you. She should be resting and trying to recover from what that bastard did to her but instead, she's pacing and worrying about you."

Adam sighed. "I get that you want to keep her safe. So do I. But you're in no shape to do that. It's time to delegate before you hurt her more than help her."

"Delegate to who? To you?" There was a derisive snort and Adam gritted his teeth. "You barely even know her! She was with *you* last night and she was hurt worse than she's ever been before."

"Because none of you bothered to inform me that she was in danger there," Adam countered. "You're right – I barely know her. But you... you've known her all her life and you still *left* her there!"

"I had no choice! It killed me to have her away from me, to ignore her when she called and watch as she withered in front of my eyes but *I* didn't have a choice. I couldn't do anything else."

"So what makes you think you'll make any difference now?" Adam asked her unsympathetically. "You're risking three lives right now. Yours, hers and your baby's."

The blood drained from Shaida's face. "Get out," she whispered. "Get out!"

Adam did as he was told. He'd done all he could, cruel as it had been. Now all that was left to do was wait.

CHAPTER FIFTEEN

"You should go see her. Just give her a few minutes first." Adam said as he closed the door behind him.

Iman's heart sank. "You didn't...?" she asked, needing to make sure.

"I don't know," was the quiet answer. "I tried my best but... it depends on her now. I'm sorry it's not better news."

That he'd done anything at all had been a pleasant surprise. "Thank you for trying," Iman whispered gratefully. She squeezed his arm tightly, enjoying the contact. A loud, gurgling noise made her glance down in alarm.

Adam's cheeks turned bright red. "I... uh. I seem to have forgotten to eat."

And sleep and shower. Iman looked at him properly, for the first time noticing just how run down he looked. "You should go home." She felt a peculiar sense of loss as she said it.

Adam shifted uncomfortably. "I don't particularly want to leave you alone right now," he admitted, studying the wall behind her head.

"Oh," Iman breathed, suddenly feeling warm. She clamped down on the urge to give in and persisted. "But you're tired and hungry. And I'll be with Shaida anyway. You should go get cleaned up and get some rest. But-" She stopped herself, feeling foolish.

"What?" Adam looked at her intently.

"You could come back when you're done?" Iman offered hesitantly.

"Of course." Adam's tense posture relaxed. "I'll be back soon." He hesitated for a moment, looking at her oddly, then left.

Disappointment curled in her gut as she watched him walk away, along with a longing for something she couldn't quite identify.

"Iman? Are you still out there?" Shaida's muffled voice stopped her from exploring that puzzling feeling any further.

Iman hurried to Shaida's side. "What is it?" The normally vibrant woman looked lifeless and dull

"Come sit with me." Shaida patted the side of her bed gently. "I need to talk to you about a few things."

Iman tucked her hair behind her ears, still leaning over the older woman. "What's wrong?"

"Just sit," Shaida took hold of her wrist and tugged weakly.

They sat in silence for a while. Shaida had a faraway look in her eyes and a wistful smile on her face. "Do you remember how we met?"

"You found me hiding under a table, crying. I wouldn't talk to anyone else but you managed to get me out."

"That's right. You were such a cute little kid with that

ridiculous pageboy haircut. You looked like a little boy."

Iman blushed.

"You were a spoilt little brat too! You had everyone in this house wrapped around your little finger, sneaking you candy and making you laugh. And then," she sighed. "And then you had to go."

Iman looked away. "Shaida, don't-"

Shaida patted her cheek. "Let me finish?" she requested.

Iman nodded silently.

"You had to go," she repeated, "and it broke my heart. I was furious with everyone and everything for a while there. It took me a long time before I could even be in a room with your grandfather without yelling at him. I thought you were safest with us and he disagreed. He had his reasons, I understand that now. But it didn't make it any easier for me to swallow."

Shaida paused, taking a deep breath as if to steady herself. Her eyes were wet. "And then you came back and you were suffering.

But it wasn't enough for us to bring you back. We thought it was better for you to be a little unhappy and safe rather than letting you stay where it was dangerous."

She gripped Iman's hand tightly. "We had no idea," she sobbed. "I had no idea what was being done to you. I should have known. I should have – I should have realized! I'm so sorry, Iman. Believe me, I-" She broke off into sobs.

Iman's own eyes began to water sympathetically. "Shaida, it's okay. Please, don't do this to yourself! It's okay." She put her arms around the sobbing woman.

"I forgive you," she whispered. And she did. The hurt that she'd been holding onto for such a long time was not gone. But it had begun to dull. The wound had finally been treated and now, now she could finally begin to heal.

Shaida sniffed lightly and mopped at her eyes. "I'm a mess," she said ruefully. "This pregnancy has turned me into a tap."

Iman gave a ghost of a smile.

"I'm glad I told you all of that. But it wasn't what I'd called you in here to hear. I got a bit side-tracked."

Shaida took a deep breath. "I'm going to go to my mother's."

Yes! Iman smiled so wide her cheeks immediately began hurting. She hugged Shaida tightly. "Thank goodness," she murmured. "I'm so relieved."

"Oh, what have I been doing?" Shaida mumbled reproachfully. "He was right, I *have* been selfish."

Iman lifted her head and pulled back. "Who?"

"Your Adam. He was very rude to me."

Iman's mouth dropped open. "He was?"

"Oh, yes." Shaida chuckled. "Don't look so horrified. It was a good thing. It made me think."

She got a satisfied look on her face. "He really was the best choice of them all."

Iman cringed remembering those frantic days when she'd had men paraded in front of her like clothing options. "If only I'd realized that immediately." They would have saved so much time.

"Things happen as they're meant to," Shaida reminded her. "Now listen – if you need anything at all-"

"Call you," Iman completed the familiar refrain. "I will," she promised, feeling incredibly fond.

Shaida glanced at her. "How are you feeling?"

Iman looked away. "That's not important right now."

"Of course it is! Iman, you went through a terrible ordeal last night."

Iman's throat felt tight. "I know. But-" she sucked in a breath. "I'm handling it." Badly, but that was no one's problem but her own.

"Okay," Shaida said simply. "I'm here if you need me."

"Thank you."

-

"You're leaving tomorrow?" Iman repeated incredulously. She stepped further into the bedroom, carefully avoiding the haphazard pile of books stacked near the door.

Fareed nodded. "If I'd had it my way, we would have left a month ago," he grumbled. "I don't want to waste any more time."

"I know, but... so soon?"

"You can come visit as much as you want," Fareed reminded her, ruffling her hair as he walked past to a large, open suitcase that lay on the bed. "But Shaida needs to be settled as quickly as possible."

"You're right." Iman went to the open drawer and pulled out a stack of neatly folded shirts. "Here."

Fareed nodded his thanks. "We'll be back soon enough." He added in several pairs of shoes to the already full suitcase then began struggling to zip it.

"You're taking most of your clothes and an entire library," Iman pointed out.

Fareed had the grace to look chagrined. "I don't want to bring a newborn back here," he admitted. "We have at least three knives and a gun in every single room – even the bathroom. I want to keep them away from it as long as I can." He looked down at the zip he was still tugging, shamefaced.

"Shaida doesn't know any of this, does she?" Iman guessed.

"No, she doesn't. I've been waiting for the right time to talk to her about it but there's always been something or the other that urgently needed either my or her attention. This poor baby's been neglected so much and it's not even born yet!"

Fareed slammed a fist down on the suitcase, cursing. "And now this stupid thing won't close! Argh!"

"Why don't you let me do that?" Iman suggested. "Just take a minute and take a breath."

Fareed cradled his hand to his chest. "That's probably a good idea," he admitted. "I didn't mean to scare you," he added, for Iman had jumped when his fist had made contact with the hard plastic.

"It's okay. I'm just a little on edge."

"Understandably." Fareed paused for a second, visibly bracing himself, then opened his mouth again. "I've been talking to your grandfather a lot in the past few days, Iman. I suggested something to him this morning and he dismissed it but it's more your choice at the end of the day."

Iman let out a low noise of triumph as she finally succeeded in zipping the bag shut. "What did you suggest?"

"Therapy." Fareed held up a hand. "Just wait," he pleaded. "Don't just dismiss it. I know that secrecy is a huge concern for everyone here but that's not a good enough reason to let you all just languish and eventually completely ruin your mental health."

Iman sighed. He meant well, she reminded herself. "Fareed, security isn't just a huge concern, it's the biggest concern. And I wouldn't feel comfortable talking to a stranger about *anything*, much less... that."

Fareed looked resigned. "Just think about it? It could help."

"I'll think about it," Iman agreed, to pacify him.

She patted the suitcase lightly. "What time are you leaving tomorrow?"

"First thing. But we'll wait to say goodbye first."

Less than twenty four hours. "I'm going to miss you both so much. At least James is due back soon."

Fareed scowled suddenly and Iman remembered that he'd always held a dislike for James. "He's not that bad," she assured him. "Really. He's a flirt but he doesn't mean any harm."

Fareed's expression didn't change and Iman sighed. "Well, at least you won't be here by the time he gets back."

"That's what I'm afraid of," Fareed said grimly. "That's just what I'm afraid of. Excuse me for a second?"

"Yeah, sure," Iman responded, taken aback. She walked to the door of the little apartment and added; "I wanted to call Adam anyway. I'll see you later."

She'd been telling the truth – she did want to talk to Adam. But as Iman made her way up to the floor she shared with her grandfather, she wasn't anticipating a phone call. Instead, she typed out a short text to Adam, letting him know that she wouldn't be available for a while then headed out in search of her grandfather.

She'd barely spoken to him at all in the past two days and worry for him had wrapped around her heart. He seemed to have aged a decade in the past forty eight hours and her brief conversation with Fareed had reminded her that she needed to make sure he was alright.

She rubbed the back of her neck with a groan. Why was everything happening at once?

-

'Come by later please? I have some things to sort out.'

Adam glanced down at his phone, relief and disappointment mingling within him. He typed out a quick affirmative then tucked the device back into his pocket.

He'd been eager to go and see Iman, to make sure that she was still alright, but he had his own mess to sort out. And it was waiting right outside his front door, kicking said door hard enough that he was surprised it hadn't dented.

Kat had been waiting in his apartment the second he'd gotten back and it had taken a good few minutes of yelling to get her to leave him alone even long enough to take a shower.

Mercifully, his stepfather had responded to the outraged barrage of texts he'd sent by distracting Kat long enough that he'd been able to get a few hours of sleep before she was back and nagging him for answers.

Of course, she was in a foul mood now, but it had been worth it.

Maybe...

Adam looked the angry brunette over and hastily revised his previous opinion.

Kat looked ready to breathe fire.

He let her in silently.

She stalked into his kitchen, began helping herself to whatever took her fancy and then, once she'd loaded up on food, seated herself comfortably on the counter and began her interrogation.

Adam's head began to throb. He should have just jumped out the damn window and escaped to the Khans' mansion.

"I cannot believe," Kat began, prying open a tub of ice cream, "that I had to learn from the *clean up crew* that you killed someone last night. Without any kind of plan, without a go ahead, you just murdered someone and I had no idea until I heard them gossiping about it."

She stuffed a spoonful of ice cream into her mouth and gestured to him with her spoon. "You look remarkably happy for what you did. I saw the body, you know."

"He deserved it." He'd deserved worse. For a moment, all Adam could see was Iman, crumpled on the floor and struggling to rise.

Kat dropped her spoon. "You really believe that," she marvelled. "Did he murder a school of babies?"

Adam looked away, reluctant to tell Kat the truth. It wasn't his secret to share. "He got what he deserved. That should tell you enough."

"He choked to death on a mixture of his own blood and vomit."

"I know."

"Tell me what happened," Kat demanded. "I've never seen you in a state like this. You don't regret it at *all*? What happened to not causing unnecessary pain and suffering?" She'd gotten to her feet and was standing right in front of him, condemnation clear in her eyes.

"It wasn't unnecessary, Kat!" *Let go!* Iman begged in his mind, sobbing and fighting to get free. *Tell her, make her understand.*

He opened his mouth.

No. He wouldn't do that to Iman. He *couldn't* do that to Iman.

Kat's face fell. "I'm gonna go," she whispered. She lifted her jacket and headed for the door.

"Kat, don't-" He reached for her and she ducked away, shaking her head.

"You've changed, Adam. And this isn't a good look on you. Not at all." The sound of her heels leading her away from his door echoed loudly in the empty apartment.

Adam bit back a curse and collapsed into the nearest chair, burying his face in his hands. A wave of exhaustion hit him and his temples throbbed.

Kat's reaction shouldn't have shocked him. But it had. He'd grown so used to her being the one person he could always count on, whose support was a given, who knew him well enough to give him the benefit of the doubt...

It seemed that without him even noticing, that had changed.

And yet, he couldn't be angry with her.

Memories washed over him. Suddenly, he was fifteen years old again, terrified and raging. He'd just made his first 'soft-kill'. Ostensibly, a cause for celebration – he was almost ready to start going out on real jobs.

Adam had never felt less like celebrating in his life. His stomach lurched again and he heaved, bringing up nothing. He'd long since emptied his stomach but the cramps hadn't stopped. He wondered if he'd ever stop feeling sickened by what he'd been forced to do.

That was his only consolation – he'd been forced to do it. When he'd first been brought in front of the stray creature, he hadn't understood. He was just concerned for the poor thing. It wasn't until Ali had hauled him directly in front of it and handed him a gun that he'd understood.

He was meant to kill this animal. It had been taken off the streets and brought here, chained up so that it couldn't flee for its life, so that he could kill it and earn the *privilege* of moving on to killing humans.

He'd refused.

For a moment, there had been relief, as Ali nodded and accepted the gun back from him. Right up until he'd instead turned the gun on Adam, pointing it between his eyes. "You have a choice," he'd said in that charming voice, "You can kill the dog or I can kill you. What'll it be?"

Adam had no doubt that he would have done it. It didn't matter that Adam was his wife's only child. Ali would have killed him and it wouldn't even have bothered him enough to wipe the smile from his face.

He'd done it. Had forced himself to look into those innocent, oblivious eyes and watch as the light drained from them.

Ali had clapped him on the back afterwards and congratulated him, as though murdering an innocent was something to be proud of.

"Keep it together."

Adam lifted his head. Kat. He didn't bother asking how she'd found him. "What do you want?"

"You've been holed up in here for fifteen minutes. I was starting to get worried."

"I'm not going back out there."

Kat sighed. "You have to. Just like you had to kill that dog. You don't have any other choice. None of us do."

"How can you just stand that? Doesn't it even bother you?"

Kat looked taken aback. "Of course it does. I don't like all of this any more than you do. But you saw what happened when you tried to refuse. He wasn't bluffing, you know."

"So, what do we do?" Adam whispered, sagging against the wall. "How do we get out?"

"We don't." Kat said matter-of-factly. "There's no way out. All we can do is make sure we don't become like the rest of them."

In her eyes, Adam had done just that. He'd killed without being commanded to and just like that, he'd gone from a helpless tool to an active participant.

Kat had only ever been able to live with herself and her guilt by constantly reminding herself that she had no power to change things. She did as she was told and kept herself as far away from the rest of Ali's killers as she could manage.

Now that he'd lumped himself with the rest of them, she'd stay away from him as well.

He'd just lost his only friend.

The table was still piled high with all the food she'd raided from his fridge and Adam couldn't stop a fond smile. She always ate when she was nervous. He'd taken to making sure all her favourite things were on hand just in case she decided to escape the compound and camp out with him.

That would never happen again now.

He'd ruined it.

-

She looked terrible and he had no idea what to do. Adam stared at the blonde hair spread over the pillows and clenched his jaw. Even her hair seemed less bright. Iman was withering faster by the day and it was infuriating him that he could do nothing to help. The culprit was dead but that didn't help her nightmares.

It had been just over a week and already, he could see a difference in the way she stood, in the set of her shoulders. The lack of sleep wasn't helping either. She'd woken from nightmares almost every night – twice screaming so loudly that it had made his own heart race to hear it.

All he knew was the advice Kat had once given him – to talk about it. He didn't see how reliving the experience yet again would help but he was almost desperate enough to try and suggest it.

Thinking about Kat was like picking at a scab – painful and likely to leave a scar. But he couldn't help it. He missed her. He'd picked up his phone countless times, wanting to talk to her, had even gotten as far as dialling a few times. She'd never answered.

As if all of that wasn't enough, his month of holiday time had ended and Ali had just let him know that he was expected to leave for the other side of the world in a week. He couldn't turn it down but the idea of leaving Iman while she was in such a state was almost painful.

He was running out of time.

There was a whimper from the woman lying in bed next to him and Adam quickly reached out an arm, hoping that she wouldn't scream herself awake this time. Feeling restrained seemed to make the nightmares worse so his first action was always to remove the covers that she somehow always trapped herself in.

He held his breath, waiting. Sometimes that was enough to stave off the worst of it and allow her to stay asleep.

Tonight was not one of those nights.

Iman let out a sob and yanked at invisible hands. She screamed when he tried to touch her and he cursed, shaking her too roughly in his haste.

"Iman, wake up!"

She screamed again and wrenched her eyes open, gasping.

Adam immediately retreated, giving her space.

Talk about it. That's what Kat had said.

Iman pulled her knees up to her chest and sniffled.

Enough. He had no idea how else to help. There was no harm in trying this, surely?

He opened his mouth. "Do you want to talk about it?"

-

Her throat was raw from screaming. Iman shivered, her skin clammy with sweat. It was the third time this week that she'd woken in the middle of the night, tormented by her dreams.

At least she hadn't vomited this time.

Adam had been the one to bring her out of the dream, just as he had every other time she'd begun thrashing and moaning in her sleep.

Iman felt her cheeks burn with shame. She'd offered to sleep on the couch so that she wouldn't keep disturbing his sleep but Adam had refused. When she'd persisted, he'd simply declared that if she went to sleep on the couch, he'd follow her and all she'd accomplish was making them both uncomfortable for the night.

Exhausted, Iman had dropped the issue. But she still felt guilty every time she saw that pinched, exhausted look on his face.

"Do you want to talk about it?"

Iman lifted her head. "What?"

"Do you want to talk about it?" he repeated. "The nightmare? It's... supposed to help. When you talk about it."

The sheer panic she felt at that question must have been obvious because he quickly backtracked. "Never mind. Maybe you should just try to go back to sleep."

But Iman's curiosity had been piqued. "Does it help? You don't have any – nightmares, I mean. Is that because you talked about them?"

Adam shifted uneasily. "Well... no. I do have them." His face turned haunted for a second as he remembered some past horror. "But my nightmares are a little different to yours."

"So... you do have them then?"

"I do," Adam confirmed. "I had to learn to be quiet which is probably why I haven't been the one waking you."

Distracted now, Iman unconsciously began to relax. "That's awful." she mumbled.

Adam shrugged. "It's how we were trained. Showing weakness

wasn't tolerated well – or at all. Nightmares, injuries, phobias... We were made to act as though they didn't affect us. And if we ever slipped, those weaknesses were used against us until we'd learned better."

"Why would you keep training then?" Iman wondered, trying to wrap her head around it. "Surely people would just leave instead of subjecting themselves to that?" Adam laughed darkly. "Because the only way to leave was – and is – in a body bag. You can't really change your mind."
Iman didn't know what to say.
"I take it your grandfather does things differently?"

"I've never really thought about it," Iman whispered, horrified. "God, I hope so." She knew her grandfather had killed people, but she'd never truly thought about it before. She'd always been content to stay away from that side of his life and see him only as the loving grandfather who doted on her.

It was jarring to remember that technically, he was a criminal. As was Adam.

"Iman?" Adam shifted to look at her. "I didn't mean to upset you."

"It's fine," Iman said automatically. "I just... I'd forgotten."

Adam nodded understandingly. "The grandfather you know is very different to the person the rest of the world gets to see. That's not such a bad thing."

Iman lifted her hand to her mouth to cover a yawn, suddenly feeling sleepy. "I guess not," she agreed as she closed her eyes and settled into the pillows.

She vaguely heard Adam say something else but she was already too far gone for it to properly register. Moments later, she was fast asleep.

CHAPTER SIXTEEN

Iman stared at the beautiful house, unable to move. It had been close to a month since she'd last stepped foot in it and she could hardly believe that she was about to do so again. A part of her shrieked that she didn't owe her mother a single thing, that Aasia had *never* been there for her and there was no reason Iman shouldn't return the favour.

But the thought of leaving Aasia to her grief made her stomach clench. She'd called herself ten types of fool on the drive but had kept going anyway.

No one knew where she was. Adam had left early that morning, unable to put his stepfather off any longer, and Iman was only expected at her grandfather's in two hours. Misleading them both had made her feel almost as guilty as abandoning her mother and she'd spent the morning anxious and miserable.

Iman looked at herself in the rear-view mirror. She looked just as bad as she had during those long, awful days when she'd been lucky to catch an hour or two of sleep in between nightmares, before they'd figured out that talking to Adam until she dozed off seemed to help keep the night terrors at a manageable level.

She still hadn't managed a single night's worth of unbroken sleep but she was at least now getting enough rest that she could function.

There was a knock on her car window and Iman started. A guard was crouched in front of the door, indicating that she should roll the window down.

"What is it?"

"I just wanted to know if everything was alright, Ma'am? You've been in your car for the last fifteen minutes. Are you coming inside?"

"Yes. Yes, I am. You can call the house and let my mother know I'm here."

The man's eyes widened. "Oh, I'm so sorry, Ma'am! I didn't know, I didn't mean to rush you at all! Really, I'm just new, I didn't mean to offend!"

Iman cut him off when it looked like he wasn't going to stop. "It's alright. Please just let my mother know that I'll be coming up in a few minutes."

He nodded eagerly and scurried off.

Iman sighed, wondering at the man's solicitousness. Had he simply been thoroughly warned about the tantrums that Aasia and her friends would throw at the drop of a hat or had he been unfortunate enough to have already experienced one for himself?

Speaking of tantrums... If Aasia thought she'd been kept waiting, there'd be hell to pay. It was too late now to back out, she just had to get out of the car and brave the house.

Iman took a deep breath and tried to ignore the dread that had begun creeping up on her.

It can't be as bad as last time.

-

Or maybe it could.

She didn't know what she'd expected to see when she walked inside but it hadn't been this. Aasia looked less like she was mourning and more like she was celebrating.

Iman watched silently as her mother danced around a huge table, every inch of which was covered with vases of gorgeous flowers. She'd search for the card, add it to the stack already in her hand without bothering to read it and then move on to the next one, a satisfied grin growing larger on her face with every new card.

Iman cleared her throat and Aasia immediately assumed a distraught expression, tucking the cards behind her back. Her eyes found Iman. "Oh, it's just you." She dropped the sad expression immediately.

"I came to see if you were alright," Iman explained, wanting to give her the benefit of the doubt. "How are you feeling?"

"Terrible," Aasia said immediately. "It's awful."

"I'm sorry, it must be hard to have lost him." The words tasted like ash in her mouth. *She doesn't know,* Iman reminded herself. *She has no idea.*

"What? No, don't be silly. I'm talking about having to stay at home like this. It's such a bore. If people wouldn't talk, I'd be out right now, enjoying myself. Ugh, it's so ridiculous that I have to be cooped up like this."

Iman couldn't believe her ears. "Your husband is dead," she

reminded Aasia. Her husband whose misdeeds she had no idea about. "Shouldn't you be mourning?" That she even had to ask the question was shocking. How could someone be so shallow?

Aasia rolled her eyes. "I see you still haven't learned anything of substance. This is an investment that has just matured. There's nothing to be sad about. I can now live my life just the way I want without any interference. No more problems. I'll even have a better time with the staff now that he's not around to play with the girls. They're so sensitive," Aasia huffed. "Quitting over a few pats and kisses."

Iman felt ill. "What?" she croaked. "What did you just say about the staff?"

"Hm?" Aasia was counting her condolence cards. "Oh, your stepfather liked to play with the staff. Especially the young girls. Don't look so horrified," she added. "They're just staff."

"You knew?" Rage was beginning to make Iman's voice shake.

"Of course I knew. The stupid things would come to me to complain about it. Honestly, can you believe it?"

"You're despicable. And so was he!" Iman screamed. "You knew he was attacking women and you did nothing? What the Hell is wrong with you?"

Aasia took a step back. "Don't you take that tone with me! How dare you yell at me! Have some respect, I'm your mother!"

"You are not a mother. You let him hurt people. You let him hurt me! How could you?"

Aasia froze. "Your stepfather... You?" She began to look horrified.

"Yes," Iman felt a moment's hope.

That hope shattered a moment later when Aasia shrieked and

lunged for her. "How could you?" she howled. "You tried to steal my husband from me?! You selfish little bitch!"

Iman shoved her away, breathing hard. "Did you not listen to a word I said? *He forced himself on me.*"

Aasia wobbled, trying to regain her balance. "You led him on. You must have. You just wanted him because he was mine, didn't you? Well, you didn't get him in the end. He was mine, do you understand? And every single last penny of his *is mine.*"

It felt like she was finally seeing Aasia clearly. "You're sick," Iman breathed. "You're – something is wrong with you. You're broken." It hit her then. "It wasn't me. I didn't do anything wrong, you're just broken. You didn't love me because *you're* broken, not because there was something wrong with me."

Aasia shrieked in fury. "There is *nothing* wrong with me! It's you! You, you ungrateful little *parasite*. You should never have been born. I didn't even want you," she said viciously, intending to wound. She panted, waiting for Iman to break.

But something had happened. It felt like there was a shield around her. She heard every word but it no longer hurt. Iman smiled. Her mother's venom had lost its power to hurt her.

"Your beloved grandfather had to pay me to keep you and it wasn't even worth it in the end. You just got everything, you *took* everything and it was MINE!" Aasia was beginning to look deranged. "Stop smiling! Stop smiling at me like that, wipe that smug look off your face! You did not win, do you understand me? You got your father and your grandfather but *I won.* Me!"

Iman felt like she was watching a train wreck. "I'm going to go," she said calmly. "I'm sorry that you're so unhappy." She got two steps away before she felt a tug on her hair holding her back.

"Don't you dare walk away from me!"

–

Iman touched the throbbing bruise on her face lightly and winced. It had taken four guards to get Aasia off her and the older woman had done her best to do as much damage as she could to her daughter's face. Iman was sure she looked hideous.

The young guard she'd spoken to earlier came up to her and handed her a glass of water. "We put your mother in her bedroom," he said reassuringly. "She won't be able to get back out. And I called the police."

"What?" Iman gasped. "Why?!"

"She attacked you," he said, looking confused. "I heard some of the stuff she was saying, it was awful. Is she... sick?" he added delicately.

"What? No, she's just always been like that. There was no need to call the police," Iman added.

The guard looked unconvinced. "Um, okay. Well, they're already on their way..." He trailed off.

Iman got to her feet slowly, wincing. "I'll deal with it."

The two officers were far easier convinced, especially once she'd mentioned her stepfather's recent murder a few times and talked about how on edge Aasia had been as a result. They left once she promised to have a doctor check her mother over to make sure everything was alright, after taking a brief detour to admonish the guards for wasting their time.

Iman breathed a sigh of relief. If she left now, she might just be able to make it to her grandfather's before he began to worry. Her appearance, she'd worry about later.

The young guard came up to her. "Is everything okay?"

Iman nodded. "Yes. Could you please get a doctor here to check her out? I need to go."

"Of course. Are you... gonna say goodbye?"

"I don't think that's a good idea." She held out a slip of paper. "Here, my number. If there's an emergency, please let me know but I won't be coming back. And you can pass it on to the other guards as well."

The guard nodded. "Yes, ma'am. I'll do that."

As she got into her car, Iman thought about what she'd said to the guard. How many times had she sworn that she'd never come back? But she always had. She'd always clung to the hope that Aasia would change.

But even she had her limits. Aasia Rahman had run out of chances where her daughter was concerned. Iman had finally spoken the truth – she wouldn't be coming back, not ever again.

-

James whistled as he took her in. "Do I even want to ask what the other guy looked like?"

"Girl," Iman corrected crankily. "And she looked just fine."

James assumed a sorrowful expression. "You got your butt kicked?"

"I got my everything kicked." Iman limped into the house and groaned at the sight of the stairs.

A hand closed over her wrist and she hissed in pain. James let go immediately and held his hands up. "Sorry! Sorry."

"What, James?"

"That." He pointed at her face. "You need to get all of that cleaned up or you're gonna give your old man a heart attack." The infirmary was on the other side of the house, a five minute walk that would probably take Iman twenty in her current state.

She groaned and James laughed. "Come on, I've got some stuff in my room."

"Thanks," Iman said gratefully.

"You're so close to the entrance," Iman remarked as he led her to the small suite. Iman took it in, mildly surprised at how sparse it was. It looked like James was still living out of his suitcase.

"Yep," James agreed. "I'm the newest guy back so I get the cannon fodder room."

"Cannon fodder?"

"You know... if something happens, I'm the first guy who'll have to deal with it. Cannon fodder. Right up at the front. Whereas you are in the heart of the house, the most defended spot." James indicated a little stool tucked away in a corner. "Sit on that."

Iman sat. "Oh. Why is it like that?" she asked, meaning his living arrangements.

"Because you are the heart. For your grandfather, at least."

Iman shook her head. "I meant for you. You've been working for my grandfather for so long. Don't you get a better room?"

"I wasn't here for a while, remember?" James began cleaning up the marks on her face. "What happened here, anyway? Scratches, cuts, did you get in a fight with a cat or something?"

"Or something," Iman replied tartly.

James rolled his eyes. "How witty you are, little girl! Seriously, what happened?"

"Don't worry about it. Thanks for cleaning me up." Iman got to her feet.

"There's nothing else?"

"Just some bruises." A lot of bruises, if she was honest.

"Okay," James relented. He took hold of her wrist and studied her fingers. "You fought back. Not well, but you tried."

"I know."

"If you ever wanna learn how to fight back and win, let me know," he offered.

Iman was taken aback. "Really?"

"Yeah. I'll teach you if you want."

"You're not busy?" Iman checked.

"Not really. I'm assuming you don't wanna train like we do, right?"

Iman shook her head emphatically. "No way. But a little self defence might be useful."

"Will be useful," he corrected. "There's no downside to learning how to defend yourself."

He was right, Iman realized. Maybe if she'd known how to defend herself, he wouldn't have...

She jerked her thoughts away. "When can we start?" she demanded.

James didn't blink. "Tomorrow. Meet me in the gym at five."

-

Ibrahim took one look at her and knew exactly what had happened. "Why did you even go near her?" he shouted furiously. "How many times has that woman hurt you already? Why would you let her do it again?"

Iman's eyes filled with tears and her grandfather cursed. "At least tell me you're not going to go there again?" he pleaded.

"I'm not," Iman confirmed. "I just thought... She was all alone."

Ibrahim pinched the bridge of his nose. "There's a reason for that, sweetheart. She drove away every good person in her life. The only one who's still giving her the time of day is you. And she's not going to change. She's..."

"Broken," Iman finished.

"Yes. You know then."

"I realized today," Iman admitted. "When she was screaming at me. There's something wrong with her, isn't there?"

Ibrahim sighed. "I don't know. Your mother would never agree to see a doctor, let alone a psychiatrist. But she was always very self-centred and possessive of anyone she deemed to be hers. Your Dad... he wasn't in love with her. But he thought that they could be happy together. And they were, in the beginning. But when your Dad began to focus on other things – work, his friends, spending time with me – she couldn't handle it."

He was mine, do you understand? And every single last penny of his is mine.

A flash of insight hit her. Everything had to be Aasia's. *She couldn't share,* Iman realized pityingly.

-

There was a bandage on her face. He'd only been gone for three days. How had she managed to get injured again?

He was so preoccupied with the way she was walking – as though it hurt her to move – that he didn't realize she'd reached out, and up, to hug him until she'd begun to pull back, wrongly assuming that she'd upset him.

Adam wrapped his arms around her gently, careful not to use too much pressure. Up close, she felt even tinier. He had to stoop to hug her properly and his back began to complain almost immediately. He caught a whiff of her scent and pulled back in surprise. She smelled like... gingerbread?

Iman let out a giggle and he realized that he'd voiced the question out loud. "It's my shampoo," she explained. "It's scented."

"Like gingerbread?" Why would a cleaning product smell like food?

"It's pretty," she said simply. "And it's better than a lot of other scents. I've always loved gingerbread. I used to make myself sick eating it when I was a kid."

Adam pictured an even tinier blonde, curled up next to a plate of cookies and had to fight the urge to laugh. "I bet you got it whenever you wanted anyway."

Iman wrinkled her nose. "Not *every* time. Just almost every time." She put a hand to her face and grimaced, the strange expression she'd made having obviously upset whatever wounds were hidden underneath the white gauze.

Adam couldn't keep his eyes from it. He opened his mouth to ask but Iman pre-empted him. "I'll tell you later?"

Adam nodded. He could wait if she needed him to. It wouldn't make much of a difference in the long run, after all.

Iman had taken a shower she didn't need, eaten a meal she hadn't wanted and unpacked a bag that hadn't needed unpacking. She would need to repack it later, in fact.

She was moments away from faking a yawn and attempting to escape to the bedroom to pretend to be asleep when Adam reached out to her across their table and took one of her hands in his. "You don't have to tell me if you don't want to," he reminded her. "I won't push."

She knew he was telling the truth. Adam hadn't pushed at all. Even the first few days when she'd been waking him all night, he hadn't gotten angry or insisted that she try to talk when she wasn't ready. He'd given her the option and when she'd rejected it, he'd accepted it.

More than that, once they'd realized that she slept better when he talked to her, he'd done that willingly. He'd shared so much about his past with her and hadn't complained once when she hadn't been able to do the same.

He'd told her enough about his stepfather that Iman had finally understood her first, unsettling reaction to the man, and had explained enough about the training he'd been subjected to that she knew she'd always hate Ali Cassim for being the one to dole it out.

The night he'd told her about his first kill, she'd been so angry on his behalf that she hadn't known what to do with herself.

Adam's thumb rubbed a slow line across her knuckles. "It's okay. Some other time."

He made to pull away and Iman tightened her grip on his fingers. "Just... give me a minute?" she pleaded.

"Sure." He settled himself back down. "Whatever you want."

"The day you left, I went to see my mother."

Understanding began to dawn on Adam's face. He said nothing, waiting for her to continue.

But she couldn't. Unconsciously, she shook her head, her mouth open but silent.

"You've met my mother."

Iman nodded, confused. "She's nice," she said lamely.

"She is. She's one of the most important people in the world to me. But there was a time that I hated her."

Iman lifted her head and stared at him in shock. "What?" she breathed.

"I've told you some of what the past seven years have been like for me. What I never told you is what my mother did about it."

Iman knew the answer to the question even as she asked it. It was written in the lines of his face, the downward twist of his lips. "What?"

"Nothing. She knew what was happening but she never tried to stop it. I asked her a few times but all she'd ever tell me was that I'd understand some day. I don't understand. Not in the least. And there's a part of me that still resents her for not saving me." Adam cleared his throat.

"I didn't even... I'd forgotten that your Mom was there with you. Do you think she... could have?"

Adam looked at the floor. "I don't want to believe that she could have," he said finally. "It's easier to believe that she had no power. It gives me a way to absolve her. But she could have done something, if she'd tried. At the beginning, if she'd asked, he would have stopped. But she couldn't find the courage and afterwards, I wouldn't have agreed anyway. I was too busy punishing myself."

"For what?"

Adam took a deep breath. "When I was sixteen, I made a huge mistake. And I wasn't the one who paid for it. Other people died and my stepfather had to spend an incredible amount of money fixing things. After that... I never really complained about anything. It felt like a kind of penance, to stop trying to get out. That's pretty stupid, isn't it?"

"No, it's not." The force in her voice surprised them both.

Adam looked bemused. "You're nicer than I am."

Iman looked at him, feeling a rush of affection go through her. He'd shared yet another piece of himself to make her feel better.

She leaned forward before she knew what she was doing and pressed her lips firmly to his.

He pulled away a second later, eyes so wide with shock that she could see the whites around them. "You kissed me."

He didn't *sound* disgusted. Courage came from a place deep within her and Iman found herself saying, "Yes. I did."

-

"Is that okay?" Iman stared up at him with big green eyes, biting her lip in concern.

Of course it was *okay*, Adam wanted to shout. Instead, all he managed was to nod dumbly.

"Oh," she smiled happily. "Well then... Can we do it again?"

This tiny woman was going to kill him, Adam realized with sudden clarity. And he had absolutely no problem with it.

"Yes," he murmured, leaning forward. "We can do it again."

CHAPTER SEVENTEEN

How had everything gone so wrong so fast? His best friend, his stepfather, his colleagues... They were gone. Taken by surprise in the very place they'd thought they were safe. In a place that should have been safe. That wasn't safe only because of him. Because he'd been stupid and trusting and had again cost other people their lives.

Her face flashed in his mind, mocking him with its feigned innocence. He'd been so enthralled by her that he'd refused to believe it at first. He'd yelled at the two remaining men who were lucky enough to survive that they were wrong. He'd insisted that there had to be some kind of mistake. The Iman he knew was kind and sweet and didn't even know the first thing about the world they lived in.

She'd only been to the compound once and she'd been asleep for most of the trip. She probably didn't even remember how to get there. It must have been someone else. He'd been so blind that even when his own mother told him otherwise, he'd still believed in her.

Finally, thoroughly fed up with him, they'd pieced together the remnants of the security footage to show him a single face. It had been enough.

Iman's new best friend. James Blackwell. Adam had seen his face often enough that even the grainy, salvaged images had been enough for him to recognize Blackwell.

And then, he couldn't deny the truth any longer.

He'd been told that the first thing Ali had done was to secure his mother's way out to safety. That, despite everything, was enough for Adam to forgive Ali everything else the man had done to him.

And Kat. The loss of his best friend Adam felt more keenly than any other. She'd never liked Iman and she tried to warn him but he'd brushed her off. He'd picked Iman over her and he knew, deep down, that that was what had led to her death. Kat should have been with him. She *would* have been with him if she'd been able to stand being in the same room as him.

Instead, he'd gone alone. It had cost his friend her life.

Mercifully, the footage had been too degraded for him to see just how they'd lost their lives. They hadn't even been able to find bodies to bury – everything had gone up in flames.

Adam knew what he had to do now. There was no way for him to redeem himself this time. The people who were dead lay on his conscience and there was no way to bring them back.

But there was one thing he could do. He could – and would – repay them in kind.

Ali had made sure that his mother would be taken care of, in the event that something happened to him. She had enough money to live on for several lifetimes and a handful of aliases to choose from. She would be fine without him.

It was better this way. She could barely stand to look at him now. He would do this one, final thing and then disappear.

-

Iman's hands were stained red with blood. She'd scrubbed them so hard she'd half thought that the skin was going to come off but the blood refused to leave. She could still feel it, still see it flowing, spilling out from her grandfather's chest onto her, tainting her.

She waited for nausea or tears but neither came. She was numb. It was as though someone reached inside her and ripped out her soul, leaving her a broken doll unable to function as a person any longer.

"Iman?" James crouched down beside her.

Iman tried to lift her head. "What is it?" she whispered. A bolt of panic hit her and she jerked. "Is there news?"

"No, he's still in surgery."

"Oh." She returned to her crouch, folding her arms across her knees.

She caught the concerned frown James gave her and felt the beginnings of guilt. She was being rude, she knew. He had to be exhausted as well and she wasn't making any effort.

She couldn't. She was drained.

"...go home and clean up? Iman? Did you hear me?"

"What?" Iman blinked her eyes blearily.

"Do you want to go home and clean up?" James repeated slowly.

Home. What home? She didn't have a home, not any more. The apartment had been his.

She said as much and James winced. "I meant your grandfather's," he said gently. "You don't look good."

Iman's stomach churned. "I'm never going back there," she whispered. Images began to flit through her mind. The ruined floors, ugly pools of red staining them like some macabre design. Her grandfather, lying crumpled against a chair, his skin so white she'd been terrified to even look for a pulse. And him. Adam. Looking at her with such hatred that she felt it right down to her bones.

He hadn't hurt her. He hadn't had to. The accusations he'd hurled at her made no more sense now than they had God knew how many hours ago. All that Iman understood was that he'd done this to hurt her.

Now you get to see how it feels, he'd hissed, before shoving her out of his way.

Hands shook her roughly and Iman's eyes cleared.

James let go of her. "Back with me?" he asked unnecessarily.

Iman nodded. "I – think so." Her voice was raspy with disuse.

"I think we should have a doctor check you over," he suggested, yet again.

"After I see my grandfather," Iman repeated, as she had every other time.

James eyes brightened. "They won't let you in like this."

What? Why not?

"Honey, you're covered in blood. You need to get cleaned up so you don't take any germs in with you when you see him."

He was right. Iman got to her feet, a sudden energy filling her veins. "Let's go," she said simply. The sooner she left, the sooner she could come back.

"I'll just go tell the nurses," James straightened out of his crouch. "Wait here, I'll be back soon."

A thought occurred to Iman. "Won't the house be sealed off? The police... I thought they'd..."

Jake nodded. "I'm taking you to a hotel," he explained. "Wait here, okay?"

Iman nodded obediently, already beginning to feel that energy fade. She's just sit down for a second. Just until he got back.

The next thing she knew, she was being laid on a bed.

Adam?

Relief flooded through her. It had been a dream? An awful nightmare that her subconscious had come up with to torture her?

Iman wrenched her eyes open.

She was in an unfamiliar room and the man who'd set her down wasn't Adam. It was James.

It had been real.

-

It was supposed to be his penance. And deep down, he'd hoped that it would help absolve him.

It hadn't. The guilt was just as suffocating now as it had been that awful, blood soaked day. It was the least he deserved for yet another betrayal.

He hadn't been able to kill her. She'd been standing right in front of him, utterly defenceless and still – *still* – spewing lies. But he hadn't been able to do it. His rage had been so powerful he'd nearly choked on it but he hadn't been able to pull the trigger.

He was pathetic.

His only consolation was that despite being entirely incapable of killing her, he'd at least made certain that she would feel a fraction of the pain he was feeling now. He slammed down on the small, traitorous part of himself that ached for the woman he'd thought he'd known, for being the one to take away the last remaining family she had who'd truly loved her. He forced himself to recall what she'd done.

She deserved every bit of pain she was experiencing.

And he deserved worse for being weak enough to still hurt for her.

Time passed oddly. He ate and slept only when his body's needs became too overwhelming to ignore and spent the majority of his time trying to work himself to exhaustion.

He rarely succeeded. He'd collapse into bed, aching and drenched with sweat, and would lie there for hours, unable to escape his ghosts.

Ugly scenes flashed before his eyes whenever he dared to close them. Kat featured prominently, her body twisted into grotesque shapes and marred in unsightly ways by methods he himself had employed on others.

He spent most nights curled up in the tiny bathroom, retching until his throat was raw and cursing himself in every language that he knew.

Something had to change, and soon. He was running out of money, food and energy at an alarming rate and he hadn't yet found it within himself to commit to ending things for good.

He needed to find a way to function. A way to dull everything so that he'd stop tearing his insides wide open every time he closed his eyes.

Dull.

Never go near alcohol or drugs, Ali's voice lectured sternly. *You'll dull your senses and make yourself stupid.*

Sounded good.

-

The slim, bearded man was examining a file and listening intently to the nurse holding it out to him, nodding as he scanned the page in front of him.

A bubble of happiness formed in Iman's chest at the sight of him and she was moving before she knew it. She flung herself at him and he caught her gently, his arms coming up to pat her back and ruffle her hair.

"Thank God you're here," she whispered fervently, tightening her hold on the back of his shirt. "Thank God."

Fareed pulled back, gently disentangling her but still keeping her close while he spoke to the nurse who'd tactfully backed away to give them a moment of privacy. "Thank you for all the help," he said politely. "I'll come find you if I need anything more."

"Of course, Doctor," she murmured, before darting away.

Fareed turned his attention back to her, his polite smile giving way to a concerned frown as he studied her. "When was the last time you ate something?"

Iman couldn't remember.

"I'm glad that you at least went home to get some rest," he

commented. "Did you drive yourself back here?"

Iman remembered James for the first time. She looked over her shoulder, scanning the corridor. "He was just here..." She trailed off. Where had he gone?

"Who?"

"James. He took me to a hotel this morning to get cleaned up and I fell asleep. He was right behind me..."

"I'm sure he'll be back soon," Fareed said soothingly. "Don't worry."

"But..." Iman glanced behind her doubtfully. "...Okay," she acquiesced eventually.

Fareed led her to a chair and made her sit. "How much do you know about your grandfather's condition?" he asked.

"Nothing," Iman said miserably. "They wouldn't tell us anything."

She swallowed hard. "Is... will he?" She couldn't get the words out.

Fareed sighed. "It's hard to tell right now. The biggest problem right now is his lungs."

Dread froze Iman's heart and memory washed over her. She was tiny and her eyes stung. She had cried and cried, had refused to eat a thing or listen to any of the ways Ibrahim had tried to pacify her. She'd only relented when he'd sworn he would stop smoking immediately, right then and then.

"He hasn't smoked in years," she protested feebly.

Fareed squeezed her hand sympathetically. "I know. And he's strong. His doctors are optimistic. But... he did a lot of damage to himself. You need to be prepared, Iman."

"Can I see him?" Iman begged. "Just for a few minutes."

Fareed nodded. "Only a few minutes," he agreed. "But you can see him. Do you want to be alone with him?"

Iman shook her head immediately. "Come with me?" she pleaded. "Please?"

"Of course. Come on. We'll go right now."

Fareed led her into a sterile room and patiently took her through the process of scrubbing and covering up then took her gloved hand in his own. "He's got a lot of machines and tubes surrounding him. They look pretty scary, but they're helping him. Okay?"

Iman nodded, her throat tight. "Okay. I'm ready."

He looked frail. Her grandfather had never looked frail. He'd always been so strong. She looked down at his hands, studying the wrinkles and the harsh ugliness of the tubing that dripped medication into his system.

How many times had those hands held her? Would they ever do it again? She couldn't even remember the last time she'd hugged him, much less told him she loved him. What she wouldn't give to have him wake just so she could whisper it to him one last time...

Iman felt something break within her as she looked at him in that bed, fighting for his life.

Gentle hands took hold of her shoulders and began to urge her away. Iman struggled, clutching onto the bed rail. "Wait, wait, not yet!"

"Iman, we have to go. The nurses are waiting," Fareed explained, gentle but firm. "Come on, let's go."

"But-" Iman reached a hand desperately towards her

grandfather.

"I'm sorry," he said simply. "But we have to go."

Iman felt tears prick her eyes. "What if something happens to him?"

"The nurses will call me," Fareed promised.

"But..."

"They'll call me," he repeated. "Come on, it's time to go."

Iman didn't fight him as he led her out. She kept her eyes on the bed her grandfather lay in for as long as possible, craning her neck to keep him in her sight for longer. When they finally had gotten too far for her to see him any more, she felt the flood of tears she'd kept dammed up inside begin to overflow.

They'd barely taken five steps by the time she was leaning against Fareed for support and sobbing into the cotton of his shirt.

He held her patiently, handing her a handkerchief when she'd recovered enough to be able to mop herself up.

"There's a bathroom over there," he said tactfully, pointing it out.

Iman murmured a thank you and went to splash some water on her tight, aching face.

She caught sight of her reflection in the mirror and winced, finally understanding why people had been looking at her with such concern all day. She looked terrible.

Her hair hung in limp clumps on each side of her face and her eyes were so bloodshot, the green was almost overwhelmed by red.

It looked like blood in the dimness of the badly lit bathroom.

Her stomach turned. She was halfway to scooping handfuls of water directly into her eyes to frantically try and remove the red when her mind caught up to her body. Slowly, she forced herself to open her curled fingers and allow the water to drip down into the drain.

Iman bolted out of the bathroom, deliberately keeping her eyes on the floor. She was moving so fast she nearly walked right past Fareed, only stopping when he called her name and grabbed her arm.

She gasped, lifting a hand to her chest and looking around wildly. "What? What is it?"

"It's alright. Take a deep breath," he instructed.

Why?

"It will help your chest," he added when she did nothing.

How did he know that her chest was hurting?

Iman obeyed, filling her lungs with as much air as they could hold, then slowly letting it out. She repeated the motion several times as Fareed directed her.

The painful fluttering in her chest slowly began to ease and she felt her shoulders slump.

Fareed gave her a concerned look. "Iman, can you give me a minute?"

"Sure," she said, her voice scratchy. "Don't worry about me, I'm fine."

Fareed gave her a disbelieving look that he couldn't quite hide. "Right," he said. "I'll be back in a few minutes. Why don't you call James and let him know where to find you? He's been waiting in one of the waiting rooms."

Iman blinked. "Okay," she agreed. She watched Fareed walk away then began to fumble in her pockets for her cell phone. It was nowhere to be found and she furrowed her brow, trying to remember when she'd last seen it.

On the floor, she realized. Next to her grandfather's blood. She'd dropped it after she'd called for an ambulance, while she was fighting to keep all of his blood where it belonged – within his veins and not decorating the floors.

She shuddered, clenching her fingers into fists as she remembered that disgusting warmth flowing over her skin.

"Iman?" Fareed had returned. He glanced around. "Where's James?"

"I couldn't find my phone," Iman said dully. "It's with the blood."

"What?"

"I dropped it."

"We'll get you another one. Don't worry."

She wasn't. She had begun to return to the place where she was numb and nothing got through to her any more. She welcomed it, craving the numbness.

"... be alone."

Fareed knelt down in front of her and his hands landed on either side of her face. "Iman? Focus on my voice."

She was so tired. "Can't," she whispered.

"Just a little longer," he insisted. "Focus. Please."

Iman waded through the fog. "Okay."

"I don't think you should be alone right now," Fareed began. "Shaida can't come to be with you right now," he continued regretfully. "She can't leave the baby. But-"

The fog began to leave her. "Is she okay?"

"They're both fine," Fareed said comfortingly. "But it's too dangerous here right now. But Shaida wants you with her."

"I can't leave my grandfather," Iman said, for the fourth time that day. "I have to be with him."

Fareed sighed, tugging on his short crop of hair. "Iman... you can't stay here. It's not safe."

Panic began to burrow under her skin. "I need to be here."

"I know you want to be with him. But we can't spare the people to be with you."

Iman furrowed her brow, fighting to make his words make sense. "What do you mean?"

"I talked to Waseem earlier," Fareed explained patiently. "Your grandfather is in no shape to be moved. He has to stay here for a while until he's stable enough to be transferred to the hospital I've been working in. But you being here makes it that much harder for us to handle things."

Iman zeroed in on the most important part of that speech. "Waseem's okay?"

Fareed looked taken aback. "He's fine. We only lost six people last night."

"Only?"

Fareed winced. "I didn't mean it like that. I just meant... it could have been a lot worse."

Iman nodded wordlessly in agreement.

"James didn't tell you that Waseem was alright? He's been going insane worrying about you. He asked to talk to you."

Iman shook her head. "I don't remember. Why do I have to go if we have people left?"

Fareed frowned at her. "That's a little callous of you, don't you think?"

Shock made her jerk her head up to stare at him. "What?"

"You want people to risk their lives for you unnecessarily," Fareed pointed out.

Iman shook her head vehemently, beginning to feel ill. "No!" she shouted. "No, I don't. They'll be here already. Why can't they be with me?"

"They can't be in two places at once, Iman." Fareed sighed and got to his feet. "Your grandfather can't be moved and so his people will stand guard over him. They will do it for you as well if you ask. But you don't need to be here. And it is dangerous here. Waseem is working incredibly hard to get the police under control and Adam-"

Iman flinched at the name.

"He could come back. When he realizes that he made a mistake, he will want to fix it. It's not fair to ask anyone to take that kind of risk for you."

He was right. Obstinately, refusing to accept it, Iman shook her head.

"I know you want to be with your grandfather. I know you're terrified and you want to stay with him. But it's not fair. It's cruel."

She'd already cried so much it was impossible that she should have any tears left in her. But there they were, wetting her face as she finally, *miserably,* nodded.

CHAPTER EIGHTEEN

His throat still burned but this new burn was far easier to bear. Adam poured the remainder of the bottle straight down his throat, grinning viciously as his insides objected to the fiery liquid. He tossed it to the side, relishing the discordant crash as it shattered against the remnants of its brothers.

He'd spent the past week in a haze, experimenting with the amount of alcohol he needed to find that beautiful numbness he'd been craving without drinking so much that he couldn't see straight.

He'd hated the taste of it at first but now he'd come to relish the bite for what it brought with it – an escape.

-

Kat looked at him pityingly as she crouched next to his prone form. "You're killing yourself."

Adam nodded lethargically. "Yep."

"Do you think this is what I'd want, Adam? For you to piss your life away?"

A bolt of pain cut through the haze. Kat seemed to waver. "You don't want anything. You're dead. Maybe if I die, I'll get to see you again. Get to apologize."

"No," she whispered. "You won't."

She was right. He was going straight to Hell and he refused to believe that Kat – bright, sweet Kat – was destined for the same. She had worked so hard to try and be better... Surely – Surely, that made a difference.

His temples began to throb and he reached clumsily for one of the bottles scattered around him, putting it to his lips. He was tired of thinking.

-

Adam groaned, resting his head against the cool porcelain of the tiles. His stomach churned and he fought the urge to vomit. There was nothing left in him to bring up but his body didn't care. It punished him for the poison he drank by forcing him to endure almost constant aching. He couldn't remember the last time he'd been in no pain at all.

He needed to eat. He'd forgotten again. Food would help the alcohol work its magic without condemning him to hours spent in front of a toilet, trying not to crack his head open on the tiles.

There was no more food in his little room. That wasn't surprising, he hadn't stepped foot out of it in days. He'd need to go out if he wanted anything – the cheap little room he was paying for didn't include luxuries like room service.

Adam struggled to his feet, using the sink for leverage and stood there, waiting for the dizziness to subside. He couldn't drive like this. He had no problems risking his own skin but he wouldn't risk someone else. Not again.

He sank back down. Food could wait until he was sober. It wouldn't take long – he was out of alcohol too.

-

Crappy, hole in the wall motels weren't supposed to have standards. They especially weren't supposed to have staff who stared at him and made comments about his drinking and offered to call him someone to help.

He needed to leave. He'd lost it with the short little receptionist and by the terrified look on her face, he knew to expect security at his door soon.

Adam felt guilty about scaring her. It wasn't her fault that she looked like...like... He still couldn't say her name.

Hatred overwhelmed him, vicious and consuming.

He wondered where she was, whether she was in the same shape he was. He had killed her grandfather, killed several other people she'd told him she'd known all her life. He'd wanted to make them suffer, had taken a grim pleasure in knowing that every bullet was slowly balancing the scales.

The Khans had killed more than he had by far. He still didn't know what the exact body count was. But Ali's compound had been home to over fifty people. Three had made it out on their own power. Just three.

And to add insult to injury, they'd then torched the place. Adam hadn't gone near his apartment but he was sure that they'd ransacked that as well. Thank God he hadn't let her anywhere near any of the other properties Ali kept maintained. All of them would have been gone.

He'd wanted to, he remembered. In those few wonderful, *fake* weeks when he'd thought they'd been getting closer – after she'd gone and kissed him that day and gotten him to completely let his guard down – he'd had half-formed plans in his mind.

She'd told him once that she'd never gotten to travel much. He'd wanted to fix that. He'd wanted to show her his favourite places in the world.

If she'd only waited a little longer, he'd have given her even more to cripple him with.

God, what a fucking *idiot* he'd been.

She'd ruined everything. Everything.

No. He refused to give her the satisfaction of taking even that from him. He'd loved to travel all his life and she *wouldn't* take that from him. He wouldn't let her.

-

Little Uwais was adorable. Iman may have been biased but she thought that he looked just like Shaida, with her large brown eyes and the beginnings of her curly brown hair just starting to grow on his tiny head.

A wave of affection for the older woman rushed through her. Iman had no idea what she would have done without Shaida. She'd been there, ready to help and hold Iman through the grief and anger that had finally come crashing down on her.

Shaida had been infinitely patient with her, treating her as much like her own baby as she did Uwais.

Iman cuddled the little baby close, delighting in his solid weight and soft, satiny skin. In the three weeks that she'd been staying with Shaida she'd fallen deeper and deeper in love with the little boy and Shaida had begun to joke that Iman was acting as a substitute parent for Uwais while Fareed was away.

She sighed regretfully, making Uwais wrinkle his nose at the sudden gush of air. Fareed had been as good as his word – he'd stayed with Ibrahim the entire time and would stay with him until he was ready to be moved.

He'd missed so many of Uwais's firsts in order to make sure that Iman's grandfather was being given the best possible care. He would likely miss more in the next week until he was finally able to return.

She had no idea how she could ever possibly try to repay either Fareed or Shaida for all they'd done and the one time she'd tried to bring it up, Shaida had immediately called her an idiot and assured her that they were happy to do it.

They weren't the only ones. She received calls from other members of her grandfather's staff wanting to make sure she was alright, the most notable of which had been the half an hour long call she'd had with Waseem who'd asked her every question under the sun trying to make sure she had everything she needed.

Iman had expected them to be angry with her – she was the one with a tie to Adam. But she'd been met with a crowd of assassins and other sundry criminals anxious to make sure that nothing had happened to the little girl they'd watched grow up.

Uwais wriggled, letting out a plaintive little wail and she felt laughter bubble inside her. He wasn't happy that she was ignoring him.

She held out one of her hands making sure to let the bracelet she wore catch the light. The baby cooed happily and reached for the shiny piece of jewellery, grasping it with his tiny fingers. He was enchanted.

Iman allowed herself to be distracted but in the back of her mind, it nagged. So many people had sacrificed for her. How would she ever be worthy of it?

-

Iman stood rooted to the spot, afraid to move for fear that she'd find she was dreaming.

"I can really see him?" she asked, half terrified of the answer.

Fareed laughed. "Yes, you really can. He's right in there."

It was an effort to make her feet move. She had longed to see him for so long, to make sure that he was still alive. But now... She was scared, Iman realized. Scared to see what had happened to the strong man who'd taken care of her all her life.

How would she cope if he was different?

She knew one thing for sure – no matter how things had changed, she would find some way to cope. She had to.

Iman took hold of the handle and pushed open the door.

"There you are," a warm voice said. "I've been waiting for you." Iman burst into tears.

She felt like a small child who'd gotten lost and had just been found. The panic and fear that had been her constant companions for almost a month now evaporated and were replaced with a relief so strong it made her dizzy.

"Oh, sweetheart," Ibrahim made an aborted movement, as though to get up and then cursed. "Help an old man out and come a bit closer please?"

Iman went, hiccuping and sniffling. She hovered awkwardly within touching distance, wanting so badly to hug her grandfather but afraid that she'd somehow hurt him.

Ibrahim solved the problem for her by taking hold of her closest arm and pulling her down onto the bed next to him. "Much better," he said in a satisfied tone.

Iman sat stiffly, hesitant and Ibrahim sighed. "I'm not made of glass," he reminded her gently. "I won't break."

But he nearly had. "You almost died." Fresh tears welled up in Iman's eyes just saying it but she dashed them away impatiently. "I was so worried about you!"

"It's alright now. I'm alright."

"You're in a hospital bed!" Iman couldn't seem to calm herself down. "You've been in a hospital for over three weeks now. They said... they told me they weren't sure you were going to survive." Her voice wobbled.

Her grandfather scowled. "Who on Earth told you a thing like that?"

"Fareed." Iman drew back. "He wasn't lying to me."

"No," Ibrahim agreed reluctantly. "He wasn't. But he shouldn't have told you something like that. I'm fine now. Just fine." He rubbed her back lightly, trying to soothe her.
Iman was having none of it. "You're still in a hospital," she persisted. "You're still hurt. You almost died!" She looked away. "And   it's   my   fault."
"What? What on Earth do you mean?"
Did he not know? Had he not seen who had attacked him?
Iman opened her mouth, struggling to find the words to explain. Before she could, her grandfather spoke.

"That Adam shot me is not your fault, Iman," he said patiently. "You don't have to take the blame for everything sweetheart. I made a bad choice when I picked him for you and we'll have to deal with the consequences of it."

Iman wasn't comforted. "He told me," she got out. "He told me that he was doing it to hurt me. It *is* my fault. Why are none of you mad at me? Waseem, Shaida, Fareed... all of you are being nice to me when it's my fault that all of this is happening!"
If she hadn't begged her grandfather to find her a husband... If she'd just agreed to one of the men Aasia had tried to pawn her off onto... Everything would be different. It was all her fault.

"Iman," Ibrahim's voice was steely. "What do you mean 'He told you'? When did you talk to Adam?"

Iman frowned in confusion. "That day. After he... you know. He found me and he was yelling... He told me..." She struggled to remember. "He said he wanted me to feel the same way he did."

"He didn't hurt you?" her grandfather asked urgently, tightening his grip on her arm.

"No. He just... left."

Ibrahim pursed his lips. "Hmm. Do you remember what else he said?"

"N-not really. Why? Does it make a difference?"

"It might," Ibrahim told her. "It just might. Could you get Waseem for me sweetheart?"

-

Italy was just as beautiful as it had always been. Adam had only been there two days and already, he was starting to feel better.

He'd forced himself to remain sober for a large part of the past two weeks and it had forced him to find another way of keeping himself numb. He hadn't had to look too far. A few little pills were far easier to swallow than the bottles he'd been throwing back, even if they were harder to get access to.

He knew he was playing with fire. He'd heard horror stories of men who couldn't function without some kind of substance in their system and had scoffed, finding them weak and arrogantly thinking himself so much superior.

Now he knew better. He was weaker than any of them.

He'd tried, last night. Tried to end things for good. He'd had the gun in hand, loaded and ready. And he couldn't pull the trigger.

For the second time in his life, he had failed to kill someone.

He felt disgusting. He hadn't shied away from killing an innocent animal. He'd been too much of a coward then, too afraid to stand up for what was right. But his own life... Her life... Those he couldn't bear to take.

He was hopeless.

A thought occurred to him and he suddenly felt a jolt of excitement, waking him up.

He couldn't kill himself, no. He'd tried and failed.

But maybe someone else could.

He was in Italy. He'd been there enough times that he knew exactly where to go. *And* where not to go.

All he had to do was wander down to one of the seedier parts of town.

He'd find someone looking for a fight eventually. And he'd give it to them just long enough to make sure they stopped him for good.

He'd been walking up and down the city for most of the night and somehow, despite the fact that it was almost dawn, he was still completely unscathed. Naples was the most dangerous city in all of Italy, was in the top ten for all of Europe, and yet he'd been walking around for six hours now and nothing had happened to him.

It was past dawn now. The darker parts of Naples were being put away, retreating from the light to bide their time until night fell again.

Adam debated going back to his little hotel for the day but the scent of freshly made coffee changed his mind. He'd get some coffee first. It wasn't like he had anything pressing to do.

Five minutes later, coffee in hand, he began to make his way back. He'd walked all the way to the other side of the city in his preoccupation and he'd finished the large cup of coffee long before he'd made much progress.

The city got busier as he walked and soon the morning rush was in full swing. Adam enjoyed being able to lose himself amongst the crowd and let his feet guide him while he watched the people milling around him.

What were their lives like? Had any of them ever had to fight for their lives?

He doubted it. They weren't like him.

Adam watched a young mother lean down to lift her son, dredging up a rusty smile from deep within him as saw the little boy reach out with a chubby hand to tug on one of his mother's blonde curls and lift it to his mouth.

The colour made him jerk his eyes away, his fingers itching as he remembered other curls that he'd tangled his hands in.

When would she leave him alone?

He turned, and saw something so confusing he initially

thought he was somehow hallucinating.

-

Iman couldn't remember when last she'd been so tired. She desperately wanted to just collapse onto the nearest soft thing and stay there until her exhaustion somehow disappeared but she couldn't get her mind to quiet.

She thought back to the conversation she'd heard that afternoon, trying for the fifth time to puzzle it out. She'd sought out Waseem as Ibrahim had requested and had settled herself in a seat in the corner.

A few minutes later, she'd had the uncomfortable realization that they'd forgotten she was in the room. She'd only caught bits of the conversation but that had been enough to thoroughly confuse and worry her.

She wasn't sure exactly who or what Waseem was on his way to track down or why the man who'd been a surrogate uncle to her was so upset about it but Waseem wasn't one to be overly dramatic. If he was this upset... The implications made her stomach twist.

She'd questioned her grandfather once his Second had left but Ibrahim held firm and refused to tell her a thing.

She looked around the small room she'd been given. Shaida's mother wasn't one for 'clutter' and the room, while neat and comfortable, was sadly devoid of things for her to fiddle with.

She eyed the lone item on her night stand. A copy of the Quran, in its original Arabic. Shaida had taught her the language – and the basics of Islam – when she'd been tiny but it had been years since Iman had prayed. At least until she'd met Shaida's mother.

The fussy old woman had left her alone for a while, doubtless due to her daughter insisting. But a week after Iman had arrived, it seemed she'd finally lost her patience. Iman had been painting when Shaida's mother had walked into her room and asked her point blank why she did not pray.

After listening to Iman's stuttered response, she'd nodded once and announced that anyone who lived under her roof would pray. Did Iman know how?

Shaida had come in moments later, somehow sensing trouble and had hurried her mother away. Later, she'd told Iman not to feel pressured, that her mother meant well but she could be a bit forceful.

Since then, Shaida's mother had developed a habit of calling Iman when she herself went to pray in an effort to either guilt her or encourage her into doing it herself.

Seeing no harm in indulging the old lady who – despite admittedly being a bit abrupt – was very sweet, Iman had found herself praying fairly often.

It made her nostalgic for a time when she'd been too little to know just what kind of a world her family lived in and too loved to ever have much to worry over.

She looked around the room again and gave a mental shrug. Her Arabic could use some practising anyway.

-

Adam began to run, shoving people aside in his haste. He still couldn't believe what he was seeing, was certain that his mind was playing tricks on him, but he was determined to make sure and if he made a fool of himself in the process, so be it.

She slipped through the crowd faster than he could, her smaller frame far easier to get through the gaps. He almost lost her several times and by the time he'd closed the distance between them he was gasping and sweat was pouring down his face.

Out of shape, he thought in disgust.

He pushed every last bit of strength into his legs, forcing himself forward. He noticed with grim satisfaction that he wasn't the only one tiring. Her stride had shortened considerably.

He was almost on her.

Almost.

There.

He reached out and grabbed her shoulder, yanking her around to face him.

He wasn't hallucinating.

She looked just as shocked as he felt and as he stood there, the shock morphed into panic.

"Kat?" he whispered, needing to make sure.

"Let go of me, Adam. Let go of me now!" Her voice rose. "You need to go. Go now."

"What?" He felt like he was wading through fog.

"Let go," she said.

"No." The shock was beginning to fade and rage, always close at hand now, had taken its place. "Come with me." He began to lead her into the closest alley.

"Adam, it's not safe here!" Kat sounded truly afraid.

He looked down at her. "Then tell me where to go. But I'm not leaving you alone without some answers. You owe me *at least* that."

Adam knew by now that she wasn't a hallucination. Enough people had reacted to her as they'd made the trek to his hotel that he would have been convinced even if his body hadn't ached hard enough that he knew he couldn't be under the influence of anything.

He shut the windows and dropped the blinds, the light slipping from the room as they lowered. He flicked the switch on the lamp conveniently positioned on the night stand and then turned to the woman standing awkwardly in the middle of his hotel room."Well?" he prompted, looking her dead in the eyes. "Aren't you going to explain?"

Kat shifted her weight from foot to foot. "What do you want to know?"

The question made Adam clench his teeth. "I don't know," he hissed. "How about, maybe, *how are you alive?*"

Kat flinched and eyed the door. "Keep your voice down."

"Answer my question," Adam countered. "And while you're at it, tell me why you're so jumpy. Who are you running from Kat?"

She shut her eyes for a moment, putting a hand to her temples. "How much do you know about what happened?"

"I-" Adam cleared his throat. "Iman gave the compound to her grandfather and he, for whatever reason, had it burned after sending in some of his people to kill everyone they could find."

"You don't know anything then," Kat said matter-of-factly.

"What does that mean, Kat?"

She shook her head and he pressed. *"What does that mean?"*

"It means that you're being led around like a puppet and you don't even know it!" she yelled. "Why would your little wife give up the compound? Why now, months later? After you've killed for them, even!"

The old hurt twinged for a minute but Adam was quickly distracted by more important things. "Then who?" he croaked. "No one else knew!"

"Exactly!" Kat threw her hands up.

"Exactly *what*, Kat? Who was it? And why did I see one of Ibrahim Khan's men on security footage with my own eyes?"

Kat blew out a sigh, pulling out the lone chair and straddling it. "Blackwell doesn't belong to anyone," she said softly. "He's made a career out of stepping on as many people as he has to to get what he wants. If the Khans thought he belonged to them, they were wrong."

"Then Iman..." Adam's voice gave out.

"She didn't do a thing," Kat confirmed.

The implications of that one little sentence were too overwhelming for him to bear. Adam shoved it all to the side. "How did you get out? I saw the compound, it was ashes."

Kat gave him a pitying look. "You still don't get it, do you?" She pushed herself to her feet. "There was no attack, Adam. No one is dead except the people you killed when you went to get revenge for something that didn't even happen."

No.

Adam shook his head.

Oh, God, no.

Kat came up behind him and handed him a glass of water. "I'm sorry, Adam. I really am."

"Why?" he gasped. "Why would you... I don't understand." He coughed.

Kat spoke in a monotone. "You were supposed to kill them all," she explained, her eyes dead. "You were supposed to kill every single one of them."

"And then what? You'd come back and I'd just fall in line?"

Kat nodded.

"How could you think that would work, Kat? How could you even..." He stared at her, unable to believe that she was the same woman he'd mourned for nearly a month now.

"It wasn't me!" she snapped, with sudden energy. "This has been killing me! You have *no* idea." Emotion made her voice thick and her eyes were glassy.

Adam didn't care. "I thought you were dead!" he yelled. "I thought fifty people were dead, because of *me*! You know, you've always known what that would do to me. How could you just let me believe that?"

"I didn't have a choice!" Kat flung out her hands. "If I hadn't gone along with it, he would have killed me!"

"Who?" Adam bellowed, fed up.

"Ali!" Kat sniffed and rubbed at her eyes. "I told you," she went on, "there was no attack. Ali... I don't even know why. But he's been planning this since before you got involved with the Khans. Not to make you kill them. But to get rid of them. I think his plans changed when you got married but I don't know. It's not like he tells me stuff."

Adam felt cold. "And my mother?" He almost didn't want to hear the answer. Lina had chosen Ali over him before but he didn't know if he could bear hearing that she'd done it again.

Kat lowered her eyes to the floor, looking regretful. "She has no idea what's going on. She's as clueless as you were."

There was a moment of relief before the guilt set it. How could he be happy that his mother was in mourning for her still very alive husband?

Again, he pushed it away in favour of more pressing issues.

"Why did you tell me to go when you saw me?"

Kat squeezed her eyes shut. "Ali is furious with you. For messing up. You didn't kill Ibrahim Khan. You – you missed. He's still alive and he'll make a full recovery. He's been raging for a while now about it. He almost sent me to get rid of you. I convinced him that I'm needed here but you need to go, Adam! If he finds out that you're in Naples, he will either make me kill you or do it himself. You need to go and you need to go fast."

Kat looked down at her phone. "And so do I. I've been gone for too long. I need to get back."

"Wait!" The plea was out before he could stop it. "Kat..." Adam hesitated. "I'm sorry for the way we left things."

Kat gave him a ghost of her usual smile. "So am I."

He didn't ask for forgiveness and she didn't offer it. And as Adam watched her leave, he knew – if Kat had to, she *would* kill him.

CHAPTER NINETEEN

Dead people haunted his dreams.

Adam rolled out of bed and directly onto the floor, catching himself on his arms and beginning a set of push ups.

The urge to swallow a handful of pills or down a few bottles of disgusting spirits was strong but he fought it. He needed a clear head.

The only way he'd gotten through the past few days was by promising himself that it would only be for a little while. He just needed to function for a little longer and then, he could descend back into the haze he'd been living in.

He'd been mourning people who still breathed for a month and now he mourned the strangers he'd killed to avenge them. In the space of a few hours, everything had changed.

His arms were beginning to ache. A wave of exhaustion hit him but Adam kept going. He knew well enough by now that if he tried to sleep, he would lay in bed tossing and turning until dawn.

The only way to win himself even a few hours of rest was to

work until he was shaking and could barely move.

His thoughts turned to the plane ticket in his name that was waiting to be picked up. He'd booked it scant hours ago and he was already having second thoughts.

Was he ready to go back? Could he handle what he was stepping back into?

-

Iman was curled up with her feet underneath her, watching Uwais as the little boy tried to push himself off of his stomach, wriggling his limbs. He whined, lifting his head up to stare at her with a scrunched face.

Shaida came in, braiding her long hair as she walked. She smiled down at her son, "Are you having fun, sweetheart?" then turned to Iman. "Do you mind if I steal him back from you?"

Iman lifted the little boy and handed him over. "Fareed?"

Shaida smiled indulgently. "Yeah," she sighed. "I'd love to spend some time alone with my husband but all he wants is to stare at our son. I suppose I can live with it." She bounced Uwais. "He is pretty adorable, I guess."

"He looks just like his mother," Iman grinned.

Shaida wrinkled her nose. "Flatterer. Thanks for taking care of him."

"It was only for five minutes!"

"Still, it's pretty early. What were you even doing up?"

"I wanted to paint the sunrise," Iman lied. She had, in fact, painted the sunrise that morning but she'd woken for a far less pleasant reason – Adam. He haunted her all night.

"Show it to me later," Shaida requested distractedly.

"Sure." Iman watched the brunette leave, keeping a smile on her face that immediately dropped once Shaida had pulled the door shut behind her.

She sighed and looked at the canvas she'd left in front of the window to dry. It was one of the worst paintings she had done in a long time – bad enough that she'd probably paint over it – and a clear indicator of how shaken she'd been when she was painting it.

There was a click.

Shaida stood there with a hand on the door handle. "Ready to talk?"

Iman stared. "About what?" she stalled.

Shaida narrowed her eyes, looking unimpressed. "I've known you since you were a little girl. I've even bathed you," she reminded Iman. "Did you think I wouldn't notice how off-balance you've been?"

Iman looked away. "You should be with Fareed and Uwais."

Shaida rolled her eyes. "Neither of them even noticed me leave. Will you talk to me, please?"

"I'm fine."

Shaida pursed her lips. "Good try. If I'd lost my mind, I would believe you. What's going on? I thought you would be having a good day today, at least. Are you worried about leaving?"

Iman hesitated. She'd been too preoccupied by other things to think about it much but she *was* a little apprehensive about leaving the little bubble she'd been in for the past month. But her grandfather was insistent that he wanted to be back in his own home and so Iman would bear with it.

"Iman? You know you can stay here for as long as you'd like, don't you?"

"I know." Iman smiled gratefully and hugged Shaida. "But..." she trailed off.

"But you want to be with your grandfather, I know." Shaida frowned thoughtfully. "Do you want me to come with you?"

Iman's eyes widened. "No, no, you should be here."

"Are you sure? I have more than enough time," Shaida joked.

"I'm sure."

"Alright. If you change your mind, at any time, tell me and I'll pack a bag." Shaida sighed. "I'm going to miss you, you know. I've gotten used to you being here all the time."

Iman had deliberately avoided thinking about leaving Shaida behind and now a knot began to form in her stomach. "You're not coming back, are you?"

Shaida's eyes darkened with sorrow. "No, sweetheart, we're not. Before... It was different before. But now, I just can't bring myself to let that world touch Uwais."

"I understand." And she did. Iman swiped a hand across her cheeks.

There was a knock at the door. "Shae?" Fareed called. "He's hungry." As if on cue, there was a little wail.

Shaida looked between Iman and the door, a torn expression on her face. "Oh-"

"What are you waiting for? Go feed him!" Iman injected humour into her voice.

Shaida squeezed her hand. "We'll spend time together tonight when he's sleeping," she promised.

-

He was home. It felt strangely unreal to be back. Even though his entire life had been turned upside down, nothing else had changed.

Adam had been second guessing himself for the entire flight. Now that he was here, about to knock on the front door, he felt even less certain than he had before.

What was he doing? Was he going to tell his mother the truth? Would she even believe him? He didn't know.

Kat had warned him that his life was in danger. His stepfather wanted him dead.

Would going to see Lina get him killed?

The part of himself that had been in control when he'd wandered through a city looking for someone to kill him reminded him that maybe that wouldn't be so bad.

Adam walked down the driveway, deliberately letting the guard who was stationed at the door see him.

Lina gasped at the sight of him. "Adam! What are you doing here?" She didn't sound particularly happy to see him.

"I... wanted to see how you were doing." He shut the door behind himself, leaving the guards at their posts.

His mother's eyes hardened. "You wanted to see how I was doing?" she repeated. "Adam, it's been over a month! *Now* you want to know how I'm doing?"

Adam winced. "I'm sorry," he said helplessly.

Lina waved off his apology. "Where were you?" she demanded.

"What was so important that you left me alone all this time?"

He had no answers for her. The justifications he'd spouted off to himself when he'd left seemed hollow now. He'd been furious and guilty and he'd wanted revenge on the Khans.

He...

He *hadn't* been thinking of her, Adam admitted to himself. He'd been trying to find a way to make himself feel better and it had been easier to convince himself that she'd be fine without him than to keep worrying over her.

"I'm sorry," he repeated.

"Did you even think about me all this time?" She looked so disappointed in him.

"No. I was trying not to think much at all."

"And why are you here now, Adam?" Lina's frustration was palpable. "Why did you come here?"

Adam opened his mouth. "I – found some things out." Most notably that his stepfather was a monster. He looked at his mother, trying to find the words to tell her what had happened and experienced a moment of clarity.

He couldn't tell her.

If he did... If he even attempted to give her hope... He didn't even know what Ali's actual plans were. All he did know was that he needed to stay far away from anyone even vaguely connected to his stepfather until he got his head on straight.

He was in no shape to deal with Ali Cassim in his current condition. He'd be dead in minutes.

"I just wanted to see how you were coping," he told Lina. "If you needed anything?"

She crossed her arms, unimpressed. "What would you even be able to do, Adam? You were barely a part of my life as it was and now... I don't even know if I'm happy you're back. You've always kept yourself away from me. If I hadn't kept pulling you back, I suppose this would have happened a long time ago. Maybe that would have been better. Clearly you didn't care enough to try and stay a part of my life."

That wasn't fair. Adam opened his mouth to protest then shut it and shook his head. What good would arguing with her even do?

"I'm sorry," he said, for the third and final time, and left.

He ended up at his old apartment. He'd long since lost the keys but it was the work of a moment to retrieve a spare set that he'd kept hidden in an alcove by the elevator on his floor.

Looking at the familiar door, he took a deep breath and turned the key in the lock.

He'd prepared himself for a mess – he wasn't naive enough to believe that the Khans would leave him be after what he'd done to them. But the apartment was untouched.

It was even clean. The service he used must have come by fairly recently.

It hurt, being there without Iman.

There were paints and sketchbooks scattered around and he could see canvases that she'd left out of the way to dry, leaning against the balcony doors.

He scrubbed a hand over his face and suddenly felt anew just how grimy he was.

A shower, he decided. Maybe it would help him feel a bit more human too.

-

There was a letter on the floor by his door. Adam lifted it, thinking of the other two he'd received just like it.

Why a letter?

Why not just kill him and end things?

What was Ibrahim Khan doing?

He slit the envelope open with a nail and pulled out the letter, his nerves jangling.

Blank. It was blank?

He was still puzzling it over when he heard a knock at the door.

Adam lifted his head, debating... Run or open the door and try to fight?

He was in terrible shape for either.

-

Iman walked slowly, carrying a laden tray in her hands. She was about to call out and ask for the door to be opened when she heard a slam.

Startled, she jumped, making the tray rattled. The door was yanked open and she found James glaring at her on the other side.

"I-is everything okay?" she asked when he remained silent.

"Not really," he muttered. "Here, let me take that." He took the tray and stepped aside, letting her into the room.

Iman went over to her grandfather and kissed his cheek. "I heard a noise. Is everything alright?"

Ibrahim smiled. "Just a bit of a disagreement," he said lightly.

Behind them, James snorted. "It's a little more than that."

Ibrahim glared at him warningly but James ignored the look. "I just don't get why you haven't snapped his neck already," he complained. "He deserves it – he made a huge mess!"

"I would like to talk to him first," Ibrahim responded, clearly annoyed. "As is *my* prerogative, James."

"What are the two of you talking about?" Iman asked absently, focusing on fixing cups of tea to their liking.

"It's not important," her grandfather assured her.

"Your *husband*," James said at the same time, rolling his eyes.

"What?" Iman lifted her head. "Adam?" The smile dropped from her face.

"James, go and get me a cup of coffee," Ibrahim instructed.

"There's tea," Iman said blankly, still holding the cup she'd been stirring sugar into.

Her grandfather ignored her. "Go. Fast."

James left immediately.

Ibrahim focused on her once James was gone. "I'm sorry about that."

"It's... fine." Iman swallowed, her mouth dry. "You're... he... you're trying to find him?"

"Yes, I am."

"To – to kill him?" She fought to keep her voice level.

Her grandfather looked intently at her. "Not immediately," he told her.

"But eventually?" Her voice cracked.

Ibrahim nodded.

"Oh. I-" She put a hand over her mouth.

Why did it hurt so much?

He'd killed people she cared about. He hated her. He was an awful person and he'd hurt her worse than anyone ever had – even her mother.

"Iman?" her grandfather said gently. "Are you going to be alright?"

Iman nodded silently, unable to speak. It made sense, logically. It was safer to have Adam killed.

It shouldn't even hurt.

But it did. Thinking of him dead hurt so badly it took her breath away.

"Can you... not do it here?"

"Of course." Ibrahim took her hand. "Why don't you drink your tea?"

Iman took the cup. It rattled, sloshing tea on the carpet. "I – I think I need to go," she heard herself say.

CHAPTER TWENTY

A portly man stood on the other side of Adam's front door, glaring so hard Adam half thought he'd burst into flames soon.

"You opened the door," the man commented. "You're either exceptionally arrogant or terminally stupid. Based on your actions, I'd say it's both."

Whatever Adam had been expecting, this wasn't it. "Are you here to kill me?"

The man snorted. "Unfortunately not."

Adam stepped back. "Then you should probably come inside."

His uninvited guest stalked past.

"Why are you here?" Adam asked curiously once they were seated in his lounge.

"My name is Waseem. I met Ibrahim Khan the first day he stepped into our world. I have known Iman since she was an infant. Make no mistake, I would very much like to kill you for the havoc you've caused but Ibrahim would like to talk to you first before he makes a decision. He seems to think there's something redeemable about you."

"Why?" Adam snapped his mouth shut, cursing internally.

Waseem's eyes gleamed. "Ibrahim has his reasons." He studied Adam frankly. "I knew all six of the people you killed and you don't look capable of besting even one of them. How did you do   it?"
Faces swam before Adam's eyes. "I was a lot different back then."

"I believe you. But I'm not the one you have to convince."

Waseem stood. "I trust you remember where the mansion is?"

Adam nodded mutely, keeping his eyes on the other man as Waseem opened the front door.

"Good. Be there tonight at eight. *Don't* be late."

Waseem crossed the threshold then, as though something had just occurred to him, turned back. "Oh, and Adam?"

"Yes?"

"Don't run from me. It won't end well for you." He smiled cruelly.

-

Iman lay on her bed, a cool linen cloth covering her eyes to try and reduce the swelling that had come from her earlier crying jag.

There was a knock at the door and she lifted her head. "I'm sleeping," she called in a thick voice.

The handle turned. "May I come in anyway?" her grandfather requested.

Iman hastily stuffed the cloth underneath her pillow. "Of

course." She straightened up. "What is it?"

Ibrahim sat at the edge of her bed. "My granddaughter cried today for the majority of an hour and now she's trying to hide the evidence."

Iman blushed and studied the embroidery on her sheets. "It's nothing."

"It's Adam," Ibrahim corrected gently. "I hadn't realized that you'd grown to care for him this much."

"I don't," Iman denied, feeling like a traitor. "He hurt you. He's a murderer." The words rang hollow.

"So am I," her grandfather pointed out. "And you love me."

Iman couldn't say a word.

"I'm sorry that you're so unhappy sweetheart. Truly, I am. If I could fix things for you right now, I would."

Iman hated the sad look on his face. "I'll be fine." She took his hand. "Really. I'll get over it." She'd make peace with this eventually. "And Adam did something unforgivable. There's no way to fix that."

"Maybe not." Ibrahim looked thoughtful. "Did I ever tell you why I became this?"

"No." Iman had asked – had nagged, in fact. But no one would ever tell her the story. She'd eventually stopped asking, her curiosity overpowered by the sadness and grief she seemed to cause Ibrahim to relive each time.

"I think you're ready to hear it. No, you've been ready to hear it for a long time. But I think I'm finally ready to tell you."

Ibrahim cleared his throat. "I was only three years older that you, Iman. Your grandmother and I had been married for a while and your father was a newborn – less than a month old."

"I never met her," Iman murmured.

"No," Ibrahim agreed. "She died long before you were born. You're a lot like her, you know. And you look like her too. You have her build and her eyes."

Iman was fascinated. All thoughts of Adam were forgotten as she listened to this most important piece of family history.

"I worked ridiculous hours when I was younger. I was a lowly assistant then, at the mercy of my boss's whims. I had a new baby at home but it didn't matter – I was still expected to be at work day in and day out and I often came home to a sleeping wife and baby because of the hours I was expected to keep."

Ibrahim cleared his throat. "One day, Yaseera went out. She needed something – groceries or something for your father. I still don't know what it was. She left the baby with her best friend and she went out into the city in broad daylight. She didn't know but she was followed."

Iman's heart twisted.

"I came home to an empty house that night. Hours after she had been attacked and left in an alley to die. I told you that I was a lowly assistant. Because of that and more importantly, because the man who'd stalked Yaseera was wealthy and powerful and a member of the police force, I was advised to let it go. There was no way that any of the several witnesses who'd stood by and watched would testify in court. Even if I did find a way to convince them, no judge would convict the monster who'd killed her. His pockets were too deep."

Tears dripped down Iman's cheeks. "Then what happened?" she managed to ask, holding tightly to Ibrahim's hand.

"I refused to let it go. When the law couldn't help me, I turned to the only place that didn't run by the law – the criminal underworld. I had a new baby at home but my only thoughts were of revenge. I could barely remember my own name but every detail about what had been done to your grandmother was crystal clear in my mind. I trained until I had everything I needed and then I murdered every single person who had tried to manipulate the truth. It took me two years."

Ibrahim sighed then. "It came with costs. By the time I was done, your father was a toddler and I was a stranger to him. He'd been living with Yaseera's best friend all that time. He didn't know me and he didn't want to at first. It took me a long time to get him back. By then, I had seen more than enough of the corruption and greed that ran this country to ever have faith in the law again. I'd built up a reputation. It was too late for me to go back to what I had been so I didn't look back."

"I had no idea," Iman whispered. She'd known that whatever it was, it would be awful. But this... She looked at Ibrahim. "Why did you tell me this?"

"To show you that people can do terrible things out of grief. Most of the people I killed had families that adored them. I was causing those innocent people the same grief that I myself had experienced and I didn't particularly care as long as I found a way to dull my own pain. And I've come to think that Adam was doing the exact same thing I did so long ago."

Iman reeled. There had been too many shocks for one night and her mind was struggling to process this final revelation. "Who? Who was he... mourning?" And why did he blame her?

That night, all those weeks ago, he'd blamed her. He'd told her that he wanted her to feel the pain he was feeling. She hadn't understood then and she still didn't understand now. Had someone close to Adam been murdered?

-

Walking back into the Khan mansion was harder than Adam thought it would be. He'd never gone back to a place he'd killed someone before. He'd even refused to train in the room he'd been forced to kill that poor dog in. Ali had let him do as he pleased, content to ignore the small rebellion – after all, Adam *had* pulled the trigger.

As it always did now, thinking of his stepfather made his cheeks burn with humiliation. Kat was right to pity him. He'd been so damned foolish, so easily led. If he was walking to his death right now, it was nothing less than he deserved.

If.

Adam still couldn't understand why there was even a question about it. He'd left bodies in his wake, had pointed a gun in Iman's face and terrified her – for it had been terror on her face that day, not the contempt that his mind had tried to convince him it had seen – and he had come close to ending the life of Ibrahim Khan. Had the old man suffered some kind of brain damage from his injuries?

Adam didn't know.

He'd been thoroughly searched before being allowed to get past the front door and there was a large, angry man pressing the barrel of a gun directly into his spine as he walked. They were at least taking some kind of precautions.

His shadow rapped on the door with a scarred fist and then urged him through the door with a shove. "No weapons," the man announced, shutting the door behind him as he left. Adam heard no footsteps and assumed that the man had taken up position right outside as a guard.

Ibrahim Khan sat at his large desk, looking as whole as ever. Adam blinked and the image of Khan crumpled to the floor overlaid reality for a moment. His stomach turned.

"Take a seat," Khan instructed calmly. "And tell me why you tried to kill me."

Adam saw no reason to lie. He told Khan everything. He had no way to back up his claims but Khan didn't seem interested in proof.

The old man questioned him repeatedly before finally sitting back with his hands folded together, seemingly satisfied.

Feeling brave, Adam ventured a question of his own. "Why am I here?"

"I wanted answers."

"There are other ways to get answers."

"Yes," Khan agreed. "There are. But I have the distinct feeling that my granddaughter would be displeased with me if I had you worked over."

Iman was soft-hearted, Adam reminded himself, beating down the hope that had begun to fill his chest.

"Don't you want to know why?" Khan asked pleasantly.

"She's a good person," Adam replied dully.

"Yes, she is. But that's not why she cried for you. You've somehow managed to make my granddaughter care for you and I can't decide whether I should kill you or congratulate you."

He was lying. Ibrahim Khan had found the perfect way to torture him and he was using it to great effect.

"Six of my people are dead. That needs to be accounted for. The fact that Iman may want to keep you around doesn't change that – letting you get off scot-free is just not in my nature. But I dislike the idea of even more death. Instead, you'll pay me back by getting rid of this."

Adam was handed a sheet of paper. There were six names, in no particular order that he could see. He recognized all of them. Every single person on this list was one Khan had warned him to keep Iman away from months ago. People who would hurt her or worse if given the chance.

"Kill them and you're in no debt to me. Fail and there will be the usual consequences."

He would be lucky to kill one of them without dying horribly. Khan was creative, Adam had to give him that. He'd die for the destruction he'd caused but Khan had found a way to get some use out of him first.

"I'll need some things," he said, feigning a steadiness he didn't feel. "I don't have access to the resources I'm used to."

Khan nodded. "Of course," he agreed. "Waseem will make sure you have everything you need."

Adam hesitated, weighing up the risk he was about to take. "May I see her?"

"Who?"

"Iman. I need to... I'd like to apologize to her." As he'd apologized to Khan himself, almost as soon as he'd gotten into the room.

"If she's willing to see you, I will not stop her." Khan went to the door and had a quick conversation.

They sat in silence until moments later, when there was a single knock. The guard poked his head in. "She said no," he announced with a grin. "Sorry," he said to Adam insincerely. "Such a shame."

Adam gritted his teeth.

"Dismissed," Khan said casually and the irritating man disappeared. "There's another name I want to add to that list. And I don't think you'll mind this one."

He was right.

James Blackwell. Adam had assumed that Blackwell was in Italy but he'd been wrong.

"James has always been greedy and opportunistic. But I never thought he'd be this foolish. It's your prerogative to do what you'd like with him – interrogate him or just get rid of him, whichever you please. All I want is to ensure that he's dead by morning. He's been creeping around Iman far too often for my liking."

The creep would be dead as soon as Adam could find him. Worry for Iman twisted his gut but he shoved it aside. He needed to concentrate.

"You'll be paid for this," Khan assured him, "as it's in addition to what we originally agreed on."

"Keep the money." Just the thought of being paid for this particular job made him feel dirty.

A pleased look entered Khan's eyes. "I have one final question for you, Adam. You couldn't kill my granddaughter even when you thought she'd betrayed you. Why is that?" He pinned Adam with a knowing gaze.

Adam's temper finally slipped its leash. "You know why," he snapped.

"Yes, I do. And I want to hear it from you."

Fine.

"I love her. I love your granddaughter so much that I couldn't make myself pull the trigger."

CHAPTER TWENTY ONE

"Another one." Waseem announced, walking into Ibrahim's study. "That's four in less than a month and a half. Doesn't this kid sleep?"

"You almost sound concerned," Ibrahim eyed his old friend knowingly. "You're starting to feel bad for him, aren't you?"

"Can you blame me? He's like the road kill you see on the highways – too pathetic to not feel bad for." Comprehension dawned on Waseem's face. "That's why you helped him back then?"

"He did look remarkably pathetic." Ibrahim thought back almost two years. "But back then, I was curious more than anything. He had a lot of potential. I wanted to see what he'd do with it."

Waseem hummed. "Looks like all he's doing is trying to get himself killed. If he doesn't slow down he's either going to burn out or die over something stupid and careless. What a waste."

It was a waste, Ibrahim agreed privately.

"Has Iman agreed to see him?"

"No. Your granddaughter is as stubborn as you when she's got it in her head to be."

Of course she was.

But that didn't solve their problem.

Ibrahim looked at his Second. "Talk to him," he instructed.

"What?" Waseem looked taken aback. "Me? I don't even like him! And he's well aware of that."

"Exactly. He won't think you're just being nice."

Waseem threw his hands up in exasperation. "You don't really think I can influence this boy, do you?"

"No," Ibrahim admitted. "But it's worth a shot. If he kills himself somehow, Iman will be very upset."

And that, it went without saying, was to be avoided. His granddaughter had suffered enough.

-

Adam was here again. Five times in six weeks, Iman thought grumpily. What was he doing?

He hadn't asked to see her after the first time. But Waseem continued to inform her every time Adam made an appearance – waiting, it seemed, for the day that she finally agreed to see him.

He'd be waiting a long time.

She couldn't bear the thought of Adam dying. But seeing him? Forgiving him? That was another matter entirely.

What he'd done... it had changed things. Permanently.

She finished tying the laces of her shoes and pulled her hair into a quick ponytail, shaking off the gloomy thoughts.

She'd discovered that she liked running quite by accident. James had suggested it to her as a way to get her stamina up and Iman had been hooked almost immediately. The runs were a way to distract her when she was too fidgety to paint and they worked fantastically.

A run would help her clear her head.

She walked down the stairs planning her route in her head, so absorbed that she didn't initially recognize the hard, familiar body she'd crashed into.

Adam.

She lifted her head and her mouth dropped open. "What happened to your face?" she shrieked.

-

Adam didn't realize what she was talking about at first.

In his defence, he was preoccupied. Iman's hands had landed squarely on his chest and he automatically grabbed her around the waist to steady her when she wobbled.

The last thing he was thinking about were a few old bruises.

He blinked at her dumbly and she lifted a hand, carefully tracing the worst mark. Adam winced as she disturbed a cut, causing it to start leaking again.

Her eyes widened comically and she drew her hand back as if it had been burned.

He'd been waiting so long to apologize to her. "Iman," he began.

Her lips thinned. "Don't."

Adam stopped.

"Don't apologize," Iman continued. "If I have to hear that you're sorry, I might scream."

"What do you want then?" He'd do it, whatever it was. He owed her at least that.

"I-" Iman looked conflicted. "I don't want to see you again," she whispered.

"Okay," he heard himself say.

Mechanically, barely paying attention to where he was going, he left.

-

Waseem found her curled up on the stairs, staring at the doorway Adam had disappeared through.

"Oh, dear." He settled himself next to her. "Is that really what you want?"

Iman should have known he'd be listening.

"No," she admitted. "It's not. But he can't give me what I want." She wanted time to rewind. She wanted Adam to not be a killer. She wanted... she wanted to be with him and not feel like she was betraying the people he'd murdered – the ones she'd known for years, who'd only been trying to protect her.

They'd died through no fault of their own. How could she forget them? How could she let their sacrifice be meaningless and be with their killer? They deserved better.

"Be careful," Waseem warned, "not to punish yourself for crimes you haven't committed.

"I'm punishing him too," Iman told him. "That makes it worth it."

"Do you think this is what anyone would want?" Waseem looked honestly curious.

How could it not be? "Yes."

"You're wrong," he told her. "They wouldn't want you to twist yourself in knots like this. I may not like that boy but you care for him a great deal. And what happened was a tragedy, but it was a misunderstanding."

"Shouldn't he pay for what he did?" Shouldn't they both pay?

"Yes." Waseem reached out and tucked a stray lock of hair behind her ear. "But you shouldn't."

"But it's my fault!" Iman snapped irritably. Why did no one seem to understand that?

"No, it is not. Many people are to blame for this mess. But you are not one of them." He took hold of her shoulders. "You did nothing wrong, Iman. Let go of the guilt – it's not yours to carry."

Iman ached to believe him.

Waseem read her refusal in her face. "You are just like your grandfather," he told her, audibly frustrated. "He still blames himself, you know? I could never get him to forgive himself either, no matter how hard I tried."

"For what?"

"Your grandmother. He still believes that her death is on his hands. I suppose he does have a point," Waseem added.

"That's ridiculous!" Her grandfather had had nothing to do with his wife's death. She glared at Waseem. "He did nothing wrong!"

Waseem made a non-committal sound. "If he'd been there..."

"He had no idea what was going to happen! It's not his fault, there's nothing he could have done!" Iman's hands had clenched into fists and she felt an insane urge to hit something.

"You're right," Waseem agreed.

"I... am?" Off-balance, Iman stared at him.

"Yes. There was nothing he could do. And there was nothing you could do either."

"You... you were making a point?"

Waseem nodded. "Do you understand now?"

Iman replayed their argument in her head. "I-"

Waseem shook his head fondly. "Was your grandfather to blame?"

This, Iman had an answer to. "No."

"Then neither are you. And maybe one day, one of you will truly believe that."

-

Death was a funny thing. He'd thought that it was what he wanted. He'd tried to bend it to his will and failed. And now that death was coming for him, the fear Adam felt was all-consuming,

He didn't want to die.

He wanted to live. His life was far from what he wanted it to be.

But still.

He wanted to live.

Too bad that realization had only come now, when he could feel himself losing the battle.

When he'd been living, he'd tried everything to find death. Now that he was dying, he'd give anything to make it stop.

Adam choked on a laugh, coughing hard as his injuries made themselves known again. Blood leaked from the side of his mouth and he gasped for breath.

-

Iman paced the starkly lit corridor, the tip of a finger stuck in her mouth. She'd bitten her nails down to the quick and was now forced to be content with gnawing at the skin on her fingertips.

She'd told him she never wanted to see him again. The last thing she'd ever said to him had been an instruction to leave.

Would those be the last words he ever heard from her?

The smell of antiseptic filled her nose and she choked. For as long as she lived, she'd hate hospitals.

Iman had lost count of the hours long ago. He was in surgery. That was all anyone would tell her. He was in surgery.

He'd been in surgery for lifetimes now.

Blood, salty and unpleasant, filled Iman's mouth and she pulled her hand from her mouth, looking down at her fingers in surprise. She'd torn the skin open.

Sharp, stinging pain abruptly brought her back to life.

She'd been sitting there too long.

She'd go find a nurse and make them tell her something. She'd *make* them.

-

His granddaughter was falling apart before his eyes. Iman was seated in a chair with her legs tucked underneath her, her right index finger shoved in her mouth.

Ibrahim winced and reached to tug it away. "You'll hurt yourself," he admonished.

She didn't seem to hear him. Her lips were stained from the blood she'd already shed but still, she bit and tore at her own skin.

Had she been like this when it had been him in a hospital bed? Ibrahim didn't know. He hadn't seen his granddaughter until well after he'd been declared well and his employees seemed convinced that withholding information from him was a good idea no matter how much he threatened and ordered otherwise.

They really needed to be disciplined more.

Or maybe not, considering what 'proper discipline' seemed to have caused.

Ali Cassim needed a swift kick in the pants, in his opinion. If not for that man's craziness, his granddaughter would still have a good husband, Ibrahim himself would not be scrambling trying to patch up his ranks after losing six very skilled employees and Adam would not have been foolish enough to run himself ragged and kill himself over a kill that was not remotely time sensitive.

If the boy woke up, there would be several people waiting in line to yell his ears off for being so careless – most notably, his own granddaughter.

Whatever else it had done, this recklessness had at least gotten Iman to see the light.

Now if only that large team of doctors could make sure it wasn't too late.

-

Everything hurt.

The effort it took to open his eyes made a wave of exhaustion sweep over him and Adam nearly gave up before he was done.

He tried to swallow and began to panic as he realized there was something stuck in his throat. He was choking!

There was a voice above him saying something but Adam couldn't make out the words. He tuned them out and struggled to lift his arms, trying to clear the blockage in his throat. He was choking!

The world swam and he slept.

The next time he woke, there was a weight on his chest. Where was he? The last thing he remembered was pain – so much pain that he thought it would never leave him.

He tried to push himself up. Had he been left for dead?

No...

Whatever he was laying on was too soft to be ground.

He barely managed to get his head off the pillow before he collapsed back down, his arms too weak to hold his weight.

His struggling had disturbed the weight on his chest and it began to move. What was it?

A flash of blonde caught his eye, familiar and beloved and his heartbeat quickened. Iman?

Adam struggled to lift himself again. Where were they? Why was Iman here? Was she in danger?

"Adam? Adam, it's okay." She scrambled off of him and leaned over him. "You're okay," she told him. "You're okay." She laughed and squeezed his hand, sounding giddy. "You're okay."

-

She'd worn the nurses down until they let her see him.

He was so hurt. There was hardly an inch of him that wasn't bruised or scraped. She was almost afraid to touch him at first, scared that she'd somehow hurt him even worse.

She pulled the chair in his room right up to the bed so she could hold his hand. Her legs were numb underneath her but she refused to move. She'd sit right here until he woke up.

Just.

Just in case.

Her pillow shifted, waking her. For a moment, Iman didn't remember where she was. She breathed in and the scent of antiseptic brought everything rushing back.

Her pillow had moved.

Adam!

Joy flooded through her when she saw his eyes open. He began to move and she hurried over to him, worried that he would hurt himself somehow.

He was okay. He'd woken up and he was going to be okay.

She told him as much, grinning so hard her cheeks were aching.

Looking down at his face, bruised and swollen and lovely, an urge hit her.

Iman didn't even try to fight it.

She leaned down and planted a kiss solidly on his chapped lips. "I'm so glad you're okay."

Adam shifted and let out a groan.

She needed to get a nurse, Iman realized.

"Wait," Adam called softly. His voice was strained.

Iman was back at his side in an instant. "I'll be back in a minute," she promised.

-

"Enough!" Iman shouted, thoroughly at the end of her rope. Why wouldn't he just listen?

Adam recoiled and she spared a moment's thought to feel guilty for scaring him. "Enough," she repeated. "No more of this nonsense."

"This nonsense is my job," he countered, beginning to look annoyed himself.

"You almost died. I thought you *were* dead. If Waseem hadn't found you when he did..." Adam would have been gone. Nothing anyone could have done at that point would have kept him in the world.

"But he did find me. And I'm not done yet."

"Done with what?" Iman's voice began to rise again. He'd been saying this constantly as he tried to argue with his doctors that he needed to be released – barely two weeks after being admitted into the hospital and nowhere *near* healed.

"There's still one other person I need to go after. I have to get that done."

"Why?" Iman sat beside him, careful of his many injuries, and put her hands on his cheeks. "What's the rush? You're still so badly hurt."

Adam shook her off. "No broken bones," he argued stubbornly. "I can still walk."

"Barely, Adam!" Iman got to her feet again.

"It's better than nothing," he insisted.

"It's not good enough."

"What's the rush, Adam?" He looked away and didn't answer.

"Why can't you just wait until you're healed?"

"I'm fine. I can keep going."

"But you don't have to!" Iman cried. "Why are you forcing yourself like this?"

"Because," Adam began hotly, before abruptly falling silent when the door was opened.

"Everything alright in here?" one of Adam's nurses asked, glancing between them.

Iman looked back at Adam. Now, with her anger derailed, she once again saw the unhealthy tinge to his skin that had triggered her anger in the first place.

"I need some air," she announced abruptly.

The nurse shot her an understanding look and nodded. "It's a bit stuffy in here, isn't it?" As Iman left, she heard the curtains being opened.

Maybe the light would help Adam's mood.

Walking down the corridor to the closest waiting room, her eyes landed on a sight that immediately helped hers.

Waseem rose to hug her. "Having a debate in there?" he asked, tilting his head in the direction of Adam's room.

Iman's shoulders slumped. "You heard us?"

"I think the whole floor heard you."

"I just don't understand why he's in such a rush," Iman complained. "And he won't tell me. He just insists that he wants to get out and go... y'know." She hinted, leery of mentioning the word *kill* where they could be overheard.

"Ah," Waseem leaned back in his chair. "This again."

"Again?" Iman repeated.

Waseem looked puzzled. "Oh, you wouldn't have known. Yes, the last time he came back he was in quite terrible shape. I did tell him that your grandfather wasn't the type to insist he keep going if he was injured but that doesn't seem to have sunk in."

"What does my grandfather have to do with it?"

Iman listened quietly as Waseem filled her in on the deal Adam had made with Ibrahim. She said nothing as her legs carried her towards Adam's room or as she flung open his door. Only once she'd made sure that they were alone did she speak.

"You are *not* going to try to kill yourself – again – over nothing."

-

Adam was bone-weary. All he wanted to do was sleep but even that seemed impossible in this sterile room, filled with beeping machines and the brightest lights he'd ever seen.

He looked around resentfully. Hospitals. He despised hospitals.

And if Iman had her way, he'd be here for another fortnight.

Adam scrubbed a hand over his face. He felt bad for continuing to upset her but this fight was one he wasn't willing to lose.

The sooner he got out of this place the better.

She didn't understand. But then, how could she? She'd never been trained to keep going the way he had.

Yes, it hurt. And yes, he was probably doing some damage to himself by not laying quietly in the bed like she wanted him to.

But he was losing his mind in here.

And that last name was nagging at him like a constant itch that he couldn't scratch.

He'd been taught to finish a job by any means necessary. And this one – the most important one – wasn't finished yet.

Adam groaned. How was he supposed to explain that to Iman?

She would think he was insane – and obsessed.

The door was shoved open and he stared at her, unable to hide his surprise. How had she gotten even angrier?

"You are not going to try to kill yourself – again – over nothing."

Adam's own temper – worsened by pain, inactivity, and medical personnel who refused to listen to him – snapped. He was yelling before he knew it. "It is *not* nothing!" he hissed.

"You don't have to do this for me!"

She was right. "No, I have to do it for *me*."

263

He'd confused her. "But why?" she asked, not for the first time. "Why?" she whispered. "I don't understand why this is so important. You could *die!*"

Adam had no way to answer her. He didn't fully understand it himself. But the thought of not finishing what he'd started made him feel ill.

The door opened and Adam experienced a brief moment of irritation. "You have terrible timing," he told Waseem.

The portly man looked offended. "I have excellent timing. I waited for a nice lull in the conversation, didn't I?"

"You were listening to us?"

"You are very loud," Adam was informed. "It would have been harder to not listen."

Adam rolled his eyes.

"This problem you've been arguing about," Waseem added. "It has been solved."

"What? How?"

"We have other employees. And you were clearly in no shape to finish things. I had one of them go off and take care of things."

Adam felt his mouth drop open. He shut it and scrambled for something to say. Iman beat him to it. "Why didn't you say something earlier?" she scolded.

Then she turned to Adam. "Now will you stop trying to leave?"

"No," Adam admitted. His skin still crawled at the thought of being in this room much longer.

Iman's cheeks began to redden and he prepared to defend himself. Again.

-

"You were never this argumentative before," Adam commented later, after they'd both tired themselves out, as he tugged on a lock of her hair.

"I was," Iman told him. "You just didn't know me then. I was really worried about you," she explained.

"I was really worried about me too. Worried that I'd lose my mind."

Iman rolled her eyes. He'd gotten more worked up about recovering than being hurt in the first place. "It wasn't that bad."

"Was."

Iman opened her mouth and Adam bent down, cutting her off with a kiss.

"Did I find a mute button?" he asked playfully.

He was better out of a hospital, Iman conceded. There was colour in his cheeks and his eyes didn't look so dull any more.

Now if only the nightmares would stop...

She pushed the stray thought away. Today was a good day.

"Iman?" Adam tugged on her hair again. "Something wrong?" His eyes were dark with concern.

"Do you remember the day we met?" Iman asked, picking up the thread of their conversation. Nightmares had no place in the bright patch of daylight they lay in.

"Of course."

"What did you call me?"

A groan was the only answer.

"A spoiled princess," Iman answered her own question. "You know, if you'd met me a few years earlier, you'd have been right. I was a princess, or at least I was treated like one."

"Were you a terror?" Adam shifted, tightening the arm he had wrapped around her.

"Careful," Iman cautioned. He still wasn't fully healed yet. And he seemed to forget his injuries constantly.

"I'm fine," he said dismissively. "Tell me more about being a tiny terror."

"I wasn't exactly a terror," Iman protested. "Just kind of pampered."

"So you were just a *little* brat."

Iman caught the emphasis this time. "No short jokes."

"But they're so easy. And you have to admit, you're small."

Compared to him, she was. Lying together, she fit neatly under his chin and the tips of her toes only just grazed his ankles if he stretched. He'd carried her yesterday without being noticeably winded, even with stitched together holes in him.

She'd been scared of how huge he was before. Now, the only time she spared a thought to his bulk was when appreciating what a nice big pillow he made.

She put a hand to his chest, feeling it move as he breathed.

"Yes, I'm fine. No, you're not hurting me and no, I do not need to go back to the hospital." Adam pre-empted her.

"How did you know what I was going to ask?"

"You were fondling my bandages," Adam replied. "Stop

worrying about that. Tell me more about being a bratty kid."

"Are you sure-" Iman began.

"Yes."

"You carried me yesterday." He'd gotten out of a hospital bed to do it too. Iman scowled.

"You were the smallest thing in the room. And they discharged me after that, didn't they?"

"Yes, but-"

"So I'm fine," Adam continued.

"But-" He kissed her again.

"I'm fine. And I'm starting to like this mute button."

Iman smacked a hand against his chest without thinking about it and Adam winced. "Not that fine."

"What? Oh!" She scrambled away. There was a hole in him, she berated herself. How had she forgotten that?

-

Adam watched Iman scoot away so far she was in danger of falling off the bed and held in a sigh. No matter how many times he told her he was fine, she seemed convinced that he was five seconds from falling down dead.

He reached across and towed her back to him. "Relax. If you hurt me, I'll tell you."

"Okay," she agreed doubtfully, hesitantly laying back against him.

Adam lay there for a minute, appreciating her weight. It was still strange that he could do this again. Less than three weeks ago, he'd thought she'd never speak to him again and now, here she was worrying about hurting him.

How quickly things changed.

Things hadn't gone back to the way they were – he'd begun to understand that they never would. He would always carry guilt for the blood that was on his hands but the burden of it had slowly begun to weigh a little less with every name that he'd ticked off that list.

Only five names. And Blackwell, but Blackwell didn't count. He'd have killed Blackwell on his own if given half a chance.

That last name had been ticked off by someone else.

It was over but he hadn't been the one to end it.

Could he let it go knowing that someone else had paid the balance of his debt?

Adam was beginning to fear that the answer to that question was no.

-

He was woken by the sensation of hair tickling his face. Adam took a deep breath and his nose filled with the scent of Iman's shampoo. Gingerbread.

He'd never be able to eat it again without thinking of her.

His stomach let out a growl and Iman laughed from somewhere above him. He pried his eyes open and a smile spread across his face.

No nightmares this time.

"Hungry?" Iman asked him. "I cooked."

She could cook? She'd never told him that. He said as much

and she blushed lightly.

"I'm not as good as you. I never got much practice since there was always someone running the kitchen. But I know how to feed myself. And now you too."

She took hold of his hand and urged him out of bed. "Kitchen's on the right, come find me when you're done," she instructed, shoving him gently in the direction of the bathroom.

Adam found her in the kitchen, just where she said she'd be. "This is really nice," he told her, meaning the house. He'd taken a few detours before finally ending up at the kitchen and had peeked into most of the rooms.

She lifted her head from where she was fussing with something. "It is. My grandfather thought it would be better."

Adam wasn't surprised that Ibrahim had noticed the difficulty he had being in the mansion. "He was right."

CHAPTER TWENTY TWO

Iman drew in a deep breath, trying to steady her nerves. Adam was healed. He knew it and so did she. Soon, there would be nothing to stop him from diving back into the muck, from filling his days with even more blood and danger.

She couldn't bear the thought of having to go through it again. Iman wasn't stupid – she knew that Adam was skilled. But she had seen him bruised and bloody and torn, and she knew far more intimately that he wasn't invincible. He could break, could bleed, could die.

The thought was abhorrent.

But how could she convince him not to go back? They'd fought so hard over him just waiting a few weeks, Iman thought miserably. And even then, the only reason Adam hadn't continued to insist on risking his neck had been that there was no one left for him to risk it with.

Iman buried her face in her hands and groaned, whispering a quick prayer while she kneaded her temples. She'd been doing that so often it had become a little habit whenever she became overwhelmed. Whether or not it made a difference was another debate entirely but the soft, whispered requests never failed to make her feel better, if only a little.

The strangeness of it struck her and Iman shook her head, fighting a bizarre urge to laugh. She'd never prayed for herself. Not because she hadn't believed that there was a God – she'd never doubted that – but because she'd been afraid. She'd always thought of herself and her own problems as too insignificant to beg for help with, especially considering the fact that she rarely ever fulfilled any kind of religious obligation.

But for her grandfather, for Adam... For them, she did it. She'd beg and plead and try absolutely anything she could. She just couldn't imagine doing otherwise.

Adam came up behind her, his arms snaking around her waist. "Hi," he whispered, kissing her forehead. "Why are you up so early?"

Iman covered his arms with her own. "Hi," she returned his greeting, spinning around and rising on the tips of her toes to bestow her own kiss. "I couldn't sleep."

Adam drew back, sobering. "Nightmares?"

"No, nothing like that. I just had some stuff to think about."

"Do you want to talk about it?" Adam offered, wandering over to the fridge.

"After we eat," Iman decided. If she even could eat with the knot her insides seemed to have twisted themselves into.

"Alright," Adam nodded agreeably. "Am I cooking?"

"Please," Iman agreed gratefully, thinking longingly of a nice, hot shower.

She looked back at Adam, silently watching the way he moved

around the kitchen for a moment, *Please let him agree.* He felt her eyes on him and turned his head, offering her a quick smile. *Please.*

Half an hour later, as she sat with a still half-full plate in front of her, Iman knew that she could put it off no longer. Adam had been watching her push her breakfast around with his mouth turned down and his eyebrows scrunched together. He'd already asked her twice if something was wrong with the food and he seemed ready to do so a third time.

Iman pushed her plate away.

"We need to talk," she began.

Adam gave her his full attention, staring unwaveringly into her eyes.

The carefully prepared speech she'd crafted in her head deserted her and Iman scrambled for words. Finally, she blurted out the first thing that came to mind. "Are you still going to kill people?"

-

What?

Adam stared at his wife. Iman looked ready to bolt.

She'd been distant for the past few days and he hadn't known what to make of it. Eventually, he'd decided to wait until she was ready to talk to him before doing anything.

Well, now she had. And he had no idea what to say.

"Probably," he admitted. What else was there for him to do?

Iman's face fell. "Oh," she mumbled. "You are." Her eyes turned dull and Adam wanted to kick himself.

"I don't really know how to do anything else," he reminded her helplessly. "Why are you worrying about this now anyway? I don't have a job lined up."

"You're healed now." Even her voice was dull and Adam scrambled to find something to cheer her.

"Yes," he agreed. "I am. But I'm not going anywhere right now, Iman." He squirmed uncomfortably. "I'm not... Your grandfather runs things differently. I wouldn't be going up against anyone innocent."

"That's not what I'm worried about," Iman said immediately. "I'm worried about *you*."

This again. Adam restrained the urge to sigh. "Iman, I'll be fine. I – I'm actually pretty good at this." His one call to fame – he could kill well.

Her eyes dropped to his newest scars, almost as though she could see through his shirt.

"That was different." Adam got to his feet and held out a hand to her. She took it and he pulled her up, hugging her close.

"I was a mess. I'm still a bit of a mess but... I'm a lot better now. It turns out almost dying is good to help you see things clearly. I didn't... I didn't care much before, whether I lived or not."

Iman's head jerked up and she looked at him, her eyes filled with horror. He tightened his grip on her reflexively, hurrying to add. "I do now. This past month... Being with you again... It helped. A lot."

"Then why keep going? Why keep doing this?" she pulled away, stepping back to stare at him with big, hurt eyes.

"What else is there? I have to do something," he pointed out.

"I'm scared, Adam. I'm scared that you're going to leave again and you're not going to come back. That's a possibility every single time you leave and just the thought of it is driving me insane." She gave him a pleading look, as though begging him to fix it.

"You didn't react like this before," was all he could think to say. Even as the words left his mouth, he knew they were a mistake.

"I didn't *know* before. I didn't know what seeing you like that would do to me. I didn't even know that I loved you!" Her face crumpled and she rushed from the room.

Adam stood rooted to the spot, still frozen.

What had she just said?

By the time the shock had worn off, she was gone. The sneakers she favoured were gone too. Out for a run, he realized.

Adam snatched up his keys and phone and stuffed his feet into a pair of running shoes, intent on going after her. He knew Iman's preferred route.

He'd just crossed the threshold when familiar hair caught his eye.

"Kat?"

What was *she* doing here?

-

"Hey, Adam," Kat gave him a tight smile. "Can I come in?"

"Actually," he found himself saying, "I was on my way out."

Kat looked taken aback. "It's important," she countered, a note of urgency in her tone. She looked awful, Adam realized, now that he bothered to look closer. Her hair was a mess and the frown lines at her cheeks and forehead had deepened.

He hesitated, torn, and Kat pressed her advantage. "It'll only take a few minutes. I don't have much to say to you."

Adam couldn't hide his wince. "Alright," he agreed reluctantly. "Just a few minutes."

He couldn't help wondering as he watched the door swing shut, whether the decision he'd just made was one he'd come to regret soon.

He directed Kat to the kitchen and she took a seat at one of the stools on the island, sinking down into the plush chair with a soft sigh.

"You look terrible, Kat."

"I feel it," she said grimly. "*You* look good. Better than you did when I left you and definitely better than the last time I saw you."

Why had she said them like they weren't one and the same? "When *was* the last time you saw me?" he asked curiously.

Kat reached into her jacket and Adam tensed despite himself. The gun he'd retrieved from its hiding place underneath the little table in the entryway felt cold against his skin. "Relax," she told him. "If I was going to kill you, I'd just burn this whole place down. I wouldn't bother coming up to you and shooting."

"Good to know," Adam commented, feeling sick.

"Here," Kat passed him a photograph. "This is what I was talking about."

It was him, bloody and crumpled on the floor. He looked like a corpse.

"How did you walk away from that?" Kat asked, a thread of

worry in her voice.

"I had help."

"*Why* did you go after them?"

"Them?" Adam played dumb.

"*Them,*" Kat repeated. She rattled off five names in quick succession, crossing her arms. "Blackwell, I understood. But the rest of them... what were you thinking? Do you know what you were playing with?"

"I had debts to pay."

Kat drew back. "You were paid?"

"Other debts," Adam corrected.

"The Khans. Of course." Kat scowled. "Do you jump when she says too?"

"Don't sneer at me, Kat. Even if I did, how is it any better than what you – than what *we* – did for Ali?"

"It's not," Kat admitted, looking downcast. "But how can you be content to trade one master for another?"

"I didn't," Adam told her. "It's funny, I've heard a thousand and one stories about Ibrahim Khan and his evil but he's the only one who *didn't* try to kill me and the only one who actually has reason to want to."

"So these past few months, that's all you did? Paying debts?" Kat checked.

"Yeah," Adam said shortly. "I killed six of his people so I got to kill six people of his choosing."

"Oh," Kat whispered.

"What did you *think* I was doing?"

Kat sighed. "I don't know. Working for Khan? Going on a rampage? He never took credit for the kills. Neither did anyone else. I think I'm the only one who realized you were responsible for all of them."

"Is that why you came? To judge me?"

"I came to tell you that that photograph reminded Ali you still exist. Since that day – when you found me – I've been doing my best to make sure he thinks you're a non-issue. But that... it reminded him. He's been focused on hunting Blackwell but now that we know Blackwell is dead... Look, I came here to tell you to be careful. Ali... he's been," she shuddered and swallowed hard. "He's been different. Worse."

"Kat, do you need-" Adam began to offer, eyeing his old friend worriedly. He hadn't seen Kat about to lose it like this in so long. Ali must have done something truly awful to shake her like this.

"What? A trade like you?" She shook her head emphatically. "No, thanks. I'll stick with the monster I know."

"Thank you for coming. It means a lot."

That tight, pinched smile she'd worn the whole time eased into something sweeter. "You're the closest thing I have to family. I had to come." She drew her jacket close. "I'd better get going."

Adam walked out with her, pulling the door shut and locking it behind him. She'd begun to walk off while he was busy and he called her name, making her turn. "Be careful," he pleaded, unable to shake a sense of dread.

"Worry about yourself," she countered, finally showing a spark of her old fire. "I can handle myself."

Could she? Adam worried as he watched her disappear. Could she really?

He sighed and turned in the opposite direction. He still needed to find Iman. It had been less than an hour since she'd walked out but it felt much, much longer.

He set off at a run, enjoying the feeling of his muscles working, that feeling of dread still in the pit of his stomach. He shook his head. He couldn't keep thinking about Kat – he needed to figure out what to do when he found his wife.

-

Iman had been running for long enough that she'd begun to sweat despite the cold. She panted hard and slowed to a stop. Usually when she ran, she brought along a bottle of water but she'd forgotten it in her rush to be *away*.

She thought guiltily of Adam. Maybe it was time to go back. She'd just left him there, without even saying goodbye.

She'd just begun the slow jog back home when she felt a prickle in the middle of her shoulder blades.

Iman shook it off as nothing and carried on. Almost unconsciously, she increased her pace, her skin beginning to crawl. She gave into the urge to look back and saw nothing.

Laughing, shaking her head at her own paranoia, she set off again.

It was nothing.

Right?

CHAPTER TWENTY THREE

"How nice to see you again," a familiar voice commented.

Iman spun around.

"Hello." Ali Cassim smiled charmingly at her. His eyes were still just as dead as they always had been, ruining the handsomeness of his face.

Iman took a step back, looking around and cursing silently. No one. She loved this route because of how quiet and deserted it was and now that preference was going to kill her.

"What do you want?" she demanded, proud that her voice remained steady.

"Lots of things," Cassim replied. "Money, power, respect. For now, I'll settle for you coming with me – and not making a fuss."

"And if I don't?"

Cassim's eyes hardened. "I will have to hunt you down. And it will *not* be pleasant."

Iman looked around again, wishing for Adam.

"He's not coming," Ali told her, a sick satisfaction in his voice. "He *was* going to – that's part of the reason I took him down so easily. He was so absorbed, he didn't even notice me until I was almost right on top of him."

Ali shook his head in mock sorrow. "Such a shame. You really did ruin him, you know. I put so much work into that boy, into making him perfect and you went and spoiled him."

Anger began to overwhelm Iman's fear. She thought of the things Adam had told her about his childhood, then remembered several far more recent conversations. This man was to blame for all the pain she and Adam had been through. Ali Cassim had been the true cause. He'd deliberately manipulated her husband.

And now he wanted her.

No, Iman decided.

Ali Cassim had gotten what he wanted for long enough. She wasn't going to let him use her to hurt Adam.

She ran. Faster than she ever had in her life, praying that she would be fast enough.

There was an ugly laugh behind her. "The hard way it is then."

She ran until her lungs ached, until she was sure her next step would be her last. She pushed past it all, refusing to give in. She would *not* stop.

"Enough games."

Hands shot out and grabbed her, one wrapping around her waist while the other pressed something sharp into her side. "Look down," Cassim instructed.

Iman did.

"That is a very real, very loaded gun. If I shoot you with this, you will die. Do you understand?"

"Yes," Iman gasped.

"Good. Now, are you going to keep kicking up a fuss?"

"No."

Cassim smiled that ugly smile again and Iman tasted bile. "Excellent."

He holstered the gun and hoisted her into his arms properly. He was even bigger than Adam, Iman realized. And he wasn't even breathing hard. He'd been toying with her.

"Let's go see Adam."

No, Iman shouted silently. *No, no, no.*

Tears slipped down her cheeks as she was jostled against Cassim.

No.

-

How could he have been so *stupid*? Adam railed as soon as he'd awoken. His shoulders ached from the unnatural position they'd been twisted into behind his back and his head throbbed angrily. He had no idea what cocktail of drugs Ali had injected into his bloodstream but whatever they were, the after effects were almost as incapacitating as the dose itself.

He struggled into a seated position with a groan and turned his attention to the ropes that secured his limbs.

"You don't want to do that," a calm voice told him.

He jerked his head up wildly and saw Ali peering down at him, an indulgent smile on his face. "You'll make them tighter," he said, referring to the ropes.

"What is this?" Adam demanded. "Why did you tie me up? You don't need to do this to kill me – or aren't you as good as you always maintained you were?"

Ali swung a hand lazily and the heavy metal of the gun in his hand bit into the side of Adam's face. "Don't be rude," he admonished. "You always did have a problem with that."

"I had a problem with a lot of things," Adam snapped. He twisted his wrists again.

"Stop. That. Or that little girl in your bedroom is going to have a much harder time of it than she needs to."

Adam's blood ran cold. Iman. "What did you do to her?" he choked.

"Nothing, yet," Ali said pleasantly. "Behave and I won't have to break her."

"You're sick," Adam gasped, his heart hammering in his chest. "Leave her alone!"

"No worries over yourself?" Ali inquired.

"No. Just leave her alone!" As if he could worry about himself when she was in danger! "Please," he added. "Just leave her alone."

"How precious," Ali cooed. "But I'm afraid I can't do that. She needs to die, you see."

Adam's mouth turned dry and the scream that had been building in his throat came out as an unintelligible croak. *No,* he begged in the depths of his own head. *No, no, no.*

Not her. Let Ali kill him. But not her. Never her.

The monster standing above him sighed. "It's such a pity," he said conversationally, "that you had to go and fall in love with her. I had finally gotten you right. You were cold and deadly – a perfect weapon. And then the Khans had to go and ruin *everything*. I hadn't planned for things to go like this, you know. Originally, Blackwell was supposed to kill Ibrahim Khan. And then, of course, I would have made you kill Blackwell and take his place. You might even have gotten to keep that little girl you're obsessed with."

Adam couldn't stop the choked sound of rage that left him.

"Simmer down," Ali scolded. "Honestly, where are those manners I took so long to beat into you? You'd think we let you live like a savage."

He was the savage. No, he was a demon. How had Adam never realized?

"Where was I?" Ali mused. "Ah, yes. I was explaining to you how all of this is *your* fault. You see, Adam, if you had just killed Ibrahim Khan, I would have been happy. You would have passed my test and I would have been able to let you keep running after that little girl. But you couldn't even kill a geriatric old man right. And then the next time you pop up, you're a bloody mess. It's a disgrace and it makes *me* look bad. Now I have to fix you."

"How's that?"

"What's her name? Iman? Yes, I think killing Iman and making you watch will go a long way towards getting you back where I want you."

Ali bared his teeth in a mockery of a smile. "Ready?"

"What will it take?" Adam asked desperately. "What do I have to do to get you to leave her alone?"

Ali looked pityingly at him. "There's nothing you can do. There's nothing else that will hurt you quite this much and we both know it. Don't worry," a hand patted his cheek, "it'll all be over soon."

"Wait," Adam begged, beyond pride. "Wait, just wait!" His voice cracked.

Ali paid no mind.

Blood began to trickle down Adam's wrists. He'd been pulling so hard to try and get free that the ropes holding him had worn away at his skin.

The unmistakeable sound of a gunshot echoed from up the stairs.

Adam went rigid, his heart in his throat.

No.

He bared his teeth viciously. *No.*

She wasn't dead. She couldn't be.

He felt the ropes holding him begin to slacken and hope kindled in his chest.

Ali had wanted to kill her in front of him, he reminded himself. There was still time.

He leashed the terror and panic crippling him. Iman needed him and she needed him ready for a fight.

Adam had no illusions about what was about to happen. He had never been able to beat Ali Cassim. It didn't matter. If he could get her out, it would be worth it.

His life for her safety was a more than fair price.

He prayed that she'd be able to run.

A crash from upstairs stopped him dead for a moment, relief so powerful it weakened his knees flowing through him. She was still alive. And she was fighting.

Wait!

It took him a moment to realize that someone had spoken outside his own head.

Adam turned his head to the side, bracing himself. He pulled out the gun that still rested against his skin, preparing himself to fire it. He strained his ears, more concerned with what was happening above him.

Kat held a gun in her own hands. But not pointed at him. Instead, she held it flat in her palm, extending it out to him. An offer?

"Let me help," she mouthed. "I'll go in front of you."

Adam didn't know what game she was playing, nor did he particularly care. "Don't get in my way," he replied in kind.

He felt more than heard her fall into step behind him.

-

Iman grimaced in pain. Aasia, her stepfather, training with James. Nothing had prepared her for this. She'd never been in so much pain before. And it wasn't likely to end soon. She knew sadists, and this one was the worst she'd ever come across. He'd hurt her until she couldn't remember anything but pain and enjoy himself every moment of the way.

He was still playing with her.

The fingers on her right hand ached. She'd held a mad hope that the gun she'd found in one of the drawers would help her damage Cassim at least enough that he wouldn't get back up again.

But he'd been too fast. She'd hardly gotten one shot off before he'd wrenched it from her and tossed it away.

He had been smirking the whole time.

That smirk was gone now, replaced by a ferocious scowl. "Enough," he hissed. "No more playing."

Iman automatically took a step back and flinched as her back hit the wall with a thump.

She looked around, desperate to find something – anything – to defend herself with.

But she'd run out of time.

Hands closed around her throat. "I'm not going to kill you yet," Cassim told her pleasantly. "I need you to help me break my son. But you've lost any chance you had of a painless death. If only you hadn't decided to fight."

He looked at her reprovingly. "I suppose it's not entirely your fault. Adam does turn heads. Even Kat – my most loyal of all – decided to come and warn him. I wonder how she'll react when she learns that she's the one who brought me here... But that's not important. Now, where were we?" He grinned. "Oh, yes. I was about to do *this.*"

He began to squeeze and Iman choked. Tears began to stream from her eyes and her lungs burned. She couldn't breathe!

A gun fired and the pressure eased. She could breathe again! She gulped in air greedily, gasping when a heavy weight fell on her chest.

-

Adam rushed past Kat, shoving Ali's prone body off of Iman and lifting her into his arms. "Where are you hurt?" he demanded. He couldn't see blood on her. Where had she been shot?

She tried to speak then winced.

"Never mind. Don't talk," Adam cautioned.

She was alive. They were both alive.

He held her to him for a long moment, hardly able to believe it. They were both alive!

Movement behind them broke the little bubble they'd been in and Adam felt a sense of foreboding.

He looked up and straight into the barrel of a gun.

Kevlar. Ali had been wearing Kevlar. He wasn't dead, just winded from the impact of the bullet.

His own gun was on the floor, too far to reach. He'd dropped it without a second thought.

Sloppy.

"I really thought there was hope for you," Ali told him sorrowfully. "But now I see otherwise. You're a lost cause, Adam. There's nothing I can do but put you out of my misery."

They'd run out of chances.

Adam looked down at Iman, seeing his own horror and despair reflected on her lovely face. She was going to watch him die. And there was nothing he could do to stop it.

At point blank range, it would be a messy death, Adam thought clinically.

Close your eyes, he willed silently, shutting his own. Don't see this. You have enough nightmares.

A shot rang out and he braced for the pain.

But there was nothing.

He could still breathe.

Adam opened his eyes and saw Ali Cassim's corpse crumpled on the floor in front of him like so much garbage.

Kat. He'd forgotten she was even there.

She let go of the gun, letting it hit the floor. Her eyes were glued to Ali. "I killed him," she whispered. "I really killed him." She began to shake.

Adam met her eyes. "Thank you."

-

It was a miracle that none of them had been hurt worse.

Adam tightened his grip on Iman's waist. She was right there in his arms but still, the remnants of panic churned in his gut, making him nauseous. It could have gone so much worse.

He looked at Kat, curled up in a bar stool to their right. He'd been reluctant to let her anywhere near Iman – suspicious of how neatly she'd made her alibi – but when his wife had leaned up and whispered in his ear, he'd accepted the explanation and let her be.

She'd trailed after them like a lost puppy to the kitchen and hadn't moved since he'd directed her to the chair.

Shock, Adam diagnosed, watching her shiver. She was in shock.

They all were, he realized as he felt Iman huddle closer to him. They needed heat and sugar.

And he wanted a doctor to look at Iman.

It was a colossal effort to pull out his phone and dial but he managed it. Relating the details of what had happened was beyond him but he managed to convey enough that Waseem understood both to come immediately and to bring a doctor along with him.

The Second took one look at the three of them and went to put the kettle on. "Tea," he decided. "Sweet tea."

He went to Iman after that, tilting her head to get a look at her throat. He hissed in sympathy at the dark bruises. "That looks like it hurts." Then he turned to Adam. "Where's the body?"

"Bedroom."

Waseem nodded decisively. "Let the doctor look at her," he instructed Adam. "And finish making the tea."

It would give him something to focus on while he couldn't keep hold of Iman.

Adam had just finished handing a mug to Kat when Waseem came back down. "It's not too big a mess. The boys will be done cleaning up in an hour." Adam hadn't even noticed the extra people.

He nodded mechanically.

"It was stupid of us to forget about him. Ali Cassim always did like holding grudges." Waseem shook his head ruefully. "I should have killed him when I had the chance," he grumbled. "Before he could turn into this much of a snake."

"I didn't know you knew Ali.

"I am as old as dirt." Waseem said facetiously. "I knew everyone, at one time or another. He was young then. But still just as monstrous. And back then, he couldn't hide it as well."

"Does anyone else need medical attention?" Everyone looked round. Iman had come back with the doctor. There was a brace on one of her hands.

"No."

"Yes," Iman contradicted him. "Adam, please? It would make me feel a lot better to *know* that you're fine."

There was no way he could argue with that.

Fifteen minutes later, there were bandages on his wrists and Kat and Iman both had drained mugs in front of them.

Kat roused when he approached. "I should go," she said in a raspy voice.

"Don't."

The protest hadn't come from him. Adam turned to look at Iman.

"Don't go," she repeated. "At least, not just yet."

Kat looked like she wanted to protest. She opened her mouth. "Okay," she agreed quietly, looking shocked at her own answer.

She glanced at Adam.

"Stay," he told her simply. She was in no shape to go anywhere.

-

Twenty four hours, sleep, and a hot shower made a world of difference. Adam and Iman had slept in one of the guest bedrooms and Kat in the other.

Waseem had left soon after Kat had decided to stay, leaving behind the four men who'd *cleaned up* as guards and reminding Iman to call her grandfather as he went. The only reason Ibrahim hadn't been there along with his Second was because he was on the other side of the world.

Adam had no doubt that Iman's grandfather was already back in town by now – Ibrahim had no doubt got on a plane as soon as he'd heard that Iman was once again hurt.

Adam couldn't stop a sigh. How many times was it now?

"What is it?" Iman lifted her head to look at him.

"You keep getting hurt." He told her plainly.

"So do you." She touched the bandages on his wrist lightly.

"That's different." That was him.

"It hurts me just as much to see you hurt as it hurts you to see me." Iman shifted to kiss the edge of his jaw, right below the large bruise that had been left when Ali had hit him. "That's why..." She trailed off and shook her head. "Never mind."

"What?" Adam urged. "Tell me."

"That's why I wanted you to stop all this."

They'd been fighting about it yesterday. That was what had started it all.

Why the hell had he been fighting so hard anyway?

Self-loathing filled him. Why had he been so stubborn? He'd driven her out of the damn house, into the cold!

"Stop it," Iman commanded. "Stop blaming yourself."

"I made you leave," Adam reminded her bitterly.

"And if I'd been there with you? He would have killed me right there and then and gotten what he wanted."

"Don't," Adam shuddered, tasting bile. "Don't say that!"

"Don't say that you caused this," Iman replied. "We both know

291

exactly who is to blame and he was taken away in a body bag yesterday."

Her mouth was pressed into a thin line. She'd scared herself with what she'd said too.

Wanting to remove the fear from her eyes, Adam spoke. "I'm not going back." Even as he said it, a wave of peace settled over his shoulders.

"What?" Hope shone in his wife's eyes.

"I'm not going back," he repeated. "I'll find something else. There must be *something* I can do decently well."

"You can do anything," Iman told him. "Anything you want." She laughed. "Say it again!"

"I'm not going back," Adam said, for the third time. "I'm *never* going back."

Tears began to slip down Iman's cheeks and his smile faded.

"No, don't worry!" she shook her head. "I'm happy. I'm so, so happy."

Iman put her hands on his cheeks. "I can't believe you're really doing this." She bit her lip. "You are sure, right? You won't change your mind."

"I am sure. I'm completely sure." And he was. He felt lighter than he had in months.

CHAPTER TWENTY FOUR

Iman woke to the sounds of retching. She sighed.

Another nightmare. She still had them herself now and again but the spectre of Ali Cassim had lost most of his power for her.

But Adam was still haunted. Iman had lost count of the number of nights she'd woken to find him clutching at her, desperate to make sure she was still breathing.

She cursed Ali Cassim viciously in her head, vindictively hoping that the man was suffering in whatever grave he'd been thrown into.

The bedroom was still dark. Adam never put the lights on when he had nightmares, not wanting wake her.

She turned on the lamp that sat at her right and waited patiently. She'd learned by now that if she tried to go to him, he'd exhaust himself even further trying to pretend that he was fine and hide the worst of his pain from her.

Better to wait and let him come to her. When they were in bed, at least, he wouldn't turn her away.

As had become her habit during these nights, she began to pray, softly enough that her voice wouldn't carry to Adam and worry him.

The knot of tension she'd been carrying in her stomach began to ease and she stopped for a moment to marvel. Every time she did this, she felt better. Every single time.

She was sure she'd shocked Shaida when she'd begun to interrogate her about Islam but nonetheless, Shaida had answered every question of hers patiently – sometimes even calling over her own mother to help where her knowledge was shaky.

She was so distracted she didn't notice Adam coming back to bed. "You're praying?" he asked curiously. "What for?"

Iman lifted her head. "You recognized it?"

"My mother," he explained. "Before she met Ali, at least." Adam shook his head as though to clear it. "I didn't know you were religious?"

"It's a new development," Iman admitted. "But... I think it's here to stay."

"What were you praying for?" he asked, getting into bed.

"You." Iman settled back on his shoulder.

"Me? I don't think assassins have God on their side." His tone was light but Iman heard the self-loathing he couldn't hide.

"It can't hurt," she told him calmly.

"I guess not," he agreed drowsily.

"Besides, it makes me feel better."

"Keep doing it then," Adam told her, half-asleep.

-

The ring of a cellphone mingled with his wife's hissed curses brought Adam awake. "In the drawer," he reminded her. No matter how often he told her to put her phone away, he ended up being the one to do it after she'd forgotten.

"Thanks," she told him distractedly, yanking it open and snatching up the device. "Hello?"

Whatever she heard on the other side of the call made her sit down. Adam snaked an arm around her, squeezing once. What had happened?

"Thank you," she said eventually. "I appreciate you taking the time to call. I'll be there as soon as I can."

She dropped the phone into her lap and sat there silently.

"What happened?"

"My mother is dead," Iman told him. "She died this morning."

Adam swore silently. "I'm sorry." He'd hated Aasia but he knew Iman hadn't been able to let go entirely, even still.

Iman let out a sob. "I don't know why it hurts." She lifted her head. "She hated me. She hurt me and she hated me and if it had been the other way around, she wouldn't have blinked an eye. So why am I crying?"

Hurt for her made his chest ache. "You're a better person than she was. That's why." He brushed away the tears on her cheeks. "What do you need?"

"I need to go see... her." The body, she meant. Adam understood. She needed to make sure it was real.

"We'll go together."

She shot him a grateful look and nodded. "Thank you."

"Any time."

-

She was an orphan. It was a strange feeling. She'd sworn to herself that she would never go back. At the time, she'd finally thought that at long last, she was free.

But when her phone had rung that morning, she learned better.

Aasia had asphyxiated, they told her. She'd passed out and choked on her own vomit. An ugly end.

She'd been drinking, they thought. Bottles of alcohol surrounded her corpse along with a few scattered pills. The police had been called but they were convinced that it was just a simple overdose.

They'd expressed their condolences, commenting on the tragedy of it – only a few months after her husband had died. She must have loved him very much to destroy herself over him like this.

Iman barely heard them. She held tightly to her husband's arm and let Adam be her shield, speaking to no one but him the entire time.

He seemed to sense when she'd had enough and announced in a firm voice that they were leaving.

Thank God for him, she thought. Thank God she still had him.

-

She was about to fall asleep standing up! Did no one else see that?

He glared at the people surrounding them. Lawyers, policemen, security guards. Vultures, the lot of them. They'd offered bland platitudes just long enough to seem decent and then begun their attack.

Iman leaned further into him and his temper snapped. Enough!

They were leaving and if anyone needed anything, they were going to go through him. His wife had dealt with enough.

He guided her to the car gently and helped her in. Another minute and she'd pass out.

"Uh, sir?"

What now?

"How is your wife going to be dealing with her inheritance? We are the executors for Mrs. Rahman and we really do need to know immediately if her daughter has her own legal representation we need to contact?"

Adam glared at the simpering man. "You can contact me. I handed out my number enough today that you should have gotten it."

There was a blink. "Yes, sir. Of course. But you would like us to deal with everything?"

Whatever would get them all to leave him and his wife in peace. Adam said as much and there was a rapid series of nods. "Of course, sir. I completely understand."

Finally.

He got into the car and sighed, glancing at the passenger seat. Iman was fast asleep. She'd exhausted herself.

Adam rubbed his temples. When would the hits stop coming?

-

"A security company?" Kat repeated. "That's... different."

"It's not like I know how to do much else, Kat," Adam pointed out. "This is all I've been taught since I was fourteen. And even before that, my mother had me in any martial arts class she could find."

"I know," Kat agreed. "But... isn't it the same thing?"

Adam simply looked at her, thoroughly confused.

Kat sighed. "Not the moral side of it," she acknowledged. "You're in the clear there. But the rest of it. You'll still be in danger."

Adam shook his head. "I won't be the one on the ground."

"Staff?" Kat arched an eyebrow. "So you'll train them and send them off?"

"Pretty much."

"That's... good. It's really good. How did you come up with it?"

"*I* didn't."

"Iman?"

"Iman. She's been frantic about trying to get me something to do. I think she's afraid I'll go off the deep end if I'm bored."

Kat snorted. "She might not be wrong. I remember how you used to get when we were kids."

Adam wrinkled his nose. "Stop that. You make me feel old."

Kat rolled her eyes. "Where is Iman?"

"Out for a run." Adam scowled.

"I don't know how she can still do that. Still go running, still live in this house... I would have thought she'd want to get away. Hell, my skin is crawling being here."

"She's strong." Deceptively so. Adam thought of his tiny wife. She'd been hit so many times but she still just kept getting up.

Kat nodded. "I'm starting to see that."

Adam eyed his friend. "Well, now you know what my plans are. What are yours?"

Kat tilted her head to the side, feigning confusion. "What do you mean?"

"You're as free as I am, Kat. It's been over a month now. You must have some idea of what you're gonna do next?"

Kat bit her lip. "You're not gonna like it. I'm still not sure if *I* like it."

Adam straightened up against the cushions. "What do you mean?"

"I've been busy this past month." Kat picked at the seams on her armchair. "I've been rounding up everyone."

"Everyone?" He had to have misunderstood her.

"I thought you'd want to take Ali's place," Kat shrugged.

"I don't," he said immediately. "Not in the least."

"I know. I had a feeling you might think that way. I didn't think you'd decide to go and start a security company..."

"Kat," Adam derailed her tangent. "Focus."

"There are fifty killers waiting for you to take charge of them. Or... for us to take charge of them."

Adam looked at her, horrified. "You're not gonna... You *hate* killing."

"Times change," Kat said simply. "Seeing how the Khans work helped with that."

"Kat, what is this? I thought you'd want to get out."

"I do." Kat bit her lip. "But what happens then? I step back and some other sadist takes charge? That's not something I want."

"So you're gonna martyr yourself?" Adam was starting to get angry. "This is ridiculous!"

"I told you you wouldn't like it."

"Kat, come on! You know this is a bad idea! Will they even accept you in the first place?" They would, Adam realized. Kat had killed Ali. That, twisted as it was, would win her loyalty.

"Remember that old rumour?"

Adam did. "You're going to use it. Make them think Ali really was your father."

Kat nodded. "He might very well have been. I have no idea. Either way, the bastard's dead. He can't contradict me."

"Kat," Adam sighed. "Make sure you know what you're doing. This isn't something to do on a whim. You'll be trapped. Hunted. Just... be careful."

"You almost sound like a brother."

"Isn't that what I've always been?" He'd always thought of her as his sister. An annoying, bratty, know-it-all sister.

"Yeah," Kat said softly. "Yeah, it has." She eyed him for a moment. "Have you talked to your mother?"

Adam looked away. He'd tried, twice. Lina had refused to see him. "No."

"I'm sorry, Adam. Really, I am. I know how close you were."

"I won't force her. I just wish I could make sure she's okay."

"She is. The guards are there," Kat reminded him. "They would have let me know if anything had happened. They *will* let me know if she needs anything. And I'll take care of it."

"Thanks." It was better than nothing, he reminded himself. At least she was okay. "Kat, does she know what really happened?"

Kat froze. "I – I don't think so. Should I tell her?"

Adam didn't know. Was it cruel to show her what a monster her husband had been? Or was it worse to leave her in the dark, mourning a man who deserved none of her tears?

"Don't tell her," he decided. "It's over for her. There's no point."

Kat nodded. "If you change your mind..."

"I'll tell you."

"Can we talk about something less depressing now? And can you feed me? I'm hungry!"

Adam burst out laughing. Same old Kat.

"You have a tapeworm," he said, letting her derail him.

She grinned, recognizing the old taunt. "I'm a growing girl, is all," she responded, wrinkling her nose at him. "Now, come on, feed me!"

"Kitchen's that way," he pointed. "Help yourself."

Kat arched an eyebrow. "You want me to cook?"

Adam shuddered, remembering the last time he'd left his old friend alone in a kitchen. She'd made the biggest mess he'd ever seen, melted the handles of two pots and finished with a concoction that was so inedible Adam was sure even the roaches wouldn't go near it.

"No. No, you just sit there and don't... touch things."

Kat giggled and Adam was hit with a wave of nostalgia. How many times had he stood in the kitchen of his apartment, trading quips with her like this?

How things had changed.

The front door opened and his wife walked in, reminding him just what he'd gained from those changes.

A more than fair trade.

CHAPTER TWENTY FIVE

Iman smiled down at her laptop. Finally.

She'd been thoroughly confused the first time she'd been contacted by her mother's lawyers. They'd spoken to Adam first and he'd given her a heads up even but she'd assumed – wrongly – that Aasia had left her nothing.

Instead, she'd been informed that every one of Aasia's worldly possessions were now hers. And that included a sizeable fortune.

The news couldn't have come at a better time. Adam had been looking unhappier by the day about using the money he'd earned as an assassin – what little of it he hadn't immediately handed over to charities or Ali Cassim, at least – to fund his new business.

Now he wouldn't have to.

She couldn't wait to show him.

-

"Look!" Iman thrust a laptop in his face.

"Easy," Adam cautioned. "Don't break my nose." He took the laptop from her hands and peered at the screen. "That's a lot of zeroes. Whose account is this?"

"Mine. It's from my mother's estate," she explained. "Isn't it great?"

Adam had thought she would feel conflicted by the money. It was a weight off his shoulders to see her react this way. "Congratulations. What are you gonna do with it?"

"I'm – well, you really..." She shook her head. "Use it for the business."

"Iman, no. I'm not taking your money," Adam said immediately. It was bad enough that they were living on her grandfather, he thought irritably.

"You hate using your money for this," she argued.

"I'll get over it." And he'd do it far faster than if he used *her* money.

She sighed, taking her laptop from him and setting it aside. "But you don't have to. Just take it. There's no way I can use it all anyway – not even if I live for centuries."

How could he make her understand? He'd have to admit to her what he'd barely admitted to himself – that he was scared. He'd never done anything like this before and he had no idea whether he was setting himself up for failure by even trying.

"I love you for offering," he told her gently. "But I have my reasons. Okay?" He pleaded with her wordlessly to understand, to not be hurt.

"Okay," she sighed forlornly.

"I'm not doing it to hurt you."

Iman kissed his shoulder – the easiest place for her to reach. "I know." She bit her lip. "Why *are* you doing it then?"

She caught sight of the look on his face and hurried to add. "You don't have to tell me. Just – never mind. Leave it." She turned away.

He caught her wrist. "Wait." Just tell her. Why was it so hard?

Because he was ashamed. He didn't want her to think less of him.

"Adam, it's fine. Forget about it."

He didn't want to forget about it.

"I don't want to take your money – or your grandfather's – because I don't know if this is going to work out."

There. He'd said it.

Iman's eyes widened and then turned soft with understanding. "Well, now you have to take it."

Adam looked down at her. "What?"

"You have to," she repeated. "Because I refuse to let you believe that you're going fail. *You're not.*"

"You don't know that," he argued stubbornly. She didn't know how weak he could be.

"Yes, I do. I know you, Adam. I know how hard you work, how much you expect from yourself."

He looked away, a blush staining his cheeks. It wasn't the first time Iman had complimented him but, just as it always did, the words caused a strange mixture of joy, guilt and misery to course through him.

Immediately, he felt the urge to deny her words.

"You'll do great. I know that, even if you don't believe it yourself just yet."

Looking at her then, Adam almost did believe it.

He scooped her up. "You're pretty confident."

Iman tightened her arms around him then brought a hand up to the back of his head. "I have good reason to be."

-

Iman looked down at the date and felt a shock go through her. A year ago today, she'd finally given up the frantic search for a husband and settled on Adam. They'd been married for almost a year.

Her eyes widened and she gasped. Her anniversary was right around the corner and she'd completely forgotten about it.

She cast a guilty look at Adam who was watching her curiously. "Something wrong?"

"Just waiting to see if you'd pick up where I left off," she lied. He'd taken to sitting with her while she prayed or recited the Quran, claiming he thought it was pretty. But he'd never touched it himself.

"Honey," he said patiently, as he had several times before, "I'm a murderer. I don't think God wants to hear from me."

Irritated with herself for forgetting and racking her brain trying to figure out how to mark their anniversary, Iman's reply was uncharacteristically short. "You're a murderer," she repeated. "Don't you think you should be trying harder than anyone else?"

Adam flinched.

Already filled with regret, an apology immediately sprang to

Iman's lips. "I – I didn't mean..."

"You've never called me that before," Adam said dully. He pushed himself up. "Excuse me."

"Adam," she called after him. "Adam, I'm sorry!"

He ignored her.

Iman buried her face in her hands, groaning. How could she have been so stupid?

He'd gone into the office. She knocked lightly on the door. "Adam?"

There was no answer.

"I am so, so sorry. I should never have called you that." Tears began to slide down her cheeks as she thought of his hurt expression. "I don't know *why* I said it, I didn't mean to – I just..."

There was a sigh and the door opened. "Don't cry," he told her. "I'm not mad at you."

"You should be."

"You didn't say anything that wasn't true."

The denial stuck in her throat. "I still shouldn't have said it. I'm sorry."

Adam sighed again. "You didn't say anything that wasn't true. And... maybe you have a point."

"I hurt you," Iman argued stubbornly.

"Yeah, you did," he admitted, swallowing hard. "But you didn't mean to."

He smiled deliberately at her. "You should make it better

though."

"How?" Iman furrowed her brow.

"Kiss me."

She did. Repeatedly.

-

Adam woke to find his wife pouting at her phone.

"Iman? I don't think that look works on inanimate objects."

Iman started. "You scared me," she scolded half-heartedly.

"I'm sorry," Adam replied dutifully. "What did the phone do?"

"The problem is more what it's not doing," his wife grumbled. She glanced at him. "Give me your phone," she requested, holding out a hand.

Adam reached for the device and dropped it in her palm. "Anything else?"

Iman was already fiddling. "Thank you," she nearly squealed.

Adam blinked. "You're... welcome, I guess. Are you *keeping* the phone?"

"No," she handed it back to him. "I'm all done."

"Problem solved?" Adam checked.

"Problem solved," she confirmed, tying her hair back. "I'm going to make breakfast."

Adam watched her scurry off, puzzled. What had that been all about?

-

Iman poured pre-mixed batter into the waffle maker, laid the table and then settled in to complete her real task. She'd taken Kat's number from Adam's phone when she'd been fiddling with it and now she began to text her, praying that Kat would respond.

Iman had struggled for most of the week trying to think of a gift for Adam that would hold some kind of meaning. But she could think of nothing he wanted or needed that would make any real impact. And she wanted whatever she gave him to be special.

She'd been ready to call it quits and hand him a watch she'd seen him admiring until yesterday when they'd begun swapping stories about being little. The look on his face every time he mentioned his mother... The pain of it still took her breath away.

She would have tried to find a way to help heal that hurt whether or not she'd been desperate to find a gift for her husband but now, with the timing fall into place the way it had, Iman had already half set her heart on reuniting mother and son right in time for her anniversary.

Now, if only Kat would reply to her messages...

Adam walked in, his hair wet from a fresh shower. "Want me to finish so you can talk to Kat?" he offered.

Iman had already leaned up to kiss him in thanks when his words registered. She gaped up at him. "How?"

"You forgot to finish deleting the message," he explained, grinning. "You really did all that just to get her number? You could have just asked me for it."

Iman huffed, looking away and trying to will the blush from her cheeks.

Adam tugged gently on a lock of her hair. "Iman," he cajoled.

"What?" she said huffily, still not looking at him.

"I thought it was cute," he offered.

Iman's phone beeped then and they both looked down. She shielded the screen from him.

"Iman," Adam said slowly. "What is going on with you and Kat?"

"You'll see soon enough," Iman told him. Hopefully.

Kat had agreed easily, to Iman's relief. She sat with the other woman outside Lina's new house now, mentally rehearsing what she wanted to say.

God only knew if Lina would be willing to listen to her. But she had to try.

"Ready to go?" Kat asked, unbuckling her seatbelt.

Iman nodded. "Yeah," she said tightly. "I'm ready."

-

That had gone spectacularly wrong, Iman thought miserably. She had somehow, impossibly, made things worse.

How was she going to explain this to Adam?

Her husband took one look at her and immediately asked, "What happened?"

"I... went to talk to your mother," she admitted. And it backfired horribly.

"How horribly?" Adam asked.

Iman hadn't realized that she'd spoken the tail end of that

thought aloud. "She's angrier than she was before I meddled." Lina had refused to listen to a single thing she'd said and had demanded that she leave. But not before shouting one final thing at her.

"Oh," Adam said softly. "I see."

"But she wants to talk to you."

Adam went rigid. "She does?"

Iman nodded. "She's still angry though."

"That's understandable," her husband muttered. "What did you tell her?"

Iman winced. "Nothing." She hadn't gotten much of a chance. "Your Mom did the talking."

Adam said nothing.

"I probably shouldn't have meddled."

"Probably not," Adam agreed, his brow creased. "What were you trying to do?"

"I just thought maybe she'd be willing to talk to me. I know how much this has been upsetting you."

Adam sighed and she winced.

Just how badly had she messed up?

"Kat was with you?"

Iman nodded hesitantly.

Adam headed up the stairs to call Kat.

Iman watched him go, kicking herself internally. So much for her great plan. She should have stuck with a watch!

–

The irritation Adam felt towards his wife had quickly been eclipsed by his own nerves.

Lina finally wanted to talk to him.

He fished his cellphone out of his pocket and dialled Kat's number, waiting for the call to connect.

"Hi," she answered apprehensively. "How's it going?"

"You took Iman to see my mother?"

He could feel Kat squirming.

"She was worried," Kat defended. "She *is* worried. Hell, I'm worried."

"How bad was it? Honestly?"

"Honestly?" Kat repeated. "It could have been worse. At least she's finally willing to talk. Call her, Adam. You'll regret it if you don't."

They talked for a while longer, Adam carrying the conversation, before Kat finally grew impatient. "Call your mother," she instructed. "Hang up on me and just call her. And then go and put Iman out of her misery. She must be pacing downstairs." Kat ended the call, not giving him the chance to respond.

Adam wrestled with himself for a long moment.

Should he call? Did he even want to?

Yes.

He *had* missed his mother. Neither Kat nor Iman had been imagining things and though he could have done without their interference, a part of him was grateful that they'd tried to help.

Without giving himself any more time to think about it, Adam hit the call button.

CHAPTER TWENTY SIX

Iman looked up at the sound of his footsteps, an eager look on her face. She opened her mouth to ask him a question and then abruptly shut it as he came into view, reading the answer in his expression.

Her face fell.

Adam sat next to her and wrapped his arms around her shoulders. "I don't want to talk, okay?"

"Okay," she agreed. "We don't have to talk. We can just sit."

And they did. Adam lay his head against her shoulder and played with her hair, trying to come to terms with what had just happened. It had felt like a sucker punch to hear his mother like that, distraught and furious and so, so bitter.

"I think I would have preferred to have never spoken to her again," he said finally. "It would have been... easier."

Iman ran a hand through his hair. He saw her fight against the urge to give him another apology – refusing to put her own guilt first – and felt a wave of affection for her go through him. "You didn't make it worse," he told her.

She looked at him, clearly disbelieving. "Okay."

It was the truth. Lina's anger had already been there. She'd been told the truth some time in between Ali's actual death and Kat taking control. That was why she'd refused to let him in the last time he'd tried to see her.

"She's... angry. With me, with Kat. The only person she's *not* angry with is Ali." That had been a shock of its own – to hear his mother defend the man who'd nearly killed him, Iman and Kat. Everything that had happened – to them all – could be traced back to Ali and his thirst for power.

Adam had finally begun to accept that and Lina insisting otherwise had made him ill. He'd always told himself that she didn't know the extent of her husband's cruelty. But now... he was no longer so sure.

The Lina who had hissed at him that she wished she could trade his life for her husband's – that woman wasn't someone he recognized. Had grief made her that way or was Adam simply seeing her clearly for the very first time?

He wanted to tell himself that the mother he remembered was the true Lina, that her pain had changed her.

He *wanted* to tell himself that.

-

What the Hell had she done?

Something had broken in Adam, in those long minutes he'd spent upstairs in the study. Whatever words had been exchanged between mother and son, they'd left deep, bleeding wounds and Iman had no idea how to heal them.

She'd seen Adam bleeding, dying and suicidal. But she'd never seen him in this state before.

Why had she pried?

She listened silently as Adam talked, stroking his hair and letting him use her as a resting place.

He'd told her that he didn't want to talk and she was beginning to understand now that he'd meant he didn't want to have a conversation. He needed her to listen when he was ready to speak and be there for him.

She could do that.

It was the *least* she could do.

He'd said that she hadn't made it worse. And maybe she hadn't made Lina worse. But she had been the one to put Adam in the line of fire.

He was so hurt now.

Silent tears trickled down her cheeks as her heart ached for him.

-

Iman had never stopped caring for her mother, Adam remembered. Up to the day Aasia had died, her daughter had cared for her to the point that she had shed tears upon hearing the news of her mother's death.

Would he be the same? Would he spend the rest of his life with a wound inside him, never healing and aching whenever he thought of Lina?

Adam shuddered and Iman's hand paused its stroking. She looked at him in concern, her eyes bright with tears.

"I'm alright," he said, trying to smile reassuringly.

Her face crumpled and she turned away.

His own pain momentarily forgotten, Adam focused on his wife. "Please don't cry." He was already close to tears himself. If she kept going, he'd be right behind her.

Iman sniffed and swiped impatiently at her cheeks.

"It'll be okay," Adam told her, trying to comfort.

"I shouldn't have meddled," she argued miserably. "It wasn't my place."

Adam blinked, momentarily distracted. "You're my wife. If it's anyone's place, it's yours. I know you were just trying to do something nice."

Iman's face fell even further. "And now you're trying to make *me* feel better." A ghost of a smile flitted over her face. "How can I ever make this up to you?"

"Just... sit with me. It's helping."

-

They woke in a tangle of limbs, hours later. Sleep had allowed the ache inside Adam to dull and he even found the energy to smile at Iman when she looked at him. It still hurt, but a scab had begun to form over the new wound and he knew that in time, it would fade into a scar.

Iman yawned and he looked down at her, wincing as the movement woke the aches sleeping in such an awkward position had left him with.

"Let's go up to bed," he suggested.

Iman looked surprised. "No work?"

"It's our first anniversary. I have other plans."

She winced. "We don't have to..." she began guiltily, eyeing him like he was going to go to pieces in front of her.

"Yes, we do." Adam disagreed. "I want to. But," he allowed. "I might not be the best company."

Iman put an arm around him. "You're perfect," she disagreed. "Just perfect."

Adam leaned into her, letting her warmth distract him. "Happy anniversary."

It would be happy, Adam decided then. She deserved it. And... so did he.

He pushed the lingering thought of his mother out of his head. They'd be back eventually. But not today. Today was for good things.

EPILOGUE

Table laid, food ready, husband on his way. How different this was from last year. Her first anniversary had begun as a complete and utter disaster, and despite the fact that it had ended well, Iman was determined that things would be different this year.

She hadn't bothered to be fancy. A nice meal with her husband was all she wanted this year. She'd said as much to Adam and he'd agreed immediately. He'd been working so hard lately – putting in a ridiculous number of hours to capitalize on his company's success – that she'd barely gotten to see him.

A nice, quiet night in for the two of them was just right, Iman decided, nodding to herself.

And hopefully this anniversary would pass by without a single tear being shed.

She heard Adam's key scrape in the lock and felt a grin spread itself across her face.

"Iman?" he called. "I'm home."

She met him at the door, automatically stretching up so he

could kiss her. "Happy anniversary!"

"Happy anniversary," he echoed, smiling hugely. "I missed you."

Iman spun around, already in the kitchen. "You were only gone six hours!"

"I missed you," Adam repeated, coming up behind her and wrapping his arms around her.

She'd missed him too.

Later that night, wrapped around her, Adam asked. "What was your least favourite part of this year?"

"Least favourite?" She couldn't think of anything. This year had been the best of her life.

Adam laughed at the confused wrinkle on her forehead, smoothing it out with his thumb. "There must be something you didn't like. We changed a lot this year. New house, new company..."

"Same us."

"Better us," Adam corrected. "Well, better me," he corrected, seeing the offended look on her face.

He was better. Iman still didn't know quite how but something had helped her husband to see that he wasn't a lost cause.

"Remember back when you thought Allah was for other people?"

Adam wrinkled his nose. He hated it when she reminded him. "And you told me I needed more help than anyone else?"

It was Iman's turn to be disgruntled. "I'm sorry," she mumbled, the old guilt welling up again.

"That's... probably what finally pushed me over the edge,"

Adam admitted.

"Insulting you was motivating?"

"It was shocking," Adam corrected. "And I needed the shock. What happened after distracted me..." He swallowed hard, pain crossing his expression the way it always did when he thought of his mother. "But... when I did start bugging you to teach me, it was because of that."

"You never told me that."

"You never asked."

It was true. She'd been so excited – and so worried that she'd mess something up – that she *hadn't* wondered at Adam's sudden change of heart. She hadn't had the time.

"You never answered me," Adam prodded. "What was your least favourite part of this year?" Iman thought for a second. "My husband's company exploded," she said petulantly.

Adam threw his head back and laughed. "I have been pretty busy lately, haven't I? I'm sorry."

"That's the worst thing that happened to me this year. Having to get used to you being away a lot again." Iman curled closer to him. "Different, isn't it?" She ran a hand down the scar on his chest.

"From death and destruction? Very."

"Do you miss it?" The question slipped out without conscious permission.

"What?" Adam pulled back to look at her.

"Do you miss how things used to be?"

"Not in the least," he said immediately. "I'm happier than I ever was. By a lot."

"Do *you* miss anything?" he asked hesitantly.

"There's nothing to miss." Iman put a hand on his chest. "I have everything I want right here."

Adam smiled brilliantly at her. "I love you."

"I love you too," Iman replied, knowing down to her bones that this one thing would never change. She'd love Adam Cassim for as long as she lived and, Allah willing, even longer than that.

Faizal's Letters to Iman

Faizal's First Letter to Iman

Dear Baby,

I've been told you're the size of a peanut right now. I can barely wrap my head around that. You're inside your mother, so tiny that you'd fit on my fingernail, and in less than a year, you'll be a baby. No matter what size you are, little one, you'll always have a place in my heart.

You won't remember me, little one. By the time you're old enough to read these letters, I'll be nothing but a memory. I wish it weren't so. I wish that I could toss these letters in a fire and know that I'll be there to tell you anything and everything you want to know about me. But I won't.

Much as I'd like to still hide from it and pretend that I'm going to get better, the truth is that I am dying, my little one. I might even be gone before your mother gets to know whether you truly are the little girl I believe you are.

I have cancer, you see. And there's nothing more that can be done to keep me hanging on in this world. There's no treatment, no cure. Perhaps by the time you read this, there will be one – God knows, Dad has been tossing enough money at researchers.

My father – your grandfather! – has always believed that he would die long before me. But as much as we can assume and plan, fate is not in our own hands. I have no choice but to give in to this disease destroying me.

I am sorry. If I could hold on for you, I would. Truly, I would. I love you so much already, my darling. More than seems logical.

More than seems possible, some times. I know that you'll never feel short of love, you'll have an army of protectors ready to do your bidding from before you can even voice those demands.

It makes it easier for me to know just how fiercely the people in my life will protect you. It makes it almost bearable for me to accept that I'll be nothing but a faded memory for you. Maybe it would be kinder to leave you with nothing of me instead of these little scraps.

I am so, so sorry little one, but I can't do that. I'm too selfish to not want you to know me, to not want you to love me. I know that it will hurt you, just as it hurt me to not know my father the way I should have. And there will be no relief for you like there was for me. There will be no calling your father back to his duties.

I'll leave you a letter from me telling you everything I could ever want to until the days in this short life of mine run out. Today, I write to tell you the most important thing of all – I love you dearly and I would give almost anything to be able to meet you.

Love,

Daddy

Faizal's Sixteenth Letter to Iman

Dear Baby,

I'm sure by now, you're tired of reading these. Maybe I should have stopped at fifteen. But I can't. Feel free to not read all – or any – of these if you don't want to, sweetheart. They're selfishly more for me than you in any case.

Today was... a very difficult day, Baby. The pain is getting worse and there's only so much that can be done without drugging me into a stupor. Your grandfather has taken to looking at me with such misery that I can no longer bear it. I gave in and agreed to let him hunt down yet more specialists to poke and prod at me and say exactly the same things – I am dying and they should prepare themselves.

I'm afraid for your grandfather, little one. I know him and I know just how stubborn he is. It's a trait he's passed on to me... perhaps one I've passed on to you as well? I don't know. How I wish I did.

Dad has not accepted the inevitable. I am terrified that he will not until it's too late. I don't want my father to not say goodbye to me. I don't want him to lose himself in grief the way he did over my mother.

Being with me then, focusing on being a good father, was what helped pull him out of it. Perhaps you will be the one he pours all his love and attention into. I dearly hope so. It's funny for me, little one. I'd always assumed that it would sting when your grandfather no longer loved me best... But the thought of him loving you best just fills me with joy.

I would give you anything you wanted of me, Baby. I love you that much.

Today's lesson, Baby, is that your grandfather is a stubborn beast. But he loves you and will do anything in his power to see you smile.

He loves you almost as much as I do and I couldn't be happier about it.

Love,

Daddy

Faizal's One Hundred & Sixty Fifth Letter to Iman

Dear Baby,

This letter might be one that you never get to read. I've barely mentioned your mother less than a handful of times in all these letters which is something you must have picked up on. If by the time you read this, things are different, just know that people can change when they make the effort to.

For your sake, I hope that your mother has made the effort. If that is the case, if she's a wonderful parent to you, you have my permission to tear up this letter and toss it in the trash. I don't want this to hurt you or to ruin your relationship with your mother. If it's a happy one, I am thrilled for you, Baby. I could never begrudge you love.

If you're still reading, little one, you have some idea that your mother can be... difficult.

When we met, I wrote it off as the result of a difficult upbringing, surrounded by nannies and overly spoilt by guilty parents. Your mother was given everything she wanted no matter how bad it was for her up until your grandparents had to deal with the backlash of her wildness, as they called it. They overcompensated and she rebelled, unable to understand or accept their behaviour.

I ignored the warning signs and I shouldn't have. We were happy at first – I doted on her just as her parents had when she was younger and all was well. It was only when faced with having to share me and my attention that things began to get complicated.

We dealt with it. Not always successfully, but we did deal with it. Your mother resented my father, I know. She outright hates him now. But we were still able to pretend that things were alright.

Until you.

I am firmly convinced that by the time you are born, your mother will have come to her senses and found the love for you that she must have deep in her heart.

Right now, however... There's no easy way for me to put this, Baby. And perhaps you would prefer to be kept in the dark. But you deserve to know the truth. If your mother and grandfather still haven't reconciled, you deserve to understand why.

When your mother found out she was pregnant, she was furious. She didn't want a child – we had been using birth control at her request – and immediately wanted to have an abortion. If I hadn't been there with her in the doctor's office when she was told, I think she would have gone ahead with it and kept your existence from me forever. It is what she has told me she wishes she would have done.

I pleaded with her and we ended up at Dad's. I needed his help to try and convince her to keep you. Your grandfather shielded me from the worst of it but I know he kept guards on her for those few weeks to make sure she couldn't get the abortion she wanted.

I'd like to think that my diagnosis had something to do with motivating her to keep you. I was already visibly deteriorating when we found out and two weeks later, the day I wrote my first letter to you, I was finally diagnosed.

Your grandfather was even more determined to hold on to some part of me and he immediately offered your mother money. He told her to name her price, that he would pay anything she wanted if she just agreed to have you... She didn't need to do anything else once you'd been born.

She agreed, of course.

Your mother is not an evil woman, Baby. She's damaged and I wish I had been smart enough to realize that she needed help before all of this. Perhaps then I wouldn't see the need to write you a letter just so that you can know that any problems you may have with her are not your fault.

But I need you to know that, little one. If she's cold or standoffish, if she's not there for you all the time... It's not because of you. The fault lies with many people – her parents, my father, me. Even she holds some of it. But you, little one. You are blameless.

That's today's lesson – you are not to blame for other people's actions.

Love,

Daddy

Faizal's Two Hundred & Eighth Letter to Iman

My dearest daughter,

Happy birthday, sweetheart! I was right, you're a girl. And the prettiest, most perfect little girl I've ever seen.

I didn't think I'd get to see this day, sweetheart. I was sure that I wouldn't get to see you, not until the afterlife, at least. But I did. God has granted me the privilege of seeing you, holding you, even kissing you.

You're early, Baby. You were supposed to stay in there for another month and a bit but you were determined to come out and meet the world.

I wasn't there to see you being born. I can't stand that long any more. But I got to see you as soon as you were cleaned up and the nurses were nice enough to let me hold you.

It was the one thing that I still wanted to do. The one thing that I couldn't let go of. And now that I've been able to do it. I have a feeling the end is near. I'm so sorry, Baby. I wish I could keep holding on for you, long enough that you'll at least be able to remember me as you grow. But it's beyond me.

I don't have the strength, my darling.

Today's lesson... Today's lesson is that your Daddy adores you.

Love,

331

Daddy

Faizal's Last Letter to Iman

My dearest daughter,

It's going to be soon. Even your grandfather has made his peace with it now. I suppose I look too fragile for him to keep pretending.

Writing you this letter is taking longer than I'd like to admit. I don't know what to say to you, Iman. I don't know how to find the words to express my unending regret and my overwhelming love.

I love you more with every passing moment and I finally understand my father's desperation to find me a cure. Thinking of no longer having you with me... I thank God that I will at least be spared the pain of having to watch you die.

Iman, I still hold out hope for your mother. But know this, Baby – if she can't find it in herself to be with you, she is the one who has lost. I've been promised by several very lethal men and women that you will be protected by their hands. And I know with the utmost certainty that you've already wrapped yourself thoroughly around Dad's heart.

Surely, with all these people, you'll be alright? I'm no longer selfish, little one. I no longer want you to love me despite the hurt. I don't want you to feel the loss of me.

I love every inch of you, Iman.

I need you to do something for me, okay?

I need you to know that you're loved. I need you to know that you're important. I need you to know that I never, for a single second, wanted to leave you.

And I need you to be as happy as you possibly can be.

There's no lesson for today, sweetie. Life will teach you everything from now on. I wish I could have been there to see it. But I have faith that on the day when every soul is called to be judged, you and I will finally be together again, in Paradise where it never has to end.

Love,

Daddy

ACKNOWLEDGMENTS

I have a great many people to acknowledge as always – writing may be a solitary process but publishing a book takes a large army.

Ayesha Desai is and always has been fantastic and wonderful and this book wouldn't be anywhere close to coherent without her.

Naeelah Vally, my lunch date, my fellow cat lover, my best friend. Without her, I'd still be dithering, thinking I couldn't make it.

Rashdah Hameed, one of the most fantastic people I know who's always been there to listen when I have something to whine about.

ABOUT THE AUTHOR

Neymat Raboobee is a South African author and blogger. She has been writing ever since she can remember and being an author was a childhood dream of hers that has finally been fulfilled.

She also runs www.theimperfectmuslimah.com and spends her little free time volunteering as a social media manager for a few organizations in between studying towards a Bachelor's in Education.